THE
MERVYN
STONE
MYSTERIES

THE MERVYN STONE MYSTERIES

3

CURSED AMONG SEQUELS

NEV FOUNTAIN

First published in November 2010
by Big Finish Productions Ltd
PO Box 1127, Maidenhead, SL6 3LW

www.bigfinish.com

Project Editor: Xanna Eve Chown
Managing Editor: Jason Haigh-Ellery
With thanks to: Matthew Griffiths and Lisa Miles

Geek Tragedy
978-1-84435-530-3 (numbered edition) 1-84435-530-6
978-1-84435-513-6 (hardback) 1-84435-513-6
978-1-84435-531-0 (paperback) 1-84435-531-4

DVD Extras Include: Murder
978-1-84435-532-7 (numbered edition) 1-84435-532-2
978-1-84435-514-3 (hardback) 1-84435-514-4
978-1-84435-533-4 (paperback) 1-84435-533-0

Cursed Among Sequels
978-1-84435-534-1 (numbered edition) 1-84435-534-9
978-1-84435-515-0 (hardback) 1-84435-515-2
978-1-84435-535-8 (paperback) 1-84435-535-7

A CIP catalogue record for this book is available from the British Library.

Cover design and photographs by Alex Mallinson.

Printed and bound in Great Britain by Biddles Ltd, King's Lynn, Norfolk.
www.biddles.co.uk

Secret passcode: 5C

For my Worrier Queen

Thanks to...

Nicola Bryant, for her support and her love and her devotion. It is reciprocated in spades. Thanks for allowing me to write through Christmas, and for sitting up in the early hours saying 'I don't think this bit works.' That's a real dream girl, that is.

Big Finish Towers. Thanks to Jason Haigh-Ellery, for taking me to his expensive club and saying 'Yes please, three books by the summer of 2010.' David Richardson, Nick Briggs, Alex Mallinson, Xanna Eve Chown, Paul Wilson and Toby Robinson, for being so lovely all the way through this project's gestation.

Jonathan Morris and James Goss, for their help, their comments and their 'squee' noises.

Ian Fountain, for his extensive knowledge of cars and tube trains.

Gareth Edwards, Bill Dare, Caroline Norris and Richard Webb for allowing me, an annoying writer, to swan round the sets of their busy television shoots.

Tom Jamieson, Ann Kelly, Alan P Jack, Steve Berry, John Banks, David Tennant, Peter Ware, Steve O'Brien and Ally Ross for their help.

Simon Brett for his encouragement and inspiration.

Sheila Bryant for the use of her dining room table.

Iona, Jill and Jackie Fountain, for taking me to see Cornwall, Bob and Sue Mynett, for showing me more of its wonders, and the Falmouth Docks choir, for their voices, and Christmas time in Cornwall.

Russell T Davies, Steven Moffat and everyone at Cardiff, for making all that toast.

The Sun's Ally Ross says...

Ah yes, *Vixens from the Void*. Now you ARE talking real television.

It's been written off by the usual right-on bed-wetters, and those TV Cream dorks. But this almost-forgotten masterpiece claims a space, forever, in my TV Gold. From a time when we were actually allowed *Vixens* on the television, and everything wasn't just a void, it was wobbly sets, wobbly women, Tara Miles and ta-ra clothes.

Now this was a show with real heart and false eyelashes. And who cares if the sets looked like the inside of Boy George's head? And who cared if the hairstyles were able to be seen from space, and the make-up could have caused a slick that would shock BP? And the costumes? They may have looked daft on the outside, but as any teenage boy at the time would have told you, when it came to Arkadia's brassiere it was what was inside that counted...

When I was a wee boy with more asteroids on my face than the whole Vixen Empire, I watched it every week, and I had my posters and my customised duvet to prove it. Not that my duvet was officially customised, mind, but the glimpses of Vanity Mycroft's twin planets were enough to engage any young man's warped drive...

11 MILLION viewers and an impact like a 240-volt charge in the Groolias. Earthlings, they do not make TV shows like *Vixens from the Void* anymore. Note to telly bosses everywhere: Bring it back, you bunch of 'Ken A Wilders'...!

'Progress is a continuing effort to make...
things... as good as they used to be.'

Bill Vaughan

'There's no point just trying to recreate the past exactly.
If you do you're bound to fail.'

Mervyn Stone

AUTHOR'S NOTE

This book takes place in a weird alternative wibbly-wobbly reality where, because *Doctor Who* is the most successful show in Britain, another old sci-fi show – *Vixens from the Void* – is revived.

There are *Doctor Who* fans that already think that because *Doctor Who* is the most successful show in Britain, they're already living in that weird alternative wibbly-wobbly reality.

Because there is a blurring of reality and fiction in this book, allow me to put on my anal fan hat (not a thing you can buy at Argos) and file the 'fiction' from the 'non-fiction'.

Product Lazarus UK isn't real. There is a jolly little radio station which happens to be in Truro, but it is not inhabited by the likes of Louise Felcham or any of the characters in this book, all of which are completely made up.

Nick Briggs and Steve O'Brien are real, so they tell me, and I'm extremely grateful for their permission to be included in this book. *SFX* magazine is also real, and again, I'm grateful for the editor's permission for its inclusion.

Russell T Davies and Steven Moffat are real, thank God, as is the TV series produced in Cardiff, without whom the galaxy would be a much poorer place, and to whom this book is dedicated.

Vixens from the Void isn't real. But then again, neither is *Doctor Who*, and it certainly didn't stop me believing in any of it.

Extract from the *Vixens from the Void Programme Guide*, originally printed in the fanzine *Into the Void #55*.

```
EXPIRATION POINT (Serial 5C)


Transmitted:     13 September 1990
Recorded:        Studio: BBC Television Centre
                 14-16 Feb 1990
                 Location: Clay pit,St Austell/
                 Pendennis Castle, Falmouth,
                 Cornwall, 5-10 March 1990

Medula:               Tara Miles
Arkadia/Byzantia:     Vanity Mycroft
Tania:                Suzy Lu
Velhellan:            Jennifer McLaird
Elysia:               Samantha Carbury
Excelsior:            Maggie Styles
Vizor:                Roger Barker
Gorg:                 Kim Maynard
Styrax Sentinels:     William Smurfett
                      Danny Porter
Styrax Voice:         Arthur Stokes
Production Design:    Seb Crook
Writer:               Ken A. Wilder (aka
                      Mervyn Stone)
Script Editor:        Mervyn Stone
Director:             Ken Roche
Producer:             Nicholas Everett
```

Synopsis:

A lone Styrax sentinel crashes on the planet SCARGOS MINOR. Landing on the planet, the Vixens track it down and capture it, to discover that it has broken its programming and escaped. It is fleeing from the 'expiration point' – the time in a Styrax's existence when it voluntarily scraps itself in favour of a new, more advanced model. Realising that the Styrax may contain valuable tactical information, they decide to take it back to the empire. Then a fully-armed Styrax patrol arrives to ensure that the lone Styrax complies with its 'expiration point'...

The Styrax sentinel is taken back to Vixos, but the information it contains turns out to be worse than useless. It has been faked by the Styrax command, planted to lead the Vixens into a trap. The Styrax sentinel saves the Vixens, but at the cost of its own existence.

Notes:

- It is possible to argue that more production problems beset this episode than any other. The headaches began for script editor Mervyn Stone when the assigned writer, Dermot Costello, came to London to discuss the script. Costello was detained by police on suspicion of smuggling explosives onto the mainland.

- The 'explosives' turned out to be an alarm clock attached to a lump of Plasticine (Dermot claimed he used the Plasticine to 'cushion the bell because the ring was too shrill'). Even though he was quickly released and got to his London hotel with no further delay, Dermot demanded an apology from the British government and went on a hunger strike inside his hotel room until he got one.

- The 'script' which Costello eventually sent to the production office turned out to be 60 sheets of the hotel's headed paper, on which was written: Tiocfaidh ár lá.

- Feeling that this was an elaborate ploy by Dermot to avoid writing his script, but knowing that the BBC would never sue Dermot because of the political implications, Mervyn once again took up the writing chores, penning an episode in three days under the pseudonym of 'Ken. A. Wilder'. Stone's frustration with Dermot seemed apparent at the time. It was pointed out by Darren Cardew (*Into the Void* #7) that 'Ken A. Wilder' is an anagram of 'Idle Wanker'.

- The pseudonym was essential as the Vixens script editor had written pretty much all of the last two seasons, and the BBC frowned on such practice. Such was the corporation's alarm over how many scripts Stone was writing, the BBC's Head of Series and Serials demanded a meeting with 'Ken A. Wilder', ostensibly to discuss the finer points of the script, although many suspected the meeting was to ascertain that 'Ken' really existed.

- With no one else knowing the script well enough to pretend to be 'Ken', Stone went to the meeting himself, electing to don a false moustache and a fake Irish accent. Fortunately, the Head of Series and Serials had barely made Stone's acquaintance during the last four years and the ruse worked. Mervyn has since joked that because Dermot was an IRA sympathiser, he should have been used to his words being voiced by someone else.

- The episode required a large element of location work, and producer Nicholas Everett elected to film in St Austell in Cornwall. Disaster struck the production almost immediately when snow and hail disrupted shooting and the make-up department got stranded in their rented farmhouse. Stone was forced to pen lines for the Vixens suggesting that the Styrax patrol ship landing had prompted 'freak weather conditions' that caused the Vixens' hair to look badly tousled. Stone himself escaped serious injury during a storm when an arc light nearly fell on him.

- Director Ken Roche antagonised much of the crew with his eccentric style of filming, and Everett had to function as a peacemaker. Roche chose to ignore much of the script's stage directions, much to Stone's exasperation.

- The problems were compounded when Everett fell off a boat en route to Pendennis Castle. He became dangerously ill with double pneumonia, and Stone elected to become de facto producer for the shoot. This brought tensions to a head with the now deeply distressed Roche, who had taken to hiding in the boot of his own car.

- Roche's decision to burn the full-sized Styrax shuttle prop on location horrified Stone. The two eventually came to blows on the last day of filming and had to be separated by Gorg actor Kim Maynard. The fire spread to a nearby field and incinerated a flock of sheep. A local farmer was paid compensation as a result, which meant that the budget skyrocketed.

- Nevertheless, despite its problems 'Expiration Point' is seen as one of the most popular *Vixens* scripts among fans, coming top in that year's VAS poll and sixth overall in the 1995 poll conducted by *Vixens from the Void Magazine* and published in its final issue.

CHAPTER ONE

>CLICK<

[SIGH]

Oh God.

I'm still here.

I'm still in Cornwall.

Oh God.

I thought it was a terrible dream.

Oh...

God.

CHAPTER TWO

Mervyn Stone woke up.

The first thing he noticed was the badger's head in his bed.

It wasn't a visitation from the Cornish Mafia. Mervyn imagined they were more subtle in their methods; they probably attached threatening letters to pasties and chucked them through windows or something like that.

No, the badger's head had fallen on him, for the third day in a row. It had somehow removed itself from the hook on the wall in the night, and come the morning he'd woken up to find the furred face snarling up at him from his crotch, white pointy teeth bared and ready to attack. It reminded him of the first time Vanity Mycroft suddenly decided she was going to perform fellatio on him, whether he wanted it or not. That was in Cornwall too.

He wished there was some fellatio on offer now, badger-related or otherwise. At least it would have taken up five minutes or so. It would be something to do. There was nothing here any self-respecting writer could do to pass the time. There were no trendy coffee shops to sit and pretend to write in while watching women go by. No dubious internet sites to wallow in. No mobile phone coverage. No pay-per-view channels on the television in his room. Even Channel Five was a fuzzy incoherent blob, mocking him. He felt like he was stranded back in the 1980s.

Which in a funny way, he was.

He had been stuck in the 80s ever since 1985. That was when he started work on a BBC1 science fiction show called *Vixens from the Void*.

It was a cheery little space soap opera with wobbly spaceships and even wobblier actresses, with a not-so-subtle dominatrix subtext. Each episode featured huge-breasted women wearing very few clothes ordering about huge-breasted men wearing even fewer clothes. It was a piece of disposable nonsense, but it was a piece of disposable *sci-fi* nonsense, so of course it was never disposed of. Ordinary Earth-based dramas such as *Triangle* and *Howards' Way* could slip away peacefully in their beds, awaiting the calm oblivion of UK Gold, but space stuff like *Doctor Who, Blake's 7* and *Vixens from the Void* was chucked into bath chairs and wheeled around the grounds, prodded with sticks and asked questions about the past. So even though everything else he'd ever written had been long forgotten, *Vixens* hadn't.

It was the reason why Mervyn found himself, more than 20 years later, hollow-voiced and hollow-eyed, constantly telling crowds of smelly people in jackets covered with badges what his favourite episode was, how he felt when the series was cancelled, and how he invented the monsters.

It was also the reason why he was now in Cornwall.

He was in a place the maps said was a village, but which any sane person would have said was a bus stop with houses. Not that there were any buses. There was one minibus a day out of the 'village', which took the residents somewhere slightly larger to go shopping. Mervyn hadn't driven in years and he didn't own a car any more so he felt isolated and stranded.

Still, he was a writer (it said so on his passport), and writers work well in baroque isolation. So everyone said. Mervyn never found this the case. One thing that got the steam coming out of his ears would be girlfriends who unplugged the telly and hid the radio in the mistaken belief that he would churn out the pages of his scripts faster and they could then go out to restaurants and see movies. But on the other hand, he mused, if people kept saying that isolation was good for writing then it must be true. So, like a complete idiot, he'd brought along his laptop in the hope that it would breathe some life into his corpse of a novel.

It had been three days now, and his laptop hadn't even left its little leather pouch. It served as a coaster for mugs of tea and as a doorstop for the bathroom. He'd done nothing else since he'd arrived but watch the late-night cop shows on Channel Five through a storm of static. It was like trying to contact sailors in the North Sea with short-wave radio; sometimes the picture would vanish completely, providing Mervyn with a gripping radio play where he could guess from audio clues as to who was beating up whom. Sometimes, the cops would look almost normal, just juddering slightly like sufferers of Parkinson's; sometimes they'd morph and stretch into twitching multi-coloured monsters, hissing and spitting at each other as they investigated their homicides. Mervyn suspected that all conspiracy theory nutters watched late-night Channel Five in Cornwall. Where else would they get the idea that the royal family were secretly eight-foot-tall lizards?

The first night he'd spent in his room, he'd fallen asleep at two o'clock after watching three episodes back to back, his last memories of Channel Five bleeding into his dream. There were two cops with purple faces and green hair, investigating the murder of a woman who'd been killed by atmospheric interference. She'd been scrambled all over the pavement and forced to eat squiggly black lines until she choked. Then he woke up, and he was sleeping with the head of the badger. He'd screamed. The badger had squiggly black lines down its face – it looked like it too was being interfered with by patchy reception. Still barely awake, he braced himself for it to turn greeny-purple and hiss at him.

Mervyn wondered how many guests it had landed on over the years. Had any victim ever mentioned the kamikaze badger to the staff? He guessed not. It had probably been descending on guests for centuries. Perhaps it needed a blue plaque under it: 'This badger fell on Kenneth Grahame in 1898 and knocked *The Wind in The Willows* into his head.'

Mervyn measured his life in degrees of wrongitude and crapitude. The worse the location and situation, the higher the degrees of wrongness and crapness. He didn't want to prejudge his stay after only a few days, but at least as far as his room was concerned...

'360 degrees wrong, 360 degrees crap.'

He hung the badger up again and got dressed quickly. It was cold.

CHAPTER THREE

He was staying in a pub called the Black Prince Tavern. It was a product of 21st century rural life, where out-of-town shopping centres had scorched the Earth bare, and the remaining embers of village commerce had to become multi-skilled to survive. The pub was also a bed and breakfast, a post office, an antiques shop, a bookmakers and, Mervyn suspected from the whispered conversations at the bar, a venue for dog-fighting.

Every morning, residents came down to eat breakfast in the lounge area, passing self-consciously through the bar where they were eyed suspiciously by the pub's regular alcoholic, sipping his fermented breakfast and muttering sweet nothings to his dog. Mervyn came down at 9.30, nodded to the drunk, patted the dog, entered the lounge, sat at a table and opened up his newspaper. The headlines about the prime minister, Simon Cowell and Russell Brand reassured him; it was just like buying an English paper when he was abroad. He felt he was on his home planet again.

But Christ it was cold. All the guests were in jumpers and coats. Steam from the teapots on the tables mingled with steam from the breath of the residents. A girl rushed by with a bouquet of cutlery. He managed to catch her eye and gave a helpless smile.

'Good morning,' he said.

'Good morning. Tea or coffee?'

'Coffee please.'

'Continental or full English breakfast?'

'What's your continental breakfast?'

'Continental is over there.' She pointed to a table. A collection of freshly microwaved croissants were sitting in a basket.

'Full English please. And could I have brown toast with that?'

'Toast is over there. Next to the continental breakfast.'

There was a toaster and two opened packets of bread next to the croissants.

'Umm. Isn't it a bit chilly in here?'

'Oh. No one else has said anything,' she said in a well-rehearsed way, which suggested that plenty of people had said something in the past, but none had the courage to say anything this precise morning. 'The heating's on the summer timer. It'll come on when we get to October.'

Mervyn looked at the paper. It was the 29th of September. 'Well, I know it's not winter just yet, but it's quite cold now.'

'Yes, but it's on a summer timer.' She looked at her watch, noting that breakfast was nearly over. 'I'll mention it to the manageress.' And with that she rushed off back into the kitchen to keep warm.

Mervyn was severely tempted to forgo his breakfast and go back to the relative warmth of his room, but he was waiting for someone: someone who for the last two days had come down at 9.35 precisely.

Here she was. Right on time.

He'd noticed her when she came down to breakfast that first morning. He thought she looked slightly familiar, but perhaps she just had one of those faces; friendly, engaging, attractive but not overpoweringly so; normal enough to work in a bank, but pretty enough to be plucked from her local branch to become the face of some national ad campaign flogging ISAs. She had a lovely round nose and a generous smile; her hair was an explosion of brown ringlets that danced on her forehead, forcing her to twitch her head in an adorable fashion as she flicked them out of her eyes.

She sat down at the table next to him. This morning, she was wearing a plain tweed jacket over a silk chemise, which gaped enticingly when she bent down to pick up her bag. He glimpsed red lace. She put her bag on her knee, a large refrigerated holdall. She pulled out a tub of probiotic yoghurt, a packet of organic muesli and a loaf of soda bread and put them on the table in front of her, just like she'd done for the previous two days.

She realised he was staring at him, and grinned, embarrassed. 'Please don't think I'm some kind of big city snob or anything, but I didn't think they'd have this stuff down here.'

Mervyn grinned. He'd had the same thoughts himself. 'Disgraceful. They make documentaries about people like you.'

She grinned back, relieved she'd found a confidante. 'Anyway, it turns out I was dead right. They don't sell it in the local shop.'

Mervyn picked up the muesli box and read it. He was being incredibly forward, but what the hell, he was on holiday – sort of.

'"Genuine West Country organic muesli",' he read. 'This is where it comes from... Listen. Wheat pulverised by the calloused feet of Gweek peasant ladies. Dates dried out with the hot breath of children from St Ives and Penzance.'

'It doesn't say that.'

'Really?'

Maggie smiled. 'Yes, I *know* they make it down here. But once they do they ship it out as quickly as they bloody well can, like it's radioactive. They all eat Frosties down here, while this ends up in fancy little shops for the consumption of big city snobs like me.'

'Would you and your big city breakfast like to join me?' asked Mervyn, gesturing at the empty seat opposite him.

She looked surprised, and her head rocked back on her neck like she'd been slapped. For a moment Mervyn thought he'd made a terrible mistake (*Oh well,* he thought, *if she does scream, at least there are plenty of tables to crawl under*) but she gave a delighted grin, and Mervyn realised she was very flattered (and slightly stunned) to be asked. She'd obviously not been approached by strange men in hotels very often. 'Why thank you, kind sir,' she said.

Her name was Maggie Rollins. Maggie had travelled from London to be with her ailing mother, who was reaching the end of her life after a long illness.

'She's in a nursing home,' Maggie explained. 'Millpond Retirement Cottages. They have such mealy-mouthed names for these places, don't they? So I've had no choice but to set up camp here, stay nearby, and wait 'til the bitter end.'

Like an angel of death. The image popped into Mervyn's head the moment he heard her story. He didn't say so, he wasn't a complete idiot. His quick writerly brain thought up something else.

'How sad,' he said, trying to sound sympathetic. 'It's like you're a plane coming into land, but your life is on a holding pattern, waiting for the all-clear to touch down.'

'Oh really?' Maggie said with a cheery grin. 'I see myself as an angel of death, brandishing my scythe, waiting to swoop down and carry her off.'

Mervyn mumbled, caught off-guard. 'Well, I wasn't going to say it, but...'

She laughed at him, and in that funny English way, they subtly rewrote the DNA of their relationship on the spot. Their body language changed; they stopped being awkward acquaintances and became friends.

'So that's me.' She sighed. 'I'm stuck in the middle of nowhere waiting for an ailing loved one to give up the ghost and die peacefully. How about you?'

Mervyn smiled. 'The same, really.'

CHAPTER FOUR

Mervyn explained why he was there. He explained about *Vixens from the Void*. He explained how he co-created and script-edited the original series, writing most of the episodes in the process. He explained that *Vixens* was on its way back to prime-time TV; that after almost 20 years languishing in the 'What Was That All About?' and 'What Were They Thinking?' sections of Channel 4's Clips and C**ts shows, *Vixens* was to be a cornerstone of the schedules once more. Mervyn didn't explain to her why they were making it in Cornwall. He thought it would be more fun if Maggie tried to guess.

'Go on. Why do you think we're down here?'

'Okay. Let me think... I bet... Cornwall's good for filming space stuff?'

'Not really.'

'But the wild scenery? The Eden Project? That must be good for space landscapes.'

'No. There's nothing here you couldn't replicate in any part of the world with computers. In fact, it's more difficult to make it down here than probably anywhere else.'

'Ah... I've got it! You originally made your show here in Cornwall?'

'Good guess.'

'I knew it!'

'We did make one episode here...'

'Ah-a!'

'But it was an utter disaster. At the time I pledged never to make any more television down here as long as I lived.'

Maggie frowned, and became slightly cuter in the process.

'Right. Oh. Yes. That's it. This TV company that's making it...'

'Product Lazarus Media. Yes?'

'They're based in Cornwall. I bet they are.'

'No. They're based in Los Angeles.'

'Not in the UK at all?'

'They have got a UK division.'

'Yes! In Cornwall!'

'No, in London.'

'But they do a lot of filming in Cornwall.'

'No. They haven't done anything here before. They're having to rent special offices and they're bussing all the equipment from Bristol.'

'All right. I give up. Why Cornwall?'

'Because this company wants to resurrect a long dead British science-fiction show – like *Doctor Who* – and they think that doing it in the middle of rural Britishness is the way to do it. And Cornwall looks enough like Wales for any American. '

'Okay, but why are you here?' she said.

Mervyn shivered. 'Let's go to the toaster. We might be able to keep warm if we stand round it.'

They went up to the self-service buffet, where there were tiny little pots of jam and tiny little squares of butter and tiny little boxes of cereal. British hotels specialised in breakfasts for midgets. Mervyn picked up a thick slice of bread and popped it in a toaster, and Maggie reached across him to pluck an apple from a bowl; she was so close her left nipple was practically brushing one of the knuckles of his right hand. Mervyn was momentarily caught between two delicious smells; warm bread and women's fancy soap. He felt quite intoxicated.

Mervyn tried to explain again.

'Okay, look at this toaster.'

'Right. I'm looking at the toaster.'

'This toaster is a television.'

'It's a television?'

'Yes.'

'What kind of television?'

'Um... It's your basic toaster-stroke-television. With two settings. Dark brown Terry Wogan or light brown Terry Wogan.'

'Oo, I like him dark brown. Okay, the toaster is a television. Now what?'

'Okay. Television commissioning is like a monkey with a toaster.'

'Okay.'

He pointed at the bread inside, which was nearly done.

'The lever on the toaster is the mechanics of commissioning a television show. This lever currently represents a big-budget revival of an old, fondly-remembered science fiction show, farmed out to regional programming and overseen by a famous award-winning script writer.'

'Okay. With you so far...'

'But it's the bread that's the key. The bread inside is the magic ingredient. That bread is the passion, the talent, the will and enthusiasm to do it right, the indefinable "X"...'

The toast popped up. He held it up in front of her like a referee showing a yellow card. 'This lovely, freshly-browned toast is your programme. This is the new series of *Doctor Who*.' He pressed the lever down on the toaster again.

'You haven't put any more bread in.'

'This is my point.'

'But you could set fire to yourself.'

'Well then, perhaps they'll take the hint and put the heating on.'

She laughed, a hearty man-sized laugh, and Mervyn slightly fell in love with her there and then.

'So the monkey, our commissioner, presses the lever down. The bread becomes toast. The monkey gets lovely, freshly brown toast. Yum yum. The monkey presses the lever again, because he thinks he's going to get more toast. But he hasn't put any more bread in. No "X". The monkey gets burnt crumbs. The monkey presses the lever again. He wants toast. He gets more burnt crumbs. The monkey presses the lever again...' The toaster popped up, showering the plastic tablecloth with burnt crumbs. 'Those burnt crumbs are *Vixens from the Void*.'

'Oh.'

'So imagine something becomes a huge hit. Ratings, reviews, all fantastic. Everyone's happy, and naturally they'd love to fill the schedules with more lovely brown toast, but they don't know how. They don't know why it's a success. That's the thing about my industry, they always say in television that no one knows anything – so managers, as the heads of television, have to be world leaders in knowing more nothing about anything than anyone else. The best they can do is replicate what they see on paper and hope it's going to happen again.'

'And they get burnt crumbs.'

'Exactly. There's no point to it. You can't recreate the past perfectly. If you try, you'll fail.'

Mervyn went back to the table, closely followed by Maggie. He picked up a tiny jar of jam, disembowelled it with his knife and spread it on his toast.

'So here I am, attached to a revamp of an old sci-fi show, and filming it in somewhere rural chiefly known for male-voice choirs and dairy-based puddings. Sort of *Doctor Who*, but not quite.' He shook his head disbelievingly. 'It's like I'm inside a crappy parody, like those little books you see at the tills in Waterstones, the ones called *Snored of the Rings* or *The Da Vinci Cold*. But that's what most television is; it's a crappy parody of itself.'

Maggie nodded sagely. She was on firmer ground here. 'Oh, I know. I remember when ITV brought out that talent show for groups, Star-Spangled Ballads. I remember thinking it was such a rip-off of *X Factor*. Which was a rip-off of *American Idol* anyway.'

'*Pop Idol*, I think it was.'

'Oh yes. Not that I didn't watch *Star-Spangled Ballads*, I was glued to it every Saturday. Watched the final – and I voted! Couldn't stand the two boys that won it, in their chunky jumpers. The Stepford Wagz – they were much better. Spunky. I liked them from the start. Glad they did well, and had all those hits, but I was annoyed all at the same time, you know? You like them when they're not popular, but when they become really successful you feel that something is taken away from you. You know what I mean?'

Mervyn knew exactly what she meant. He had already attended science-fiction conventions in the past few years where *Doctor Who* fans grumbled to him about how it 'wasn't the same any more', about how 'the books were aimed at kids' and 'internet chat had been ruined by teenagers and their text speak'. Marginalisation and obscurity were great comfort blankets to a certain type of fan. Mervyn was about to explain to Maggie about fans, when they were interrupted. The girl had returned, heroically venturing into the freezing lounge like Scott of the Antarctic. Mervyn's breakfast was laid before him.

The menu said it was 'home-sourced'. The sausages were from animals killed up the road; the eggs freshly extracted from the chickens down the lane; the black pudding derived from – well, he didn't know what they'd derived it from, but the insides had a red-grey diseased look, just like the complexions of the pub's regulars. Perhaps there was a discreet soundproofed room at the back for when they passed out at closing time.

There was far too much freshly-killed flesh in front of him. Mervyn tried to soften the effect by covering the whole thing with gobbets of tomato sauce, which only succeeded in making it look like a motorway pile-up. He was about to pop a bit of startled pig into his mouth and get it out of sight when Maggie looked into his eyes and rested her hand on his wrist. The warmth from her created a charge that flooded his whole body.

'You didn't quite understand my question. What are *you* doing down here? You, Mr Mervyn Stone? Because forgive me if I'm wrong, you don't sound like the one who wants to make this thing. Or even be here.'

Mervyn had thought long and hard about the question himself. Why was he here?

'I haven't the foggiest idea.'

CHAPTER FIVE

There must be a reason, but for the life of him he hadn't worked it out yet.

'They've got me down here as 'Programme Consultant', but I don't know why. They haven't exactly asked me anything since I got here. They've just ignored me. I haven't even been to the Product Lazarus offices they've set up in Truro.'

'Do you own the rights to the show or something like that?'

'No. I came up with it while I was a staff writer for the BBC, contracted to the drama department. Everything I came up with was BBC copyright. Well... all except one thing, which I craftily did as a freelancer. Basically, I sacked myself, rehired myself as a freelance writer and came up with a monster that proved very popular in the show.'

'I hope you gave yourself a bonus.'

'Oh definitely. As I did it as freelance, the copyright stayed with me – and the royalties. Product Lazarus have already contacted me and asked me if they could use them for the new show.'

'Then that's the reason. They need your monsters.'

'But they've already got permission from me. I told them they could use the Styrax on the strict condition that they give me some money. I'm very precious like that.'

'Oh.' She looked disappointed. 'Well, let me know when you find out why you're here. Maybe we'll celebrate with a drink in town.'

She was coming on to him.

Definitely.

She finished her breakfast and packed it away in her cold bag for next morning.

'Right. I'm off to see mum. Maybe this time she won't keep calling me Bernard.'

'I've finished too. I'll go up with you.' He hadn't finished at all, but he wanted to be with her for a few more precious seconds. He realised he was developing a crush.

'Great,' she said.

They walked through the pub, past the drunk and his dog, and out into the car park, where Maggie unlocked her dented Volvo. 'So what are these monsters of yours like?' she asked. 'Are they Orcs or Klingons?'

'Neither. The Styrax are... well, they're robots. They were a kind of future supercar that became so powerful that they subjugated their drivers and took over. They killed every pedestrian they could find and tried to take over the galaxy. It was a dire warning to us all not to rely on the motor car.'

'Oo, very prescient. I can see why they want to use them.'

She climbed into her Volvo and pulled out, leaving Mervyn standing forlornly at the door. She noticed his bereft expression, stopped, and opened her window.

'Are you okay?'

Mervyn looked embarrassed. 'Um. Could you give me a lift into Falmouth? I need to buy more underpants.'

CHAPTER SIX

This is what Britain is like, thought Mervyn. *It's like a tatty old painting, where they can only afford to restore the frame.*

That's what he thought the last time he came to Cornwall, and it occurred to him again now. Whenever he travelled to the edges of the country, Mervyn enjoyed watching the faded grimy greys and browns disappear, giving way to vivid colours – deep blues and harsh whites and greens so bright they made his eyes water.

The day had started with a drive along the coast in Maggie's car. She kept up an energetic prattle about her fading mother, Mavis Rollins (*they share the same surname*, thought Mervyn furtively, storing the information away for future use. *That means she's either unmarried, or very attached to her maiden name. Unlikely, with a name like Rollins*), and how she had worked in the same shop for 40 years and never thought of travelling east of Bristol.

Maggie was prepared to drive Mervyn into the centre of town first, but when the sign 'Millpond Retirement Cottages' flashed up on the side of the road, he insisted she pull in to the car park and let him walk the rest of the way. He watched her go in with a cheery wave, and then set off for the town.

It was a fresh, face-stingingly cold day in Falmouth. Mervyn was swamped by different sounds and smells. He certainly wasn't in London any more – that much was certain. Instead of a background wail of police cars, there were seagulls shrieking in the distance. Cars trundled along the high street like golf carts, nudging gently through pedestrians who wandered randomly off the pavements. He could imagine what would happen if flocks of pedestrians wandered into the road in his neck of the woods. It would look like his breakfast.

He couldn't get used to the fact that Cornish people looked each other in the eye when they passed in the street. For the first hour, he was constantly looking at his reflection in shop windows, checking he hadn't left a bit of home-sourced sausage on his face.

Even though change was as good as a rest, Mervyn was reassured by the names of the shops, which were omnipresent in the UK. *Thank heavens for the faceless corporations,* he thought. *The fifth emergency service. In case of breakdown from culture shock, they made sure you were never more than a couple of minutes from a bad celebrity autobiography, a crappy DVD player or a piece of over-fried chicken rectum in breadcrumbs.* WH Smiths, Currys, Vodafone, McDonalds, Argos... they were all there. So too, thank heavens, was good old Marks & Spencer.

Mervyn went into M&S and looked through the underpants, trying to decide which shade of grey would suit his bottom. He had just decided on 'battleship' when he heard a shout.

'Mr Stone?'

Mervyn looked around and couldn't see anyone he recognised.

'Mr Stone? Is that you sir?'

There was, however, a man he didn't recognise, looking straight at him and calling his name in an American accent.

The man surged towards Mervyn and gave him a kind of power hug; grabbing his hand, pulling him forward and giving him a pat on his right shoulder. Mervyn guessed it was an American thing.

'It's so good to finally meet you, Mr Stone.'

The man was wearing a tailored grey suit and white shirt, both of which barely covered a compact, muscled body. His green tie was the only splash of colour – it was a customised design, decorated with the word VIXENS in the classic 80s blocky font, and dozens of gold and silver Styraxes arranged in a chessboard pattern. His large head was fringed with a fuzz of receding brown hair. His teeth were two shades too white, and they glowed even brighter because they were sitting under a heavy dark moustache.

'Glad to meet you too.'

'Glad you got here. This country may be small, but it sure is hell getting across it.'

'It was no problem at all.' It actually took nine hours on a freezing train which stopped every half-mile, but lying was easier. It involved less conversation.

'Hey, where are my manners? I'm Randall. Randall Angelford. My PA exchanged e-mails with you last week.'

Of course. The man from Product Lazarus Media.

'I tell you, Mr Stone, I'm such an admirer of your work. I saw *Vixens from the Void* on PBS reruns and it just blew me away.'

The words didn't compute. 'Seriously?'

'Oh yeah. Just loved it.'

'Seriously?'

Randall caught Mervyn's tone. 'Oh sure, it was cheesy and the effects were cheap, and the acting was... odd, but it had real balls, you know? A real one-off! I can't believe the BBC let the rights go so easily...'

Can't think why, thought Mervyn.

'It was really ahead of its time in its sexual politics. You must tell me your secret.'

'I could tell you. But then I'd have to kill you.'

Randall barked with delight. 'Come on, I'll buy you a coffee.' He practically pushed Mervyn out of the shop. Mervyn had no time to protest, and was forced to drop his yet-to-be-purchased underpants onto a nearby shelf. The American guided him up the picturesque high street. Opposite an indoor market was the Cavendish Coffee House, and Randall ushered him inside. There were wooden chairs and tables, waitresses in uniform and cakes under glass. 'You know that cliché about not being able to find a cup of decent coffee in England? It's bull. You just got to know where to go.' He looked around and caught a waitress's eye. 'Their lattes are to die for.'

'I like your tie.'

'Thanks.' He stroked his tie proudly. 'I always get a tie that fits the project I'm working on. When I produced *Corpse Cops*, I had a tie made with bullet holes and coffins on it. When I exec'd *My Electric Girlfriend*, it was robots and hearts. When I produced *The Sex Lives of Henry the Great*, I, well...'

'Well?'

'I didn't wear a tie.'

Mervyn laughed.

Randall looked at him, and shook his head in wonder. 'Mervyn Stone. Mervyn friggin' Stone. I'm so excited that you could be part of this project.'

'Yes I know. I read the press release.'

Before he came down to Cornwall, Mervyn picked up *Broadcast* and read the announcement. It was a typical collage of quotes from people he'd never met, and probably wouldn't want to. It read:

The classic BBC science fiction show 'Vixens from the Void' will be given a 21st century makeover in the new year.

Last seen on our screens in 1993, the programme was an exciting galactic romp which dominated Thursday nights in the 1980s with ray-guns, big hair and studded leather space suits.

This feature-length episode will be made by US Company Product Lazarus Media (**Jason and the Astronauts, Jelly Farm, Buggins the Bucket Bear**) and will update the story of intergalactic warfare and make it relevant to today, say the show's producers.

'They were the first Spice Girls. Or should I say "Space Girls"', quipped 'Vixens' show-runner Glyn Trelawney (**GSOH, Dog the Wagz**). 'They combined in-your-face sexiness and female liberation years before Girl Power. It's only fitting that they come back and regain their relevance in 2010.'

'It's a dream come true to be working with Glyn,' says PLM's Executive Producer Louise Felcham. 'He brings a real passion to the project. It's a testament to the enduring legacy of the original programme that he is on board.'

Working on the project will be the show's original co-creator, Mervyn Stone. 'It's a great honour to be working with Mervyn,' added Louise. 'His enthusiasm and knowledge about what made the original show work has proved invaluable in bringing the crew of the Starship *Hyperion* into the 21st century.'

Produced by the award-winning team behind **Chavland** and **The Cliff**, this pilot will be an epic, exciting, adventure-packed sci-fi drama certain to appeal to Saturday-night audiences.

Mervyn was sure he had never met this woman Louise, and he was certain that his enthusiasm (none) and knowledge (sketchy at best) hadn't been called upon. If it had been called upon, he might have pointed out that *Vixens from the Void* was not the story of 'the crew of the Starship *Hyperion*'. She just made it sound like *Star Trek*.

He pointed this out to Randall, who waved his hand dismissively. 'Oh, that's just the usual mindless happy-clappy stuff Product Lazarus puts out for media consumption. In the world of the press release, everyone's delighted and everyone's honoured. That's just their way.'

'*Their* way? But aren't you Mr Product Lazarus?'

Randall sipped his coffee. 'I'm the new boy. Just moved from cable station Surefire TV. This is my first project with PLM. My baby! To say this is a departure for PLM is a making a huge understatement. PLM usually just buy up old kid's TV shows with strong nostalgia brand recognition and turn them into modern franchises.'

'Yes, I saw. I looked up their website.'

When Mervyn was approached by Product Lazarus, he Googled them – and found out that they were the ones who had been single-handedly raping his childhood...

He remembered watching *Buggins the Bucket Bear* as a small boy. It was a five-minute programme about a bear that sat on a bucket. Every week, Buggins would walk down to the bottom of the garden with his bucket to water the plants. He'd sit on his bucket as he talked to Shelley the snail, and then walk back again. The End. Buggin's exploits didn't exactly stretch the animators of this, admittedly cheap, cartoon.

He watched the new version of *Buggins the Bucket Bear* on Product Lazarus's website. It was a fast-moving riot of head-straining computer graphics, smeared with colour and noise. Buggins had a baseball cap,

23 new friends, a magic talking bucket, and his own hovercraft.

Randall was delighted that Mervyn had made the effort. 'So you see what PLM do normally! So you get this is a big big thing for them! It's a big thing for me too. So I really am genuinely pleased you could be here, Mr Stone.'

'Please, call me Mervyn.'

'You got it.'

'I'm glad to be here. And I'm really glad that you're glad that I'm here, but to be honest, Randall, I don't really know why I'm here.'

'Hey, you know the score. PLM have bought the rights to *Vixens*, but only you could provide the Styrax. Can't get round that one.'

'Yes, I know that, Randall, but I would have been happy to sign an agreement for the use of the Styrax in a warm comfy office in London and forget all about it. I hardly need to get paid a retainer for my services, though the fee is extremely generous. I haven't actually done anything yet.'

'Well the show's just getting started, Merv. We guys don't want to hang around during the boring planning stuff, like what colour the scripts are going to be, or where we get the cappuccinos from. We're creatives! I only just got here myself.' A thought struck him. 'Hey, if you want to get your sleeves rolled up and your hands dirty, I'm scheduled to attend a tone meeting this pm at Phoenix Wharf. You could tag along; give us the benefit of your years of expertise. Let's face it, no one knows *Vixens from the Void* better than you.'

'You could throw a rock at any sci-fi convention and hit someone who knows *Vixens* better; a theory I've often longed to test out.'

Randall hooted with laughter and slapped Mervyn on the back.

'Then think of yourself as my own personal morale-booster, Merv.'

'Morale-booster? Things not going well, then?'

Randall looked at Mervyn out of the corner of his eye, as if taking him seriously for the first time. 'Hey, you know what? For this stage in the production process, things are going just fine.'

Oh. That badly.

He and Randall drove to Truro in Randall's car (a monstrous customised 4x4 with American style indulgences: Tinted windows, i-pods fixed on the back seats, and incredibly, an 'in-flight' television which sprang out of the dashboard and played pop videos – even when the car was moving) and pulled up at Product Lazarus's offices. PLM had taken over three whole floors of a 'Cornish Business Village' – or that was what the sign on the front said. Like the place Mervyn was staying, here was another 'village', that had no business calling itself a village.

It used to be a local radio station. The last time Mervyn was here, doing some wretched interview to promote something he couldn't recall, it looked like a large grey shoebox that had been dumped by the side of the river. Now it was an incredibly large grey shoebox, some five storeys high, encased in glass and steel. Construction work was in progress, but it looked like it was going slowly; one side of the building was imprisoned in a cage of scaffolding. They went into reception, which still smelled of paint. The cheesy photos of radio DJs were gone and replaced by a collection of logos of advertising companies behind the desk, all slightly different, but all very much the same. They went into the lift and up to a large windowless room, where the tone meeting was taking place.

There was nothing wrong with having tone meetings in Mervyn's opinion; it was a new concept to him, but he wasn't some old curmudgeon primed to grumble about anything that wasn't done in His Day. In His Day, scripts were knocked together by writers who were positively discouraged from having any part in the production process. If a writer was discovered on the premises during production, rabid packs of runners were set upon him, savagely baring the teeth on their crocodile clips. In His Day, Mervyn (as script editor) was the only one designated to translate the writer's wishes to the production team, and the only one designated to explain to the writer (who more often than not, didn't watch television) what the damn show was about. He once took a day off sick and came in the following morning to find visual effects trying to make a 'spiceship'. He explained to them that it was a typo in the script, but he had to bring in the director and the producer to back him up before he could get them to put down the intricately constructed model of a clipper and turn their talents to making a 'spaceship'. The idea that there would be a special meeting of the whole production team to actually talk to each other about how to make the programme appealed to him.

His enthusiasm died when he entered the room, and saw who was sitting at the corner of the table. A middle-aged man, with grey hair perched squarely on his square head, a square jaw hanging above square shoulders. Square wire-framed glasses squatted on his square nose. He looked like a TV director made out of Stickle Bricks.

'You remember Ken Roche?' said Randall.

Ken? Ken *Roche*? An actual director from the crappy old *Vixens* was directing the brand-spanking shiny new, all-singing, all-dancing 21st century *Vixens*?

Randall realised that Mervyn wasn't speaking, and felt he needed to explain. Damn right he needed to explain. 'I'm sure you'll have lots to talk about with Ken. He worked with you didn't he? We thought it was important to have continuity with the classic series. Someone who knew how the show worked.'

Someone who knew how the show worked? Ken Roche? The worst director they ever had? The one whose attitude to special effects was the less special and the less effective the better? The one who had a mental breakdown on set, and took to hiding in the boot of his own car? The one who hated Mervyn's guts just for being the script editor and for pointing out Ken hadn't even properly read the scripts he was directing? The one who rolled around on the floor punching him while the trees around them burned?

Ken Roche?

Randall noticed that Mervyn still wasn't talking. 'You okay, Merv?'

'Can I speak to you outside for a moment, Randall?'

They shuffled outside to the corridor.

'Some kind of problem?' asked Randall.

'Yes Randall, you could say there's some kind of a problem.' Mervyn's voice had dropped down to a whisper. Because the only alternative was going up to a scream. 'That man in there is the biggest disaster ever to strike television. Ken Roche is a one-man broadcasting tsunami.'

'I'm not following.'

'Then let me explain. He was the *Vixens* director who, when advised by special effects that it would be a good idea to use a tiny model for his "exploding spaceship" scene, ignored them and built a full-sized replica of said spaceship on location. He set fire to it. He nearly burnt the OB van, and incinerated half a dozen sheep in the process.'

'You're exaggerating.'

'I wish I was. The last time I saw him was in 1990, on a location shoot in this very part of the world, where he had his hands around my neck and was being pulled off me by an extra dressed as a space gorilla. The production team found it very amusing. Some even joked that wasn't the only monkey on Ken's back during that shoot.'

Randall's face had turned unnaturally pale; even whiter than his unnatural teeth. His smile, which hadn't left his face since Mervyn had met him, stayed fixed, but it was definitely on autopilot. His eyes were full of terror. 'We're sure he's going to be great. We'll keep an eye on him. Hey, just remember. *Doctor Who* used a classic director on the new series, and he worked out superbly.'

Toast. Burnt crumbs.

CHAPTER SEVEN

They returned to the meeting room; Ken was staring at his script on the table very hard, as if trying to levitate it with the power of his mind. He looked up and saw Mervyn. His eyes blazed with a sudden fury. Then he composed himself, and returned to his script.

For the benefit of Mervyn, Randall introduced the other members sitting around the table. They greeted him with polite wariness. Mervyn didn't blame their caution. In His Day, if anyone got introduced to the production team, and no one knew exactly what his or her job entailed, they inevitably spelled trouble. The names went by in a blur; Mervyn hadn't a hope of remembering them all, but tried to squirrel a few of the important ones inside his memory.

There was Nick Dodd, the producer. He had grown the tiniest, most apologetic goatee Mervyn had ever seen, more of a hairy freckle than a beard. His tiny chin tuft, a watery grin, a crew cut and a polo neck jumper pretty much summed Nick up. He seemed a nice chap, but rather bland and shallow. The earring that dangled from his left ear was the brightest thing about him.

The executive producer, Louise Felcham, was also head of Product Lazarus UK (Drama). Mervyn had never met her, but he knew her by reputation. She was the bane of many a programme-maker's life, because once she was appointed, nothing would ever get made. She was television's equivalent of an unguided missile, an executive that bumped around broadcast media like a drowsy wasp, never staying in one job for more than six months, knowing that if she did she might be in serious danger of making a programme, or, more importantly, taking the blame for making one.

Her CV was littered with impressive award-winning shows that she had nothing to do with. They had either been commissioned before she'd arrived in a job, or she'd turned them down but got made anyway after they'd finally got rid of her. Mervyn thought it was extremely brave of her to sit there – a producer of her type associating herself with a television pilot that was actually being produced, with cameras and actors and lights and everything.

Louise's hair was dyed a silvery-white, carelessly marked with a huge pink splodge on the crown. It protruded untidily from a hairband in a fine frizz, matching her mohair jumper in both colour and texture. With her spray of artificially coloured tresses, huge round glasses and pointy nose, she looked like a thing given at a funfair as compensation for not winning the goldfish.

The first assistant director, Bryony, was a jolly little thing who looked about 12 years old. She insisted on being called 'Patch' ('Bryony Patch. Briar Patch. Geddit?'). She was from Newcastle. Her girlfriends back in the North East would probably have been disgusted at her attire as not an inch of bare flesh was on display. She wore a very sensible chunky jumper and jeans to keep out the cold.

Mervyn and Randall had obviously arrived in the middle of a discussion, which Louise was eager to resume.

'Well as I was saying. Is there any way we can we make the pilot a bit more relevant to the modern audience?' she said, idly examining her pencil. Louise had an inability to look directly at any living human being, preferring to stare at props, out of windows or through walls.

'Well, I'm not sure what more Glyn can do,' muttered Nick the producer. 'We've already done a lot to make characters much more empowered; independent females with attitude, and "real lives". They grapple with issues that affect modern women. We've already got one of the main characters wearing a space burqa, and another one's going to be deposed in a mutiny on her ship because she went on maternity leave. It feels pretty relevant to me. What do you suggest?'

'I don't do ideas,' Louise snapped, 'but it still seems a bit too "space" and not enough "now".' She examined the skirting board. 'I'm wondering if we could touch on present-day Earth in a more direct way. I wonder if one of the *Vixens* could be a 21st century girl, plucked from her humdrum life and catapulted into space.'

Nick considered this. 'That would be slightly problematic, as *Vixens from the Void* is set in the distant future and they are actually distant descendants of the human race.'

Louise gave the light fitting above Nick's head a withering stare. 'Exactly Nick, exactly. Which brings me to my second point. We obviously need to add a time travel element to it. Perhaps one of the *Vixens* owns a time machine and goes back in time, tracing her relatives like *Who Do You Think You Are?*, and she meets this young sassy girl and they could have adventures through time, something like that.'

Mervyn felt his soul shrivelling like a decomposing mouse. It was obvious they were saddled with that growing breed of television executive; the type with no imagination, no interest in television, and one single ability – to come up with 'ideas' that would be rip-offs either of films they'd watched recently or of what was successful on television that week. It was only a matter of time before she tried to make it into Harry bloody Potter.

'That sounds a bit like *Doctor Who*,' Mervyn muttered, a little too loudly.

Louise now seemed to be having a conversation with the tea things on the table. 'Well I don't need to point out that *Doctor Who* is very successful, do I? Anyway, I'm not the ideas person. I just think we should push the envelope on this one. Think the unthinkable and take risks. Why not make it a prequel? Maybe the *Vixens* could be learning how to be rulers of the galaxy in some big mysterious school...?'

'Hello, hello, hello!'

A man appeared at the door, grinning so hard the edges of his mouth were touching his ears. His blue eyes stared intensely through tiny silver-framed spectacles. He was tall and lean and had spiky hair which had been flecked with blonde streaks. He wore a hoodie with a picture of a fish on it and khaki canvas trousers that bagged at the ankles. They covered huge wedge-shaped trainers.

In decades past, he might have been mistaken for a downmarket barrow-boy or an upmarket drug dealer, but Mervyn knew this was the quintessential look of the 21st century television writer. Mervyn guessed this was Glyn Trelawney.

'Sorry I'm late, my lovelies, the bridge was down at Bristol and you were all entirely cut off for the morning!'

Well-drilled laughter saluted him. Glyn guffawed at his own joke, then laughed at hearing his own laugh, and then he guffawed again. 'Look at all your lovely shiny faces! Isn't it exciting? Fresh project! Everyone's got that new car smell!' His voice, thick and hearty, sounded weird because it was the only Cornish accent in the room

'Glyn!' said Randall, getting to his feet.

'Randall my lovely!' said Glyn, holding his arms wide.

Randall dived for Glyn and tried to give him a full power hug. Glyn neatly sidestepped the power hug, grabbed Randall's face, and gave him a power kiss on both cheeks. Randall tried to fight back, aiming a power pat at Glyn's shoulder, but Glyn was already moving on to his seat. The power pat became an ineffectual stroke sliding down Glyn's back.

Having established that he was the dominant male, Glyn sat down at the head of the table, cranked open a bulging ring-binder and beamed around the room.

'So what have I missed?'

Nick scrutinised his notes. 'Louise was just suggesting that we have a time machine and a 21st century teenager in the show.'

Glyn barked with amusement. 'Oh what larks! Oh Nick! Louise is pulling your leg, you gorgeous numpty! Of course that's not going to happen. How could it happen when there's the finished script right there under your noggin?'

From the hurt look Louise gave to the water jug on the table, she was most certainly *not* joking and she most certainly did *not* think it was the finished script, but she said nothing. Everyone opened their scripts at the same page and started looking through together. Mervyn took a new one from the table (it was yellow). He'd brought the one they'd sent him in his satchel (it was green) but this one looked nicer and wasn't covered in jam.

It occurred to Mervyn that he might have spent the last few days reading the script rather than watching cop shows. No, that was too dangerous. That might have tricked him into caring. He was too clever for that.

They'd gone barely five pages before Ken threw out a world-weary sigh.

'Something wrong, my lovely?' said Glyn brightly.

'Oh nothing...'

'Fine, on we go.'

'Well it's just... I'm not sure we need this huge dialogue scene while Arkadia and Medula are racing on these space surfboard things,' whinged Ken. 'Couldn't they just say this stuff on the bridge of the spaceship? That's the way we'd have done it on the old series.'

That's the way YOU would have done it on the old series, thought Mervyn sourly. *Some other directors tried to inject pace and interesting camerawork into dialogue scenes. Not Ken 'point and cut' Roche.*

'Perhaps we could cut the scene for reasons of time?' Nick suggested.

'Oh, you tink dat, do ya?'

Mervyn looked around. *Who just spoke?*

'You tink dat?'

That was Glyn!

'Is dat what you tink, Nick? Is dat what you tink?'

Mysteriously, Glyn had suddenly started speaking in a broad Scouse accent.He looked at Nick, eyes cold, all trace of friendly bumptiousness gone.

Obviously that was code for something horrible, because Nick suddenly jumped in like a referee stopping a particularly bloody boxing match. 'I think the guys from Clockworks have some great ideas about how this is going to look and they think they can do something special well within the budget.'

The guys from Clockworks – the company charged with producing the special effects for the pilot – all nodded enthusiastically. The chief guy from Clockworks – the one with the loudest shirt and least hair – turned his laptop around to face everyone, and the production team 'oohed' and 'aahed' as tiny CGI figures slalomed their way through the upper atmosphere of a moon, dodging asteroids and comets. Ken barely paid any attention, afraid to look at the screen in case he caught a computer virus.

Glyn started laughing again, all trace of his sudden transformation gone. Everyone relaxed.

Mervyn was fascinated with the unofficial power structure in the room; quite different to what he was used to. In His Day, the producer was king of all he surveyed; there with an occasional executive producer sitting to one side, chipping in with advice and hints on how angry/pleased the suits were, then below them would come the script editor, then the directors, all the various departments – make-up, props, effects, costumes – and then finally the writer, sulking in his hovel somewhere far, far away.

The power structure here was upside-down. More interestingly, it was quite fluid. The writer was quite definitely at the top holding court, with the director, producer and everyone else in tow. There was no script editor, as far as Mervyn could see. Randall, the executive producer seemed subservient most of the time, but he occasionally came in with something like 'I don't think the suits at Lazarus would wear that,' and everybody stopped talking about whatever they were talking about and moved on. Glyn included. Randall's body language was relaxed; he held the purse-strings, so he chose to pick his fights.

After an hour of pleasantries the meeting broke up, with a reminder that the first cast read-through would be at two that afternoon. Mervyn bent down to put his script in his satchel, and when he straightened up he was nose-to-nose with Glyn Trelawney.

'Mervyn! How lovely that you could join us!' Glyn bellowed, pumping Mervyn's hand energetically. 'A legend in our midst! My goodness, the actual writer of "The Burning Time" and "Expiration Point" is amongst us! Who'd have thought! Inventor of the Styrax and the Gorgs! The man who put words into Medula's delicious mouth! It's fantastic with a side helping of lovely to have you on board.' And then he went off, chuckling and guffawing and joking; slapping backs and rocking on his heels with boisterous laughter.

People poured out of the room after him, leaving Mervyn bemused and alone. Well, not quite alone. There was a young man in the corner, jotting notes in a loose-leaf folder. He was very thin, with long spindly arms and legs, jagged black hair and huge black boots. He looked like he'd been drawn by a five-year old. He looked up and grinned. 'Hi Mervyn. Are you busy?'

Mervyn looked at around at the empty room, and then at the open door through which everyone had disappeared, ignoring him as they went. 'I don't seem to be.'

'Great.' The young man grinned affably. 'Come on, there's a pub down the high street with 50 different types of beer. Let me buy you a lager.'

Mervyn had no idea who the man was, but it wasn't the first time he'd been approached by someone who assumed Mervyn knew him or her; usually a fan that'd met him three times in an autograph queue. In their world, Mervyn now counted as a favourite uncle, to be hugged and patronised.

Still, a drink was a drink.

CHAPTER EIGHT

The pub walls and ceiling were groaning under the weight of lobster pots, fishing nets and bits of boat hanging from the rafters, all tools of 'yer good honest working man'. Mervyn wondered if, in a hundred years, pubs would hang wheelie bins and rusting call-centre headpieces from their timber frames. While the man went to the bar, Mervyn took the opportunity to glance at his folder. Apparently, he was Steve O'Brien and he was a freelance writer for *SFX* magazine. A journalist. That was good to know. He must be on his guard.

Steve returned with surprising speed; carrying two glasses of yellow fizzy nothingness. 'There you go,' he said. 'Authentically fermented in an aluminium vat by American neo-Nazis. None of your home-brewed Cornish rubbish.'

Mervyn looked around nervously at the regulars, some of whom were looking directly at them.

'Don't worry; they won't kill you for criticising their beer. But they might have your eye out for saying Ginsters pasties are better than the home-made ones.' Steve straddled a stool and burst open a bag of crisps.

'So Steve,' said Mervyn casually. 'What's your role in all this?'

'No role as such. Purely observation. I'm writing a diary of the making of the making of the *Vixens from the Void* reboot for SFX, complete with accompanying blog.'

'Sorry, the making of the making? I think you had one too many "making ofs" in that sentence.'

'I'm afraid you heard right. I'm not on Product Lazarus's "preferred publication list". They prefer to talk to the international titles like *Rolling Stone*. So I can't shadow the production team. But I *can* shadow the production team behind the making of the fly-on-the-wall documentaries that will appear on the DVD.'

'I'm sorry.'

'Don't be. I'm learning far more from them than I ever would from the production team proper. My lot hate the proper lot with a hot passion. There's nothing more dispiriting than filming people making proper telly, and most of them are quite bitter about it. Lots of naughty gossip. So how about an interview from you? You know the kind of thing, "The old guy looking at the kids playing with the toys he had when he was young" – that kind of angle would be cool.'

'If you like. I won't say anything very interesting, I'm afraid.'

'I sincerely hope you won't. That would be very bad.' Steve started to roll himself a cigarette. 'It's my job to stay on friendly terms with the production team, keep things sweet so I get regular access to the stars and the filming. Let the fanzines and the internet blub and swear about continuity errors and betrayal of some mythical legacy; it's up to the magazines to report, inform our readership, and, if it turns out to be the worst thing ever made and gets canned, *then* we can say how shite it all was.'

'You don't seem very enthusiastic about the project.'

'Oh no, on the contrary. I really hope it's going to succeed. If it does it'll be like new *Doctor Who* all over again. I'm looking forward to celebrities suddenly remembering they're lifelong fans and getting the names of the characters wrong... Newspaper columnists explaining to us about *Vixens from the Void* and getting all the facts arse about face... New fans enraging the old fans by liking things that they're not supposed to like...' He chuckled to himself. 'Lots of fun in store.'

'Fair enough,' said Mervyn.

Steve was being cheerfully frank, but Mervyn was still wary. He knew all the journalistic tactics; he'd been interviewed many times by the tabloid press when *Vixens* was riding high in the schedules, hoping to squeeze out the latest plot detail from him, or even a detail about an actress's latest squeeze. He remembered one of their favourite tricks was being matey, buying him drinks, being his best friend and throwing him gossip about other shows, other actors, other writers in the hope that he'd join in. It was important to remember at all times that journalist's opinions don't matter; it would be *his* words that would get recorded and printed in the newspapers the following morning.

'So,' said Steve. 'What do you make of Glyn Trelawney?'

Mervyn was instantly cautious. 'Well, he seems very nice. Very positive, very enthusiastic, very jolly. A bit like...'

'Go on...'

'Well, a bit like a Cornish Russell T. Davies, really.'

'Yeah, he is, isn't he? Funny that. Why do you think that is?'

Mervyn had a pretty shrewd idea of why he was like that, but he kept playing the gullible old man. He wasn't going to give this boy any juicy copy for his sci-fi magazine. 'Coincidence?' he suggested.

'Hah! That's right. Coincidence. I met Glyn Trelawney 15 years ago. Back then he was drinking, chain-smoking, and you couldn't find a more acerbic and girl-hungry bastard in television. That's because he was "doing a Dennis Potter". When I met him five years ago he was making speeches about the Iraq war in Parliament Square and turning the air blue at the Hay-on-Wye festival. Why? Because Dennis Potter wasn't fashionable any more and he'd decided it was better to be Harold Pinter. Next year he'll probably put on a wig and be J. K.

Rowling.'

Steve placed his roll-up in his mouth and lit up. Amazingly, no one rushed up to him and told him to extinguish it. They truly were in a different country.

'Here's the thing,' said Steve, exhaling a thin line of grey smoke. 'I've met Russell T. Davies, and that's what he's like. And there's a reason why he's so jolly. He loves telly, and he loves *Doctor Who* with a passion, and working in telly making *Doctor Who* was a dream come true for him. How could you not be happy about it? But Glyn is just copying the surface without understanding what's going on underneath. So you're getting a kind of... well...'

'A crappy parody?'

'Yeah. A crappy parody. He thinks that just copying the mannerisms of successful writers is the way to get on in telly. And do you know what? He's absolutely right.'

Steve exhaled more smoke. 'The only trouble is, he's been doing it for years. And copying them all, well, it seems to have sent him a bit schizo, hasn't it?'

Mervyn remembered the odd Liverpudlian character that Glyn suddenly became in the meeting. It made sense now. It was disturbing to say the least.

They sat in silence.

'Well,' said Mervyn, trying to be positive. 'At least he's like Russell T. Davies in one respect. He's genuinely a fan of the series. That much is obvious.'

Steve guffawed. 'Glyn's not a *Vixens* fan. He barely knows the show.'

Mervyn frowned. 'I think you'll find he is. He mentioned episodes I'd done, one I'd written under an alias, the other I'd allowed another writer to take the credit for. It's only superfans that know that kind of trivial stuff.'

'He's no slouch. He gets Nick Dodd to do his research and put together crib sheets. Do you think he actually carries a script in that big red folder of his?'

'I don't see the point of doing all that.'

'So you never lied to get anywhere in television? Trelawney just pretended he was a big fan of the series to get the gig. People want big celebrity fan geniuses to come in and do the business for them. Like Russell T. Davies and Steven Moffat. They think that's the way it works now.'

Toast. Burnt crumbs.

'I heard him talking a year ago, on the set of *Dog the Wagz*. He said, and I quote verbatim, "They are shitting money into those big fucking space shows, and it's about time they pointed their arses in my direction."'

Mervyn drank his lager, deep in thought.

Steve continued. 'Randall rang up six months ago from the States, and asked if he knew anything about an old show called *Vixens from the Void* because they're going to film it down in the south-west. Nick spent two solid days on Vixipedia and then Glyn came back to Randall with a hearty laugh, a thick Cornish accent, and told him he watched nothing else as a kid.'

'Oh. Okay. So his motives aren't pure. Whose are? But he's done good work. He's won awards.'

'Oh yeah. *Chavland* and *Dog the Wagz* and *GSOH* were all great, but don't you think they got the awards because they were a bit like what had gone before but slightly different? Wasn't *Chavland* just *Shameless* with Brummie accents? *Dog the Wagz* was *Lock, Stock and Two Smoking Barrels* with hot girls. And *GSOH* was Glyn in his Richard Curtis phase, doing *Notting Hill* in a dating agency in Cobham.'

Mervyn could see what Steve was talking about, but didn't like to judge. Success was incredibly difficult to achieve as a writer. 'So what? So what if they were "a bit like something else"?' he muttered. 'So was *Vixens from the Void*. I nicked from everything I could read, watch or find at the bottom of my dustbin. And that's not an exaggeration. My "Sentrassi Plague" episode was directly inspired by an ancient yoghurt that had attached itself to the bottom of my kitchen bin and grown a beard.'

'I'm not judging him, Mr S. I'm just pointing out the facts. Glyn is looking at *Vixens* as his opportunity to do a Russell T. Davies. After all, he's already "done" every other writer in television and film. I'm just setting you straight. He's not some starry-eyed fan whose life mission is to bring *Vixens* back from the dead. He's a cynical bastard with a multiple personality disorder who's going to use you and your creation as a stepping stone to do something else.'

Mervyn raised an eyebrow. 'But you're not judging him.'

'Hey, I've been hanging around TV people for years now. I just gave the man the highest compliment I know.'

'I must say,' mused Mervyn, 'I liked *Dog the Wagz* even though, as you say, it was a bit of a rip-off of Guy Ritchie. I thought the Stepford Wagz were quite professional...'

'I bet you did,' said Steve with a dirty wink. Mervyn didn't like Steve's tone, or the fact he was dead right.

So Mervyn continued. 'Yes, they were quite good, surprisingly good, in a girl-group-who-shouldn't-be-let-anywhere-near-a-film-set kind of way.'

'I'm glad you liked them.' Steve now gave a sly grin 'It's just as well, considering.'

'I thought I read they were giving up music to take-up acting full-time.'

Steve grinned wider. 'Yeah, I heard that too.'

Mervyn grinned back. 'So, what are they doing now?'

'Oh they're doing some more acting. Well, they've just got themselves some leading roles in a major new TV project. Might be a disaster.'

'Oh. Some sepia-tinted Dickens? Or a gritty soap with lots of shouting?'

Steve saw Mervyn's grin, and raised him a smirk. 'Not quite.'

'Oh. Well, good luck to them.'

They sat there, for a while, grinning and sipping their lagers.

'Seriously though,' said Steve, 'what do you think about the Stepford Wagz being the Vixens?'

'Not likely though, is it?'

'Very funny.'

'What?'

'Seriously, what do you think?'

'What?'

'About them being the Vixens?'

'What? They're not!'

'Are you still joking now?'

'What?'

'Because they are, obviously.'

'Are you joking?'

'No.'

'Seriously?'

'You didn't know?'

'No!'

'But you were acting like you did!'

'I was going along with your joke about them being the Vixens!'

'I thought you were joking about not knowing!'

'I thought *you* were joking about knowing.'

Steve looked shocked. 'The announcement went out two days ago. I can't believe you haven't heard.'

'I'm in the middle of bloody nowhere with no internet and a phone that might as well be a tin can with a bit of string attached for all the use it's been. That's why I haven't heard. You're serious? The Stepford Wagz are playing the Vixens?'

'Yes!'

Everyone knew about The Stepford Wagz. They'd reached the semi-finals of *Star-Spangled Ballads*. The show was actually won by a couple of Nice Young Lads And a Guitar, for whom the grannies voted as fast as their arthritic old fingers could press speed-dial, but after two-and-a half-hits they'd vanished from the charts as there was ultimately nothing else to them but being Nice Young Lads. The lads were now presenting children's shows on the Disney Channel. No news on what the guitar was up to.

The Stepford Wagz, on the other hand, had something to them. They were authentic, and a bit on the rough side. They grew up together. They came from Birmingham, Stoke and Nuneaton and made no pretence of disguising their accents. They got into fights over men; they ate kebabs on freezing street corners, their underwear covered slightly more of their bodies than their outerwear. They seemed genetically bred to be a girl band. They were even three identifiable types: the Blonde One, the Dark-haired One and the Ugly One. One wore her bra outside her shirt. One wore a hat. Mervyn remembered a video of theirs. It had young near-naked women fondling each other and gyrating in cages. He couldn't *quite* recall the song, but then, he couldn't *quite* remember any of the plots of the pornographic movies he'd ever watched.

'What? This is going to be dreadful.' Mervyn had given up being cautious.

'Why? You said they were quite good in the film.'

'*Quite* good. They only had about a dozen lines between them.'

'Look,' said Steve. 'At the end of the day, what is *Vixens from the Void*? It's a programme all about hot babes. What's the problem?'

Well what exactly *was* the problem? Mervyn had to think about that. He had to admit, it was a show about young sexy women who wore impractical clothing and stomped around striking aggressive poses. God, you could edit all the Stepford Wagz videos together and make a new *Vixens* episode without all the hassle of roughing it in cider country.

What indeed was his problem? Mervyn thought about it.

'The problem is this,' he said slowly. 'In my long experience of TV productions I have discovered that there are lots of actresses about; a lot of them young attractive ones, with beautiful faces, huge breasts, shapely legs and breathtaking bottoms. They are the reason I got into television. And here's the amazing thing; they not only have fantastic breasts and beautiful faces and breathtaking etc, they can also act. Quite well, most of them. Very well, some of them. These "Wagz" have done one film that was pretty much shot around them while they stood still and didn't bump into the scenery. It's a huge risk. They haven't got a lot of acting experience.'

'There's the videos. They act in them.'

'I know Equity would argue that miming is an art like any other, but moving your lips to a backing track is not what they mean. It's not acting.'

'The blonde one used to be a pole dancer.'

'Well thank you. That puts my mind at rest.'

'Hey, just because they're pop stars doesn't mean they can't act. Billie Piper was a pop star, and she was great in *Doctor Who*. Who would have thought she could act?'

'Oh yes. Billie Piper. The pop star that spent several years acting and getting good reviews for her acting before getting cast in *Doctor Who*. Who would have thought she could act? That was completely the same thing.' Mervyn sighed. 'Toast. Burnt crumbs.'

'What?'

'Nothing.'

Steve noticed a collection of puffer jackets entering the pub. Somewhere inside them was a bunch of cold, miserable people. He swilled down the last of his lager.

'That's the production team of the DVD documentary. Duty calls. Nice to have a drink. And I'm serious about having that interview with you.'

'And I'm seriously thinking about it.'

'Cool.'

Steve swung his scarf around his neck, picked up his folder and was gone.

CHAPTER NINE

Mervyn was left with deep thoughts, clouds of foreboding swirling round him. He knew he was starting to care about the revival of *Vixens*, but he just couldn't stop himself.

Okay, the Stepford Wagz probably wouldn't be a disaster. At worst, they'd merely be competent, and a few fans would grumble about 'stunt casting'. At best, they could be really good. They could really surprise everyone, and be great publicity for the show – just like Billie was for *Doctor Who*.

They were young. They'd be keen. All they needed was a good, skilled, patient director to coax a really excellent performance out of them...

But instead, they had Ken Roche.

Oh God. Ken Roche.

This wasn't the first time Mervyn had been in Cornwall for a *Vixens* shoot. There was the disastrous experience with Ken.

Mervyn had no idea why they had to travel that far down the country just to get footage of some rocks and trees; normally they didn't venture more than five minutes from Shepherd's Bush. Mervyn suspected it was only because the producer at the time, Nicholas Everett, had bought a holiday cottage down there and felt he'd been under-using it.

It was a nightmare. Eight days of terrible weather and equipment failure, with Ken standing in the middle of it, slowly going bananas. Mervyn remembered nearly being crushed by a falling arc light on set, and the bad weather and soggy terrain immersed his car in seven shades of brown filth. His trusty old Fiesta Popular wasn't a happy car in Cornwall; it kept stalling, the windscreen wipers gave up and he crashed it into a tree.

Just when things looked like they couldn't possibly get any worse, Nicholas fell off a boat on the way to a location shoot at Pendennis Castle and caught pneumonia. While Nicholas was laid up in a virtual coma, Ken used the opportunity to run riot, making petty, bloody-minded decisions, ignoring the pleas of costume, make-up, props and cameramen alike.

Ken refused to listen to Mervyn, who was acting producer, and eventually they came to blows on location, punching and hitting each other and rolling around on the ground getting filthy, with the production team looking on in quiet amusement as they placed bets on the outcome. Mervyn sipped his lager, lost in gloomy thoughts.

He was unaware he was being glared at.

By Ken Roche.

CHAPTER TEN

Ken Roche had had the briefest of meetings with his production staff. He had finally worked out what everyone had realised hours ago; the show was going to be made Glyn and Randall's way, with or without him, so he'd plunged into the nearest pub.

While Mervyn sipped his lager, Ken stared at him for a very long time. Then he got up. Mervyn realised that Ken was behind him.

'Hello Ken.'

'Mervyn.'

Ken stayed there, deliberately standing too close. He peered over Mervyn's shoulder. On the table was Mervyn's contract permitting the use of the Styrax. Still yet to be signed.

'Oh I see. That's why you're here. Still eking out a living from your royalties? That must feel so degrading. That must feel like you're fucking a slowly cooling corpse.'

'At least I still have a career.'

'Not from where I'm standing.'

'Yes you are standing Ken, on your own. I can verify that for you. How does it feel? You haven't done it in such a long time.'

Ken actually looked down to check he was standing. *Former drug addicts were so much fun,* thought Mervyn. *So bewildered that they were still alive. So easy to confuse.*

'Fuck you, Has-Been,' Ken said.

'I hear you're sending out your old showreel tapes to every TV station in the world. A word of advice, Ken. Lay off the druggy substances when you post them off. Heads of television drama are not interested in your wedding videos.' Mervyn had actually been in a BBC office talking to a producer when one of Ken's showreel tapes arrived. The producer slipped it into the machine and was mystified to find three old episodes of *Top Gear* followed by one of the Die Hards, leading into pages from CEEFAX – clearly the video had been left running at two in the morning.

'I don't get this,' said the producer, jabbing his remote control. 'You worked with Ken. Surely he didn't direct *Top Gear*?'

'No.'

'Then surely not...?'

'*Die Hard*? Not quite.'

'Should I ring him and tell him? This tape doesn't really tell me what he's done in the last few years.'

'I beg to differ. The tape tells you *exactly* what he's done in the last few years.'

The producer realised what Mervyn meant.

'Oh. That's tragic, when directors like Ken end up as addicts.'

'Not really,' said Mervyn dismissively. 'At least it keeps him away from cameras and editing suites where he can do real damage.' That was cruel by Mervyn's standards, but he had no time left for the man.

Since then, Mervyn had heard stories of producers getting tapes of old westerns, snooker tournaments, wedding footage, even an "Xmas tape" – the first Christmas since Ken's divorce – which showed the director, naked save for a pair of flashing reindeer antlers, guzzling Cointreau from a bottle and pulling a raw turkey to pieces with his bare hands. He'd accidentally sent that one to BBC3, who nearly hired him as an up-and-coming genius, until they found out he was over 35.

'I've been clean for two years, you patronising fuck,' Ken hissed through his teeth. It was the loudest whisper in the world. The roar of conversation in the pub dropped to a dull grumble. Mervyn could see Steve and the DVD production team craning their heads over the bar to see what was happening.

Ken didn't notice – he just focused on Mervyn. 'I'm back in the driving seat of this project, so you'd better be nice to me.'

'Really? From where I'm sitting, you're going to be completely bypassed at every stage. Your only job is to sit in your chair and shout "Action!" Well, not even that. I gather the assistant director shouts "Action!" these days.'

'Just you wait. Just you wait and see. I'll prove who's the boss.'

Mervyn knew he really shouldn't have started this. He'd gone too far, but he couldn't stop. 'Yes,' he said. 'I remember you proving you were the boss the last time we filmed down here. When you set fire to the spaceship and implemented a scorched-earth policy on the Cornish countryside that Czar Alexander the First would have been proud of.'

'You'll never know how much I hated you on that shoot,' Ken said in his too-loud whisper. 'Maybe one day, you'll find out.'

The pub fell completely silent.

'Well look at that,' said Mervyn drily, looking around. 'Well done. It seems like you finally squeezed some drama out of a scene.'

Ken jabbed his finger at Mervyn's face like a rapier. He stopped it millimetres from Mervyn's nose.

'You never knew how lucky you were. But you will. One day. And that day will come soon.'

Then Ken left.

CHAPTER ELEVEN

The read-through commenced in the afternoon. It was the first meeting of all the cast, and there was a lot of excitement, not least among the runners and other young members of the production team who were profoundly impressed that the Stepford Wagz were honouring them with their presence.

Ken had resumed his place at the table, flipping impatiently through his script and making notes. He didn't look up when Mervyn entered.

It was a full 20 minutes before the Wagz arrived.

As any star knows, it is important to generate a memorable performance wherever they go – but it's left up to them as to whether that performance is a positive or a negative one. Thankfully, the Wagz were young and still excited about the business, so they were definitely into being positive. They came in like a beautifully choreographed firework display, making delighted squeals, subsiding, and then exploding in other parts of the room, throwing their arms around people they'd worked with or just each other. There was a lot of noise and colour before everything died down and they finally settled into their places round the table.

Then the read-through finally started, slowly and stiltedly. It didn't sound good. More importantly, it didn't sound like *Vixens from the Void*. Mervyn tried to pinpoint why. Perhaps it was the Vixens? He was used to hearing clipped BBC English barking across the table, not Brummie vowels sliding around the room.

No, that wasn't it. There were different accents in the old series. Suzy Lu's voice had been so incomprehensible they toyed with the idea of making her from a different planet and giving her subtitles. And as for Jenny McLaird's Scottish brogue...

But that wasn't it either. It was the script. It was the first 15 pages of the script. It puzzled him when he flicked though it in his room, and his confusion was reinforced when he heard it read out loud. There were scenes where the Vixens were arguing with men who'd treated them badly. Lots of scenes. Lots of shouting matches. Lots of plotlines about boyfriends betraying the Vixens in a variety of ways. Mervyn didn't like to make a fuss; but he was being paid to be a 'Programme Consultant', and he was determined to do something for his money somehow.

When there was a natural break at the end of a scene, Mervyn spoke. 'I'm a bit confused by all these scenes with all these boyfriends.' His voice sounded strange in the room, and he realised that he'd stayed silent for so long, he'd forgotten what he sounded like. 'They're all very dramatic and well written and all, but what have they got to do with *Vixens from the Void*? The arguments seem a bit pointless to me.'

Louise leaned forward, addressing Mervyn's shoulder. 'Well this is – we hope – just the first episode of many. And we fully expect a full series. So we think it's important in dramatic terms to explain to the audience what motivates the girls. I mean, just why do they hate men? That's what the viewers will want to know.'

'But they don't hate men. The Vixens just treat men like second-class citizens because that's their culture. That's been their religion for hundreds of years.'

Louise found a ring on the third finger of her left hand extremely fascinating. 'Oh yes, but we found that a bit dodgy. The whole "scripture tells us to treat the other gender as second class" stuff sounds like we're taking a pop at the Muslims, and that's a real no-no.'

'The whole religious angle is out, Merv,' added Randall apologetically. 'Too risky for our blood. Product Lazarus don't want networks dropping the show, or demonstrations outside Walmart just before Christmas hots up.'

Louise continued. 'It's far more satisfying in dramatic terms for their characters if they are all mistreated by bastard men, and come together to take their revenge on all of mankind. Like in that film.'

'I see.' Mervyn felt that the first third of the pilot was degenerating into EastEnders in space, but he didn't press the point. It wasn't his project. And anyway, who was he to judge? His pitch for the original series floated back to him across the years. 'Just imagine *Dynasty* meets *Dallas*... In space!'

They had a ten-minute fag break, and Nick, Louise and Randall rushed up to the roof of the building to brave the cold and pollute the clear, Cornish air with smoke. Other members of the production team chose this moment to dash in and out of a trendy Cornish coffee shop outside, which had enterprisingly sprung up within days of the announcement that a major television show was going to be filmed in the area. The Oo-ar Bar was already doing great business, with its interesting mix of traditional Cornish fare and metropolitan cool. The clotted creamoccinos were proving very popular, as were the pastinis, a strange hybrid of pasty and panini.

Mervyn had already drunk stupid amounts of coffee courtesy of the filter machine in the corner, so he didn't feel like dashing with them; he went to search for the loo. He went along the corridor, and pressed for a lift.

And there was Glyn Trelawney, waiting beside him.

Mervyn felt uncomfortable, and it wasn't just his complaining bladder. He pulled some conversation out of his throat. 'Just looking for the toilet.'

Glyn chuckled. 'Ah, the call of the widdle! Comes to us all! Just up two floors.'

'Oh. Maybe I should take the stairs. Get some exercise.'

The lift doors opened.

'It's here now.'

They got inside. The doors closed.

'Up, up and away!' chortled Glyn.

Mervyn felt obliged to say something. 'I'm sorry I stuck my oar in there. It just seemed odd to me.'

Glyn beamed voraciously. He couldn't have looked more delighted if Mervyn had offered to marry his daughter. 'Haha! Not a bit of it, my lovely. I'm delighted with your input. And that's what script meetings are for, Mervyn. To find out what's wrong with the script and change it.' Glyn had seemingly forgotten his view about 'the finished script being right under his noggin'.

'Okay. Fair enough.'

'No, don't give it another thought. I'm perfectly all right with it.' The lift doors pinged open, and he tootled off down the corridor, whistling cheerfully.

The lift doors closed. The lift moved, stopped, and the doors pinged open again.

And Glyn was standing there. He'd walked up one floor and waited for the lift.

He got back in.

It was curious. Glyn was standing differently; legs apart, his head down, his eyes hooded and malevolent. He looked like a completely different person. They stood there in awkward silence as the lift continued.

'You dinnae want tae cross me, old man,' Glyn growled at last. His voice was now immersed in a thick Glaswegian accent, all trace of jolly Cornish gone. 'They all tried to tell me how tae write ma scripts, an' they've all been verra sorry they did, every one o'them. Okay boy?'

Glyn's new voice was familiar, and Mervyn recognised it with a shock. It was the voice of another television writer, James Robert Ogilvy. Jamie was big a few years ago, seemingly managing to write half of Channel 4's drama output single-handed. He was incredibly talented, but had a huge temper. He'd actually gone to prison for taking his car and running over (and seriously injuring) a producer who'd incurred his wrath by rewriting one of his scenes without his knowledge.

The lift pinged open again.

Glyn straightened up and beamed, looking his cheery self once more.

'See you downstairs, my lovely.' The Cornish accent was back, too. He left the lift without a backward glance, whistling cheerfully.

Mervyn was stunned. He'd just been threatened, like he was a minor member of the mob who'd stepped out of line. He'd just been threatened by some bighead writer who was so insecure he needed to adopt other people's personalities to work, interact and bully to get his own way.

He was slightly scared, but he was angry too. He wasn't taking that. He wasn't some court flunky, looking for patronage. *It's fine to threaten some 25 year old who's desperate for his first job in television, but you're messing with a man with nothing to lose.*

If it's a war you want, Glyn Trelawney, or whoever you are, you've got one.

CHAPTER TWELVE

Mervyn tried out his new rebellious streak. He deliberately took 15 minutes to get back after the ten-minute fag break. He was slightly disappointed and slightly relieved to find that everyone was still talking and no one noticed. They were munching on pastinis and drinking their cider smoothies.

Nick came in just after Mervyn. 'Sorry,' he mumbled. 'Always need that extra fag or I just can't function'.

Glyn was still yet to reappear, having decided to be even more rebellious than Mervyn. The Wagz had all returned and were excitedly swapping stories of cars and pop stars they'd test-ridden, holidays and film stars they'd had. There was also a smiley bald man at the end of the table who hadn't been there before. Mervyn thought he was another runner until he got a large machine out and switched it on.

'Um... Hi everyone,' said Nick, calling the meeting to order and indicating the bald man. 'This man here is Nick. Nick Briggs. No relation...' A polite, if bemused titter came from one of the Wagz. 'He's a great voice man. He does the Daleks AND the Cybermen for the new *Doctor Who.*' There was an impressed 'oooh' from around the table. 'And he's doing the new voices for the Styrax for us.'

Nick Briggs used the machine to greet everyone in his Styrax voice. There was laughter, and a scattering of applause.

'Ooh, smashing, I'd love to have a go,' said Louise.

Nick Briggs hugged the machine close to him. 'It takes hours to calibrate the machine to my voice. It won't work for anyone else.' Mervyn suspected Nick was lying.

'What happened to Arthur Stokes? Didn't he do the Styrax voices?' Mervyn noticed Nick's anguished face, and added hurriedly, 'Not that what you're doing isn't absolutely splendid, Nick, well done. They sound like the Styrax right enough.'

Nick glowed with pleasure. It was plain that praise from the creator of the Styrax meant a lot to him.

'Arthur Stokes was unavailable,' said Nick the producer.

'Oh really? Hope he's okay. I would have loved to meet him again. Arthur was a right old character, grumpy as hell, but always a twinkle in his eye,' drawled Mervyn, extremely aware he was talking like an old fart, and probably boring everyone present; but after his encounter with Glyn he didn't really care. 'He was always hiding inside the studios with Smurf and having a crafty fag. Whenever we saw smoke pouring out of a Styrax we'd say the Styrax was giving off "Stokes signals".'

There were polite but indifferent chuckles from round the table. Obviously Mervyn wasn't important enough to be humoured, but he didn't care. He droned on. 'He used to write all his lines on the back of his cigarette packets. Just to make a point. I wonder what he's doing now?'

'He's in hospital,' said Nick Briggs apologetically. 'He's just had a tracheotomy.'

Oh God, thought Mervyn. *Sorry I spoke.*

Nick continued. 'I did go and see him, and he was very keen to continue. He pointed out that he sounds much more like the Styrax than he ever did and he can do the voices without the machine now... But I'm afraid his doctor won't allow it.'

Glyn exploded back into the room, puncturing the awkward silence and throwing mad cackles in all directions. 'Sorry I'm late, my lovelies,' he leered. 'Had a bit of an altercation with the lady at the front desk. Just one more pointless argument...'

He winked at Mervyn, and then screamed with deranged laughter.

Everyone else laughed. Mervyn didn't.

Something was wrong with Glyn. It was obvious. Something had happened to his voice and his manner. Like an old tape cassette that had worn down with age, his cheeriness had distorted into a ghoulish hysteria.

He was no longer a Cornish Russell T. Davies. He was like every actor who had ever played the Joker in *Batman*, taking it in turns to say a line each.

No one mentioned it, of course. Everyone around the table just eyed him warily as he slumped into a chair and hurled his feet on the table, still tittering, wiping tears from his eyes.

The read-through continued. Thankfully, the endless argument scenes had given way to some actual action. The Vixens were now aboard the spaceship *Hyperion*.

'We're completely surrounded by Styrax warships,' read the dark-haired one.

'Tell me something I don't know, Medula,' read the blonde one.

'Okay; I've been having an affair with three of your slaves behind your back.'

There was a polite titter from a few people.

'I said – tell me something I don't know...!'

More titters.

The ugly one piped up with her line. 'That reminds me. I haven't got my copies yet. I ordered three vid-grams of Medula with the two big guys.'

More titters.

'They're coming as fast as they can.'

'So I keep hearing. But I haven't seen the footage yet.'

A big bubble of laughter. The tension was ebbing away from the room.

Mervyn smiled; he thought it was okay. It was slightly saucier than he would have written, perhaps, but still recognisable *Vixens* badinage; still within the boundaries of the show, and a good introduction to the girls' characters.

As the scene continued, Mervyn thought the dark-haired one was definitely the best. She had real potential, she could actually act it straight off the page and sold the jokes well. The ugly one might have been good, but she had so few lines it was difficult to tell. The blonde one needed a lot of work.

On to scene 11, interior, Styrax warship. Now it was Nick's turn. He was ready, eyes clamped to the script, his mouth brushing the microphone. He had a hand on his controls, ready to become Styrax Sentinel #1.

'SENSORS INDICATE THERE ARE PEDESTRIANS STILL ABOARD THE SHIP.'

He lowered his voice slightly, as he became Styrax Sentinel #2.

'THAT IS NOT POSSIBLE. THEY SHOULD HAVE BEEN IMMOBILISED BY THE CLAMPING DRONES.'

Then he raised his voice again. Back to Sentinel #1. Mervyn was impressed. Nick had obviously been practising.

'SEND OUT ALL SENTINELS. FIND ALL PEDESTRIANS ABOARD THE SHIP AND CLAMP THEM.' Nick paused, confused, and peered at the script. 'HYOK, HYOK, HYOK.'

'Wait, wait, wait!' screamed Glyn, hands waving in the air. 'What the hell are you doing? It's not "hyok, hyok, hyok".'

Nick looked scared. He was obviously keen not to disappoint. 'It's written down on my script. "Hyok, hyok, hyok".'

'I know it is, love you, and bless your literal little mind, but "hyok, hyok, hyok" – that's just comic-book speak for laughter. Try an insane giggle like this.'

Glyn cackled madly, throwing his head back and howling into the air.

Nick tried to copy him. 'Hur, hu-hu-hu-hur.'

'Hmm... not really.'

'Heh-hehehehehe?'

'Hurrah! That's marvellous with a side order of fantastic, but you need to work on it a bit more, my lovely. Make it more mad. Much more mad. I've got some Daffy Duck cartoons in my room, I think you should watch some after the –'

'I have a question,' said Mervyn.

Heads turned.

The meeting went into spasm.

Glyn suddenly became very soft and plummy. It could have been Stephen Fry, Noel Coward, or a voice-over for a sponge cake advert. It was anybody's guess.

'Oh, Mervyn, how lovely to feel your genius presence. We haven't had a chance to do lunch yet, have we? I know somewhere in Helston where the fish is to die for.'

Mervyn was unnerved, but he was not to be deflected. He didn't fire the first shot, but this was definitely war. 'I have a question. What's "hyok hyok hyok" when it's at home?'

'Laughter, Mervyn,' said the new plummy Glyn. 'The Styrax are having a jolly good giggle at the prospect of wiping out the delegation of Vixens.'

'But the Styrax are robots. They don't giggle.'

Glyn chuckled. The Joker was back. 'Mervyn, Mervyn, Mervyn. Wouldn't it be great if they did? Just imagine. How sinister would it be if you had a giggling monster?'

Mervyn looked at Glyn. Chuckling, laughing, giggling Glyn.

'Well yes, I agree – having an evil monster that giggled would be terrifying. In fact,' he said, staring pointedly into Trelawney's eyes, 'I can picture it right now. But it doesn't alter the fact that they're robots. Why not just invent a new monster that can giggle? That would be easier all round, wouldn't it?'

There was an awkward silence. Ken was glaring at him. Nick the producer was glaring at him. Glyn was glaring at him, arms folded. Louise was glaring at his right ear. Of the senior members of the production team, the only person who wasn't microwaving Mervyn with his eyes was Randall. In fact, Randall looked almost amused, hiding a tiny smile with the back of his hand.

The supporting actors looked scared. The Wagz looked confused. They sensed there was something going on that they weren't aware of. Being clever girls in the music industry, they kept quiet and let everyone else sort themselves out.

'Wouldn't it?' said Mervyn. 'Be easier I mean. Create a new giggly monster.'

Nick the producer snatched a look at his watch and leaned forward. 'Can I just interject here, for reasons of time? Mervyn, you've signed a licensing agreement. We can do what we like with the Styrax and you really can't make any objections.'

'I haven't signed anything,' said Mervyn.

'What do you mean, you haven't signed?'

'I'm very disorganised with my paperwork. Takes me weeks to get through it all. I should be better at it, but it just sits on my desk, unopened. People are always assuming I've signed things when I haven't, but then they're even more disorganised than me.'

A one-ton silence crashed onto the table. Everyone had joined Louise in looking at the fixtures and fittings of the room.

'Gosh, you know what?' beamed Glyn. 'Mervyn, you're exactly right, my lovely! Of course you are! After all, that's why you're here, and we're all extremely grateful for your sage counsel! Of course they shouldn't giggle, what an idea! You must forgive me, Mervyn, what was I thinking?' He started scribbling chunks of the scripts out with his marker pen. 'Robots don't giggle! Why didn't you point that out to me Nick?'

Nick looked defensive. 'Well, I did suggest we cut all the giggling for reasons of time...'

'Yes, but they're robots, Nick, my lovely. Why would they giggle?'

The read-through finally finished, and there was a small ripple of appreciative applause from everyone round the table. Mervyn knew that there was always an element of that after a first read-through; mostly it was due to relief that the script held together and made some sort of vague sense rather than any genuine enthusiasm, but he had to admit that Glyn's script was a fun piece of work; a bit glib, a bit facile in places, but a witty, exciting undemanding 90 minutes of prime-time melodrama.

So at least Glyn could write, despite his 'eccentricities'. Perhaps it was worth indulging him, even with his obvious mental problems? Perhaps he should talk to Randall about the threat in the lift.

Maybe. He would think about it later. Right now there were more pressing problems on his mind. There was just too much coffee available in these read-throughs. Mervyn had over-indulged and his bladder had mutinied. He needed to go again – fast.

He bounded up the flights of steps and back into the toilet. He was in the process of closing the cubicle door when the outer door banged open.

'What the fuck is that old toot doing on my show?'

That was Glyn Trelawney's voice. The affected Cornish accent was gone again and he was channelling the usual Estuary English whine of TV people everywhere.

'Mervyn Stone. Who the fuck is he to tell me my characters can't giggle? What is he doing round my table? Why is a fat old nobody telling me what to do on my show?'

Mervyn desperately wanted to hear the rest of the conversation. If he locked the cubicle door, they'd notice that someone was in here with them and might stop talking. He stood on the toilet, quietly pushing the cubicle door to a 45-degree angle. He hoped it looked as though no one was in the cubicle.

'Randall insisted on having him on the show, Glyn,' said Nick Dodd.

'"Randall insisted, Randall insisted." That's all I hear from you these days. "Randall insisted"!'

'I'm sorry Glyn, I'm really sorry. I can't do anything about it.'

'No. I suppose you can't. You are only the producer, after all.'

'I'm sorry.'

'Forget about it.'

'But I can't. I just feel like I'm letting you down.' Nick sounded like he was on the verge of tears.

'Hey, hey. Nick. Nick, Nick, Nick. Just listen. Listen. Listen to me, my lovely.' Glyn's voice had quietened, returning to Cornish. His tone became soft, reassuring.

Mervyn pressed his eye up to the edge of the door, and could just see them by the sinks. Glyn held Nick's face in his hands, pushing his cheeks together and forcing him to look in his eyes. 'You're not letting me down. Don't ever think that. I owe everything to you, don't I?'

Nick nodded dumbly.

'If it wasn't for you I'd be in jail right now, wouldn't I my lovely? I'd be the reluctant girlfriend of an eight-foot-tall con called Bubba. Okay?'

'Okay.'

'I'd be eating fried chicken for my last meal, on my way to getting my roots done with a five-million-volt hairdryer. So I owe you big time? All right, my lovely?'

'Okay.'

Glyn kissed Nick full on the lips very hard, and released him. Nick wiped his nose with the back of his hand. Glyn pulled out a paper towel from a dispenser and gave to him.

'Thanks.'

'Thank God for paper towels, eh? Imagine trying to dry your tears under a hand-dryer.'

'Thanks. I'm better now. I'm fine. I'll be right outside. Thanks. Sorry.'

Nick backed out of the toilet, mumbling and wiping his eyes.

Mervyn moved to a slightly better position to see more clearly and nearly slipped off the toilet. He put his hand out to steady himself and let go of the door, which swung gently closed. Mervyn instinctively put his hand in between the door and the catch to muffle an inevitable clunk, but in doing so his fingers were visible from outside the cubicle.

Glyn didn't notice the door move or Mervyn's fingers appear. He gave a sigh that spoke of infinite weariness and leaned on a sink for support. He looked in the mirror above the sinks, then his eyes focused on the sign just below his nose.

'"Now wash your hands",' he muttered, reading the sign. 'I couldn't have put it better myself.'

CHAPTER THIRTEEN

>CLICK<

[SIGH]

Oh God.

I knew it.

I just knew it.

As if being stuck in Dreary in the county of Fuckall isn't enough.

Today was so full of shit.

Today I was fed a sewage sandwich, followed by turd on toast, washed down with a manure margarita. Today, I was dipped in a sty full of pigshit and while I was lying there in the shit, the biggest, stupidest shittiest pig just shat all over my head.

I mean, what the hell is he doing here? What's the point of him? I knew he would shove his piggy nose in my face. I knew he was going to challenge me.

It's no good. I'm going to have to kill him. I've decided. I'm going to kill him, I'm going to make him squeal like the piggy he is and then I'm going to shove his Styrax up his fat pig arsehole.

But first, I'm going to have a practice.

Call it a rehearsal.

I'm going to kill someone, just to see if I can. Just to see what if feels like.

And I'm going to do it tonight.

And if I like it?

Mervyn fucking shitting arsing Stone will be next.

CHAPTER FOURTEEN

'All I said was "Styrax don't giggle." They just don't.'

The long day was over, and everyone had vanished into their rented cottages, hired flats and hotel rooms. Mervyn couldn't help but notice that the 'big names' all had rooms in Truro. His room was ten miles away. He was stranded again. And this time it was getting dark.

He had to wait around for Randall to give him a lift back to Falmouth and Randall insisted on taking Mervyn direct to the Black Prince, which was a great relief. But before they left, he also insisted on buying Mervyn dinner. Mervyn was quite tired and keen to get to bed (he was also keen to get back to see if he could bump into Maggie in the bar, but he'd been in there two nights running, and she seemed elusive in the evenings), but he was a writer. He never turned down free food.

So here they were, in the Falmouth Bay Seafood Café, talking about the day's events. Mervyn wrenched a claw off his lobster.

'I mean it's not a radical comment to make, is it? They've never giggled before. Not unless they've had some personality transplant since 1993. I once owned a car that seemed to snigger behind my back when it coughed and died on the sides of busy motorways, but it never actually laughed in my face.'

Randall gave a greasy laugh. He had already disembowelled his lobster and was starting on the smaller shellfish that decorated the edge of his plate.

'Watch your lovely tie, Randall,' added Mervyn, 'I wouldn't like to see it get stained.'

Randall gave a thumbs-up and tucked his napkin more securely round his throat.

Mervyn carried on justifying himself. 'It's hardly a radical thing to say in a *Vixens from the Void* meeting. In my considerable experience as creator and writer of the classic show, I've never heard a Styrax giggle.'

'Hey, you get no argument from me, Merv. I watched the show, remember?'

'Which is more than what Glyn Trelawney ever did.'

'Sorry?'

'Just something someone told me. Sorry to be the bearer of bad tidings, but I've been told that Glyn never even watched *Vixens from the Void*. He's just pretending to be a fan to get the job.'

Randall didn't seem bothered. He wrenched a mussel apart and then shrugged, one half of shell in each hand.

'Yeah, well I kinda knew that.'

'Oh. Did you?'

'Yeah; well, I suspected. These are the games we play in television. You have an interview at a studio to script-doctor an Adam Sandler movie and suddenly you're his greatest ever fan ever, and you think he's better than Monty Python, the Marx Brothers and Laurel and Hardy put together. And it is your life's ambition, no, your life's dream, the very pinnacle of your career to rewrite one of his fart gags.'

'I wish I could do that. Lie, I mean, not rewrite fart gags. I probably would have got on a lot better.'

'Hey, you do all right. You're sitting in the middle of a large-scale TV production with big money behind it, and it's all a testament to your genius.'

I'm actually sitting in a restaurant, because the production team won't get me a car to send me back to my very cheap bed and breakfast which is stuck in the middle of nowhere, thought Mervyn.

'I don't understand what Glyn's doing,' Mervyn changed the subject. 'It would solve all his problems if he just created a new monster of his own. I could jot one down on this napkin here and I'd have something horrible with laser eyes by the time the dessert menus come round. He must like the Styrax an awful lot.'

Randall grinned. 'Glyn hates the Styrax. He doesn't want to use them at all. He wants to create his own new monster. Get all that lovely merchandise money in his wallet.'

Mervyn looked surprised. 'So why are they in the script?'

'Because my people wanted them there. That's one of the conditions for the cash we're giving to the project. The Styrax are the one thing about the series that Glyn can't get rid of. I insisted they be in the pilot, and the suits agree with me. Every one! I've convinced them all that the Styrax are essential to the success of the new *Vixens from the Void.*' Randall grinned. 'He plays games with me, I play games with him. That's television.' He waved a fork at Mervyn. 'You know, you are doing exactly the right thing by digging your heels in over the giggling, Mervy.'

'Well I wasn't really. I was just pointing out...'

'*You* are protecting your creation, Merv. I'm sure you guessed this, but what Glyn is trying to do with the whole giggling thing is to make the Styrax his property. He's trying to change them just enough so after the success of the new *Vixens from the Void* he can turn around and say "Guys, look, the only reason they're so popular with kids is the fact they giggle. I want to share copyright with Mervyn Stone on every giggling Styrax in the shops. Cos if a Styrax toy comes out and they don't giggle, then little Johnny is going to be throwing his toys at the wall, saying 'Where's my giggling Styrax?' So therefore I have to co-own them or they stay mute. QED." That's what he's trying to do, and you're doing the right thing by stopping him. Well done that guy.'

'Thanks,' said Mervyn, in a very small voice.

They climbed into Randall's huge car and set off into the countryside. The journey played out in front of Mervyn like a horror movie projected onto the windscreen. The roads were murky and the spindly trees rushed past in terrifying blackness.

'Randall, I agree that the Styrax are fun, but they're hardly essential. You've created a world of trouble for yourself by insisting on them. Your writer and show-runner hates them. He obviously hates me, because he threatened me today.'

'He threatened you?'

'Yes.'

'Aw, he probably just got a bit tense. It is the first read-through, after all.'

'But... Glyn does seem to have 'problems' with his behaviour, to say the least. There's no telling what he might do.'

'You mean the voice thing? He's like a lot of actors I know, no character of their own, so they take on different personalities to give them leverage. It's not uncommon, Merv. Glyn might have his... eccentricities, but he won't do anything stupid. He's hungry for mainstream television success. He's desperate to find a show that pours money into his pocket and keeps on pouring.'

'I hope you're right.'

'I reckon I'm a pretty good judge. And if he does do anything stupid, I'll be ready.'

'I still don't understand why the Styrax are so essential. They weren't even introduced in the original until season two.'

Was it Mervyn's imagination, or was the car speeding up? Surely not...

Yes it was. Randall was gripping the wheel with intensity, his eyes fixed murderously on the road.

'I have my reasons, Merv,' he said, barely opening his mouth. He said nothing more, and the car slowed again.

Mervyn was deposited outside the tavern and he watched Randall's car turn round in a wide circle. The headlights hit him, plastering his shadow on the wall of the tavern. His night-accustomed eyes were bathed in the glare – there was so much light in his face it was painful

– and he had a sudden flashback to the arc light that almost fell on him, back on the other Cornish *Vixens* shoot.

Another time; another life.

Then the 4x4 left the driveway and left him in darkness. It sped into the night. Tiny red lights stared at him like the eyes of demons before disappearing into the trees.

CHAPTER FIFTEEN

>CLICK<

[SIGH]

Oh shitting bollocks.

[PANT]

I did it. I just killed someone.

[PANT]

I'm sure of it.

The day had not gone well. Fucking Mervyn was laughing at me. They all were laughing at me. Even fucking Nick.

[SIGH]

He was smiling. That fucking pussy was smiling at me. Me!

You useless fucking pansy. I'll show him. I'll show everyone.

I drove back last night; in the dark, as usual. The dark is very relaxing. I keep the lights off in my room because the bulb hurts my eyes. I'm starting to like the dark.

I was driving back. The trees were glowing in the lights. They were coming at me out of the darkness, pointing at me and laughing. Just like everyone. It's not just them. I know when we start filming, those fucking Styrax will start laughing at me too.

There she was, trudging along the side of the road with her little dog. Silly cow. I wouldn't be out on a night like this if they paid me. Stupid thing to say. They do pay me, and I do go out on nights like this. I am the whore of television.

I didn't know what I was doing. Okay, I DID know what I was doing. I knew damn well what I was doing. I was doing my rehearsal for murdering Mervyn shitting Stone.

I just moved the wheel to the left, just a little, that's all it took. Just slightly to the left. I caught her with the side of my car; she spun around with her arms in the air, just like a ballerina in a music box. Flew over my bonnet waving her umbrella. It was like watching the death of Mary Poppins. I just carried on, on into the dark. It wasn't real. It wasn't real. It hadn't happened. If I couldn't see it, it never happened. Oh yeah, it's in my mind's eye. I can see her body mashed against the hedges; I can imagine the little dog sniffing her body, barking for help.

But I didn't see it, so it didn't happen.

I drove 20 miles to find an all-night car wash. Had to get the marks off the bumper. Then I went back to my room. I lay in the darkness, listening to the gurgling pipes in the bathroom. The ticking of the clock on the wall.

I realised that yes, it had happened. I had done it. I had done it. The rehearsal was over.

I liked it.

Time for Mervyn fucking Stone.

CHAPTER SIXTEEN

It was Oh My God in the morning, and Mervyn was in a taxi heading to an out-of-town supermarket somewhere near Helston.

He wasn't in the best of moods. First, he had run out of underpants. If only he had thought to pack more than three pairs. If only he had gone back to Marks & Spencer. If only he had nipped out to the shops during the read-through in Truro; but he'd been too busy lurking about in toilets. So he had been re-using old pairs, selecting them by sense of smell, least pungent first. But now he was wearing his emergency pair, which were big and baggy and looked like they'd been used for washing a car.

Second, he knew he was going to have a long boring day kicking his heels and doing nothing and the early start meant he'd missed his regular breakfast assignation with Maggie. But he couldn't cry off. He'd done nothing for his employer but piss off the writer (and he knew how pissed off writers can get), so he felt he needed to show up and look busy. He'd even punched holes in his script and put it in a binder.

He listened drowsily to the driver's low rumbling voice. It made a nice change from listening to London drivers moaning about immigrants coming from the wrong parts of Europe. Now he could listen to Cornish drivers moaning about immigrants coming from the wrong parts of England. Thankfully, Mervyn soon saw familiar luminous signs with 'LOC' printed on them, which indicated that they were getting near to the location shoot. The taxi pulled up and let him out and Mervyn found himself in a car park. A cold supermarket car park in the middle of nowhere. Thankfully there was a location bus parked nearby, with extras and crew tucking into huge breakfasts from the nearby catering van. Mervyn remembered how he used to spend a few weeks a year on location and he'd always put on about half a stone. You could always identify the hardened guys who spent their lives on the road; they waddled around like the missing link between ape and hippo.

Mervyn went on to the location bus with a coffee and a bacon butty.

'Hi Mervyn,' said everyone.

'Hi everyone,' said Mervyn.

The guys who shifted stuff and plugged stuff in were always friendly to the writers; they shared a camaraderie with the underdog. He would have talked to them in a suitably matey fashion, but that would have involved knowing their names. He sat down near the male runner and the female runner. He didn't know their names either, but at least they were young and unimportant.

In among the shaggy beasts of the location crew there were even hairier creatures – a few Gorgs at the back sipping coffee and doing sudokus trying to amuse themselves as best they could, which was difficult as they'd been in make-up for about four hours so far.

Gorgs were the subservient creatures that did the Styrax's menial tasks for them, which conveniently included picking things off the floor, operating controls, opening doors and walking across terrain that wasn't perfectly flat. Anything that a large lump of fibreglass on wheels couldn't do. Which was everything.

Mervyn hurriedly created the Gorgs after watching the Styrax flounder around on their first day on location. The Gorg's back-story was simple and neat. They were the race that built the Styrax, their original drivers. But after centuries of being dominated by their own machines they'd regressed into primitive grunting creatures. He'd got the idea after he'd needed the guttering fixed on his house and two lumbering apes in overalls turned up driving a rusty old van with the *Daily Star* on the dashboard.

In the original series, the Gorgs were little more than guys in ape costumes. The current production team had decided to update them so they looked like proper aliens – let the fans sort out why they appeared so different. Mervyn approved of the redesign. The new Gorg looked rather impressive. It was now a huge beast with a tiny trunk-like nose, like a tapir. The trunk nose had horns sprouting from it, leading all the way up its head and stretching down to its armoured neck. It looked like the product of an orgy between an elephant, a bear and a rhinoceros.

He couldn't see any senior members of the production team about outside. Wait – there was Glyn, walking across the car park with a satchel. He bounded up the steps of the bus and shouted down the aisle. 'Hello, hello, hello! Isn't this brilliant with an extra dose of terrifying, my lovelies? It's my first day, so I've got my new school bag and scrumptious apples for all the teachers.' He went up and down the bus, handing out bright red apples and goodie bags. Some smiled at the gesture, others tried to ignore him. 'Bye bye all! See you at assembly my lovelies!' Glyn gave a cheery wave, left, walked past the window and into a large green trailer.

'Who's in there?' Mervyn asked the runners.

'Glyn,' said the male runner. 'That's his trailer.'

He had a trailer! The *writer* had a trailer! Mervyn had definitely been born 20 years too soon.

Just as Glyn shut the door of the trailer, Nick appeared from nowhere as if he was lurking in the vicinity. He followed Glyn inside. No more than 15 seconds later, Glyn left again. His demeanour had completely changed. He looked tired and exasperated.

Nick appeared at the door and followed him out. Then Glyn appeared again. He'd just walked around the trailer and returned to the door. He went inside. Nick went up to the door, hovered there, but this time decided not to go in. He mooched away, dispirited and lost. It was like watching the performance of a bedroom farce from backstage.

'Do they share the trailer?' Mervyn asked.

'They did on *Dog the Wagz*,' said the boom operator. 'Unofficially.'

'Yeah,' said the unit driver. 'Now they unofficially don't.'

Randall climbed aboard the bus. His affable 'Aw, shucks' manner was not in evidence. He looked tense and angry.

'Where's Ken?'

'I haven't seen him,' said the female runner.

'Well he should be the first one here. The shoot can't function without him.' Mervyn was watching Patch, the Location Manager and the Production Designer busily chugging past the bus in puffer jackets. The shoot was indeed functioning without Ken. Ken would have probably slowed things down with his obstructive and muddle-headed instructions.

'Have you tried the boot of his car?' Mervyn muttered. Randall sat down opposite him, slumping head-first on the table. Mervyn felt guilty; Randall was obviously distressed. 'Don't worry,' he added. 'I'm sure nothing's happened to him.'

Randall looked up, and stared at Mervyn like he was just saying random words. 'Who?'

'Ken. I'm sure he'll be fine. I don't think there's been an accident.'

Randall looked darkly at Mervyn.

'There's already been an accident, Merv.'

He threw his newspaper down on the table. The headline was 'HIT AND RUN DRIVER KILLS MOTHER OF TWO'.

Mervyn picked it up and studied it. He failed to see the point.

'Who is she?'

Randall laughed bitterly. 'Don't worry. It's no one attached to the shoot. No one I know. Just some lady from Gwelk or Gwark or Gweedo or whatever they call their villages down here. Just some woman who just got unlucky.'

'Fair enough. But I don't –'

'The roads round here are really treacherous, tiny windy little tracks with blind corners, no room to pass or overtake. You really need to concentrate. But visiting drivers just don't treat them with respect. They just don't give a shit. That's why the roads are so dangerous.'

He tapped the paper. 'There. That's the reason why I wanted your Styrax on the pilot, Merv. I'll wager this asshole was just some guy down from the city, escaping to his second home, hoping to wax his surfboard and do some fishing. I bet he thought he could treat the roads round here like a freeway, take the bends at 70 miles per hour. He was wrong, and now she's dead.'

He sat, crossed his arms and stuck one foot on the edge of the table, like a watchful sheriff in an old western. 'I once lived in a little place near Mulholland Drive in the hills. It's got some nasty roads too, and some kids drive too fast round there, but not as fast as the boys on their way in and out of the big city...' He blinked furiously. 'Anyway, to cut a long story short, my friend's car got totalled by another stupid driver who didn't like waiting for stop signals and she ended up with her ass in a wheelchair and peeing through a tube.'

'Oh. I see. I'm sorry about that.'

'So am I. So, you see Merv, there's your answer. That's why I wanted the Styrax in the pilot. When I watched the reruns on PBS they made quite an impression on me. "Whoah," I thought. "Evil super-intelligent automobiles bent on killing and ruining people's lives? I can relate to that." That really spoke to me.' He stopped and frowned. 'What?'

Mervyn turned to follow Randall's line of vision. Bryony was there in the door of the bus. Her expression was sickly, like a surgeon preparing to tell an anxious father-to-be that they'd lost the baby.

'Ken's here.'

'He looks terrible.'

They watched him from the bus. Ken had arrived and had poured out of his car. His face was chalk-white and he staggered with agonising slowness to the location bus. Mervyn was reminded of a mime artist walking against a non-existent wind.

He didn't say 'sorry' for being late; in fact he didn't say anything to anyone. He grabbed a polystyrene cup, poured himself a generous black coffee, lumbered to the table vacated by Mervyn and practically fell on to it, scattering the runners like skittles.

The newspaper was still there, where Randall had slapped it down.

Ken glanced at the paper. At the headline 'HIT AND RUN DRIVER KILLS MOTHER OF TWO'.

Was it Mervyn's imagination – or did Ken flinch?

No one seemed interested in tackling Ken about his lateness; not even Randall. Perhaps they all realised that the number one priority lay in getting some filming done, not having a screaming match in a supermarket car park.

Mervyn decided to hang around the set so he went into the supermarket, doors gliding open and shut in front of him and behind him.

Louise walked up to him, swathed in a huge coat that looked like it had a tog value of 93. 'Impressive, isn't it?'

'It looks very snug.'

'Not the coat. Look what our team have done. Impressive, isn't it?' she said, gesturing at what they'd done.

'It's very surprising, what they've done.' Mervyn neatly sidestepped an outright lie.

The production team had dressed the inside of the supermarket to look like an alien battleship. They'd put fake banks of controls over the frozen chickens, taken down the 'special offer' signs and put flashing lights over the tills. Now it looked exactly like a supermarket clumsily dressed to look like an alien battleship.

'Anything the BBC can do, we can do better. We'll show them. Not that we're competing. But we'll show them.'

There was a crackle, and the supermarket tannoy system scraped their ears.

'WILL LOUISE FELCHAM COME TO THE TILLS. WILL LOUISE FELCHAM COME TO THE TILLS, PLEASE.'

'That's Nick's voice. What the hell's he playing at?'

They went to the tills where Nick was waiting for them. His face was like a naughty schoolboy's.

'What do you think you're playing at?'

'So cool. I've so always wanted to do this.'

'What the hell do you want, Nick? Or are you just playing the arsehole?'

He pressed the button again. 'CLEAN-UP IN AISLE 13.'

'Stop that!' snapped Louise. Nick pointed to aisle 13, where raised voices were heard. 'Stop messing around, Nick. Spit it out.'

'It's one of the Wagz – the dark-haired one. There's a problem.'

'Oh God. Has she collapsed in the toilets with her head in a bucket of coke?'

'Worse.'

'Oh God. She's decided she wants to *stop* collapsing in toilets with a bucket of coke? That's it isn't it? Don't tell me – she wants a week to dry out.'

'Even worse. She's asking questions about her character's motivation.

And she's asking Ken.'

'Get Glyn.'

Nick paled. 'I'd rather not.'

'Fine. *I'll* get Glyn. You wet piece of haddock.' She waddled off, like an angry Womble.

CHAPTER SEVENTEEN

The dark-haired one was standing, appropriately enough, by the frozen chickens.

She was the one with ambition. If she didn't have ambition, she wouldn't have auditioned for Star-Spangled Ballads. She was working in a sports shop in Birmingham when she saw the advert in the paper and didn't waste any time. She kicked off the expensive trainers she was demonstrating, handed in her notice and travelled to London with a tent and a Thermos. Four days later, after the rest of the Stepford Wagz joined her and the O2 arena opened its doors, they were the first in the queue.

Once in the audition rooms, she squealed and flattered the female judge, flirted with the nasty judge and bitched about the other judges with the gay one. When it came to the semi-finals, she suddenly remembered her dad was in prison and cried about him on live television. She invented hard luck stories for the blonde one's mum and hinted that the ugly one was being bullied by some of the other contestants. Unlike the other girls in the group, she didn't believe it was destiny that she would be a world megastar, she knew she had to make it happen. And she wasn't about to stop working for it any time soon.

The film was fun, yeah; a film about the members of a girl band who also happened to be hardened criminals. It traded off the Stepford Wagz's popularity among pre-teen girls and sexually awakening boys, and they all essentially played themselves. But that was just a *British* movie. To the dark-haired one, it was like appearing in British porn; sure the punters *watched* it, but it was all a bit shabby, low-rent stuff. But this pilot, this was another opportunity; this was the first step to proper acting. To Hollywood.

The dark-haired one was smiling, but it was a smile on a smooth, pointed, dangerous face. The smile was comically out of place, like the cheeky grins squaddies draw on missiles before they get launched. Tight black jeans and a T shirt with 'Get the Fun out of Here' written on it (the name of their first album) were like a second skin on her hard, boyish body. The kind of body about which men usually say 'but she's just skin and bone' when they're reassuring their girlfriends with the lie that their saggy white breasts are infinitely preferable to the leather-clad ladies gyrating on the telly.

She was talking to Ken – the worst person she could have found. Ken had somehow found his way on set, the coffee still in his hand. He looked more baffled than her, his hand cradling his forehead. She was showing him her script, which was heavily tattooed with notes and squiggles around her lines. Mervyn moved closer, and could hear their voices from the other side of the aisle.

'This is just nonsense.' Her voice sounded like it came from a woman many decades older, a low growling noise she'd cultivated by standing outside nightclubs in winter wearing tiny skirts with a cigarette in her mouth. She sounded suspicious and aggressive. 'This just doesn't make sense. I'll say it again. In scene 83 I tell Elysia I know she's an android spy, and that I always knew it, and I've known it ever since she came back from the Voidlands.'

'Okaay,' said Ken wearily. Mervyn remembered Ken's catchphrase. Every problem was met with his trademark, weary 'Okaay'. The director looked around for help, but there was none.

'But in scene 19, me and Elysia, we're both trapped in the ship by the Styrax and we surrender because the air is leaving the ship faster than rescue can get to us...'

'Okaay...'

'But I've got a space helmet. So I'm not in danger of being suffocated, and she's a robot, so neither is she. So why do I surrender? And if I know she's a robot, doesn't that make me really stupid? Isn't Medula supposed to be the clever one?'

'Well, obviously, you want to keep the fact you know she's a robot secret, so you can study her, you know, find out more about her.'

'But we're being captured by the enemy! Studying the enemy by pretending to be chummy with a bloody robot is just crap. It's mad. And it doesn't say that in the script.'

'Well okaay... If you didn't surrender, right, and you reveal you know she's a robot... then she'd obviously try to kill you.'

'Um. Hello? Got a blaster in my hand! Why don't I roast her metal arse with my laser gun, put my helmet on and sit tight until the rescue ship arrives?'

Ken looked like he would love to be blasted with a laser gun at that precise moment; anything to stop him listening to the shouty girl talking about plot holes in *Vixens from the Void*.

She continued, flapping the script back to another bookmarked page. 'Also right at the start, in scene nine there's this really stupid bit when we're alone on the bridge of the spaceship. I talk about my difficult childhood to her, I get all weepy and stuff and I let her comfort me. She cradles my head on her lap and it's kind of implied we have sex and stuff.'

'Right... Okaay...'

The dark-haired one looked aghast at Ken not getting it. 'Well where do I start? If I know she's a robot... I've, well, I've just had sex with a *robot*! And I knew she was a robot! And I just talked about my difficult childhood... to a *robot*!' She waved the script in his face. 'I mean, what am I? The kind of girl who gets her rocks off sitting on washing machines?' Ken pushed his face up through his fingers, noticed Mervyn, and threw a finger in his direction.

'Look, there's a writer. Go and discuss it with him. I've got better things to do.' Ken blundered off. The dark-haired one turned her gaze to Mervyn.

'You wrote this? Seriously? I thought Glyn wrote it.'

'Well I wrote the original version. The one that was on the telly in the 80s.'

'Oh.' The portcullis slammed down. Mervyn was no longer a person who was worth talking to.

'Where's Glyn? I want to talk about scene 83.'

'I... don't think he's about.'

'Well he fucking should be. God, fuck this shit. I want my agent,' she shouted at some random person. 'Get me my agent! No one's taking this shit seriously but me. I only did this because Glyn was the writer. *Dog the Wagz* was good, but this is bollocks!' She got out her iPhone and tapped the screen, shouting into it. 'Denise! I'm coming back to London. I want a plane here in 15 minutes.'

Mervyn was faced with a potential crisis. He saw the production crumbling before his eyes. He could finally see a way he could help, and pay Randall back for that money he'd shovelled his way. He scuttled after the dark-haired one and intercepted her.

'I think we can fix this.'

'It's way too late. You heard what I said to Denise.'

'Unless she's hiding behind that piece of scenery, I don't think she heard you.'

'What?' she snapped.

'You might be able to conjure up a private plane in 15 minutes, but I don't think even you can conjure a mobile phone signal in Cornwall.'

She looked at the useless iPhone in her hand and put it away. She actually smiled. A cute little smile. 'Okay. You got me.' She slammed the script in his hands. 'You see my problem? It's just bollocks.'

'Let me look at that. Oh, this is easily fixable. You can do it with a few extra lines.'

'You're fucking kidding me.'

'You've got three problems, here. The line in scene 83 about knowing all along that she's a robot; the scene in the stranded airless spaceship where you surrender; and the scene near the start when you get all emotional and everything gets a bit, well...'

'Sexy.'

'Right. We can change the line in scene 83 to solve the other two problems. Bear with me.' Mervyn rested her script on his knee and wrote very carefully in the margins of her script. It took a while, but the dark-haired one waited meekly, all traces of furious impatience gone. At heart, she was an insecure young girl barely out of her teens, and the strain of decision-making had taken its toll. She was tired of being in control and all she really wanted was someone to tell her what to do and reassure her.

By the time he'd finished, most of the left side of her script was crammed with Mervyn's painstakingly capitalised words. He drew a circle round what he'd written, and an arrow pointing to the circle that originated from the offending 'I knew it' line. He handed it back to her. 'There, read from line 112.'

She frowned, and then started reading aloud. '"I knew you were an android spy all along, I knew it from the start, the moment you came back from the Voidlands. I know how robots move, remember?"'

'I would cut that bit about "I know how robots move". That's a bit weak. Okay, now up there,' Mervyn pointed to his written note. She followed his arrow and kept on reading.

'"I wasn't completely certain at first, so I did my self-patented sure-fire test for android detection. I had sex with you. You were too damn good, so I'd like to thank you for that while I remember. You were a very tender lover, but I'm afraid Elysia isn't. She likes to bite. And another thing; your legs were lovely and smooth. Elysia's aren't. Scientists have managed to create robots that look exactly like humans, down to their retinas and hair follicles, but they haven't managed to do cellulite yet."' The dark-haired one laughed and read on. '"I knew you were a robot, but I didn't know if you were friend or foe. So when we were stuck in the ship I pretended I still had air in my helmet to see what you would do. If you admitted you were a robot, told me you didn't need to breathe and saved us both, I'd know you were a probably just one of Excelsior's droids keeping an eye out for me. But you didn't. So from that moment on I knew you were up to no good..."' The dark-haired one looked up from the script, face shining with delight and relief. 'Hey, this is good. This is really good. It sorts it all out...'

'And it makes Medula the clever one,' pointed out Mervyn. 'It makes you look like you've been thinking everything through all along.'

'Yeah it does, doesn't it?'

She impulsively threw her arms around him and hugged him. Inside Mervyn's prehistoric pants, his penis stirred and unrolled. She disengaged, very pleased with life, and skipped back to her trailer.

Louise came huffing up. 'I can't find Glyn. Where's she gone? What's up?'

'Don't worry,' said Mervyn nonchalantly. 'She's happy. I've sorted it.'

For the first time in two days, Louise looked directly at Mervyn. With utter disbelief.

'Okaay,' Ken said. 'This is your pitched battle with the henchman of the Styrax, the Gonks.'

The blonde one frowned and looked at her script. Then she looked at the huge hairy thing with the horns on its head, standing off set and drinking a cappuccino through a straw. The thing waved cheerily.

'The Gonks? I thought they were the Gorgs.'

'Close enough. I want you to run down the corridor...'

'It's not a corridor, it's an aisle.'

'Okaay, I want you to run along the aisle, then.'

'Which aisle?'

He checked his notes. 'Aisle seven. I want you to run along aisle seven, aim your gun into aisle eight and run along aisle nine firing at stuff as you go. Turn the corner, go into aisle ten, stop in front of the big green screen and say the line "By the saggy tits of the Allmother." Okay?'

'But... I don't know which aisle is aisle seven.'

'Okaay...'

He called over the production designer. 'Peter, can we have some kind of label above the aisles, so that Miss... the actress can know which aisle to run down? Something high up, out of shot. Do you think you can do that?'

The Production Designer looked oddly at Ken, then looked back at the pile of supermarket signs, stacked neatly in the corner. The ones he had taken down at 4am and stacked neatly in the corner. He looked incredibly anguished. The sensible thing was to put up all the signs again. But he'd been asked by the executive producer to take them down. And he knew that it was the executive producer who really gave him his orders, not Ken.

Production halted for 45 minutes while he and his team painstakingly made makeshift versions of the signs stacked neatly in the corner and hung them exactly where the signs stacked neatly in the corner were hanging at 3.30 that morning. And every morning before that for the past eight years.

CHAPTER EIGHTEEN

The makeshift signs went up, but they didn't help.

The blonde one ran up aisle eight, aimed her gun at aisle seven, forgot to fire in aisle nine, got lost, went back to aisle seven, and ended up in aisle five, near the cereals.

Ken was getting increasingly short-tempered and his edginess was making the blonde one nervous. It didn't help that after each ruined take he just read out the stage directions from the script in the same exasperated manner, slightly quicker, and it was obvious to everyone that the girl wasn't taking any of it in. She ended up further and further away from the green screen and probably would have ended up outside with the shopping trolleys if they hadn't shouted 'Cut!'

Ken slumped incredibly low in his chair. He was almost horizontal. If it weren't for his huge square head, he would have oozed out of the hole in the back and on to the floor.

After six depressing takes, an enterprising props guy ran up to Ken and hissed in his ear. 'Mr Roche, you know those coloured lines you get on hospital floors?' Ken moved his head slightly further into his neck. He seemed to be trying to nod. 'If I stick down her route with a line of masking tape, then she could follow it.' Ken moved his head again and filming halted for another 15 minutes while the props guy set to work.

Take seven, and the blonde one managed to run where she was supposed to – but she forgot to fire her gun. Filming stopped for another ten minutes while the set dresser put down helpful little 'X's and arrows to denote when she should fire her gun and in which direction. With the floor of the supermarket now resembling the tactics board in a football team's dressing room, take eight began.

The blonde one ran dutifully down aisle seven, aimed her gun into aisle eight, ran up aisle nine firing as she went, into aisle ten, turned to the green screen, said 'By the saggy tits of the Allmother!' and froze into position; the location manager yelled 'Cut!' and the blonde one – and everyone else – breathed a sigh of relief. Something was in the can, and only an hour and a half behind schedule.

On to the next part of scene 83. The dark-haired one and the ugly one were waiting to take their places in aisle 11.

'Okaay... Let's run through the dialogue before we go for a take,' said a defeated voice from somewhere near knee-height.

The blonde one acted shocked. 'There's a Styrax battle fleet out there! Five hundred ships at least!'

'I know.'

The dark-haired one pointed her gun at the ugly one.

'What are you doing? Why are you pointing your gun at Elysia?'

'Because she's a robot.'

'Don't be stupid. Medula, you're making a mistake.'

'She can't be.'

'I'll prove it... Okay, bang, I shoot you, your arm comes off...'

'By the Allmother, it's true!'

'I knew you were an android spy all along, I knew it from the start, the moment you came back from the Voidlands. I wasn't completely certain at first, so I did my self-patented sure-fire test for android detection. I had sex with you...'

The other two Wagz were looking at each other in confusion. The dark-haired one carried on. She had only been given Mervyn's rewrite two hours ago, and she was word perfect. It had taken them days to learn the lines they already had.

'Scientists have managed to create robots that look exactly like humans, down to their retinas and hair follicles, but they haven't managed to do cellulite yet. I knew you were a robot, but I didn't know if you were friend or foe –"

'Well this sounds like a *lorra* fun.' A voice broke in to the flow. It was a familiar voice; hard, northern, grating. It belonged to an angry Mancunian playwright Mervyn had seen on *Newsnight review* last week. 'Are we making another show on the quiet, lads? Because I don't recognise this bit at all.'

Mervyn turned, and was astonished to find that the voice really belonged to Glyn. *He really has got a knack for mimickry,* thought Mervyn. *If he wasn't a writer he'd make a fortune as an impressionist.*

Glyn was standing behind the camera, arms crossed. There was an unmistakable air of menace to him.

'It's a rewrite,' said the dark-haired one flatly.

'Really? Not mine. Not that I'm aware of.'

'He did it,' she pointed to Mervyn.

Glyn's eyes turned to him, as did the gaze of everyone else. He felt like a luckless peasant, accused by a village maiden of cavorting naked with her by moonlight and worshipping the devil.

'Oh Mervyn, Mervyn, Mervyn!' Glyn advanced on him. 'My trusty right-hand man. Thanks and all for filling in, geezer, with huge dollop of grateful on the side.'

'Thanks. I didn't mean you to hear it like this. I hoped we'd go through it before we got on set.'

'Let me ask you something very simple, Mervyn. Take your time to answer, it's not a trick question... Now don't you think the audience will have gone to sleep while she's saying all this crap you've put in?'

'I... well...' He rallied. 'Not really. It feels important. It's tense and funny.'

'To take all your points in order, Mervyn my son. Unimportant, flaccid and about as funny as my mum's cancer.'

Mervyn was stung. 'There are *much* longer speeches in the script.'

'But this is not a speech, Mervyn. This is fat footnote at the bottom of a very boring book. An entry in the Encyclopaedia Shitannica. A collage of words that sit there and don't do anything.'

'They explain the plot.'

'No, my lovely. They slow down the climax of *my* script with stuff that no one cares about. Television's come a long way since your day... It's not theatre any more. No more standing in sets, talking for hours on end about the weather and what they're having for dinner...'

Mervyn felt his teeth grind together.

'Well... I take your point. It is a bit wordy. It could be trimmed a little, I grant you...'

'Trimmed a little! This rewrite is a spin-off series in its own right! Perhaps you can release it as a novel.' He laughed; not a nice laugh. 'Anyway, I'll just pick the bits of my work off the floor where you left them. You were a script editor for a long time, my lovely, perhaps you forgot what it was like to be a poor struggling writer, getting his art shredded by some anonymous pen-scratcher who thinks he knows best...' Glyn's good-humoured facade was crumbling and behind it was pure white-hot fury.

Mervyn's self-confidence was meanwhile bleeding to death. Like a series of blobs which when stared at magically became a 3D picture of a dolphin, his 'expert rewrite' was morphing in his head and becoming rubbish. He was a fool. The lines were clunky and forced in with no finesse or respect for the pace of the scene. He tried to be conciliatory. 'I'm sorry Glyn. It wasn't my place... I know that. I shouldn't have gone behind your back... But you weren't around, and the actress was worried about the scene.'

'She's probably more worried about her poor tongue getting worn to a frazzle, making her say all those irrelevant words.'

'Leave him alone.' The dark-haired one had had enough. 'The script made no sense and you weren't around. Mervyn fixed it.'

'You say fixed, I say ruined, girlie. Let's work out which one of us is the writer. Ooh, I think it's me isn't it?'

'You patronising bastard. I like it. It's good. I like what he's done.'

'Well you would,' snapped the blonde one. 'It gives you an extra bit to say.'

'It's not like that at all,' said the dark-haired one.

'Where does it say I have cellulite? My script doesn't say that,' said the ugly one.

'It's exactly what it's like,' the blonde one retorted. 'You're always counting your lines.'

'At least I can count.'

'Fuck off.'

'No you fuck off.'

'Oh just admit it Chrissie, it's push, push, push with you. You won't be happy until you're doing all the acting.'

'I'm already doing all the acting. Cos I'm the one who can act, Gemma.'

'Oh piss off, you arrogant bitch.'

'Why have I got cellulite?' said the ugly one.

'No, you piss off. Slag.'

'Fuck you, I will.' The blonde one ran off.

'Aaah, fuck it,' said the dark-haired one, biting her lip. 'This isn't good.'

'*Why* do I have cellulite in the story?'

'Because you do in real life, so shut up whining, you fat cow.'

The ugly one's mouth trembled, and she ran off crying.

'Fuck, fuck, fuck!' said the dark-haired one, wondering which one to follow first. She started in the direction of the blonde one, realised she'd forgotten something, then came back and stuck her finger in Glyn's face. 'Take out that fucking bit he wrote...' she snarled, pointing at Mervyn, '... and I'm walking. And those two are as well. And don't think I can't make them.' And then she ran off to glue the fragments of her girl band back together.

Glyn gave a rueful smile to himself, and then sauntered away, patting Mervyn companionably on the shoulder as he did so.

'Good work, my lovely,' he said.

Mervyn felt like he'd been marked for death.

CHAPTER NINETEEN

The day continued. Sort of.

Ken shredded his schedule and tried to salvage the day by recording tiny ten-second scenes of Gorgs grunting at each other and looking confused.

More reports came in to the set during the day. Glyn was sulking in his trailer, refusing to come out. Nick was hovering round his door, frightened to knock. Louise had disappeared with Randall, presumably urging Randall to kick Mervyn off the project.

The ugly one cried in her trailer for an hour and then emerged, enabling Ken to record some ten-second scenes of her grunting and looking confused. She didn't seem worried about the shouting, screaming and crying emanating from the blonde one's trailer. She assured everyone this was perfectly normal; Gemma and Chrissie usually did this, and they would definitely be the best of friends in a few hours. Mervyn stayed on the set, sitting in a corner and watching the filming from a safe distance. Avoiding the gaze of everyone. Ken didn't look at him. No one did.

The day was yawning its way to the afternoon, and a caffeine craving was creeping up Mervyn's throat and nibbling his brain. He knew he could get a coffee from the location bus, but that meant he had to walk. It was the principle of the thing. The female runner walked by. He cleared his throat. Nothing. He watched her take orders from the actors on set. He walked a few tentative steps away from his chair towards her, but then she disappeared, so he sat wearily back into his place.

She got coffees for the producers. Okay, they were all very important people, so they and the actors, they were first. She obviously had a system. He didn't want to throw her system into chaos by badgering her for coffee at a delicate moment. Then she got coffee for the script supervisors, the cameramen, the set dressers, the make-up teams, even getting some for other bloody runners. He was dead certain that the last tray of lattes that sailed by were destined for a bunch of guys down the street who had nothing to do with the production, but just had nice faces.

He was already thinking that he'd destroyed the project single-handed; now his ego imploded. He felt humiliated and depressed. The fact that she wasn't getting coffee for him was absolute and undeniable proof that he had officially been ostracised by the production.

Luckily, he had his own perfect remedy for those times when he was depressed; it never failed. Unfortunately, it involved having a huge bloody coffee.

The runner was coming closer to Mervyn. Finally. She was definitely getting closer. She was making straight for him. His heart would have been pounding with anticipation, but it was so starved of caffeine that it could only plod slightly faster than normal. *Yes, I want a coffee right now. Right now. Just inject it into my eyeball and put a cinnamon patch on my arm.*

'Randall wondered if you'd like to see the new Styrax and give him your thoughts,' said the female runner. 'There's one in the back of the delicatessen if you want to take a look.'

'Oh. Fair enough.'

Not what he had in mind. But it sounded like he'd been forgiven, and it was quite flattering to be asked his opinion on something, at last. He got directions from the runner, walked through dried fruits, canned goods, condiments and spices, past the bakery and through the delicatessen. He pushed his way through the hanging tongues of plastic and felt a blast of cold air. He found himself in the warehouse; there were props for the show, guns, bits of equipment. But no Styrax.

He noticed an open door. There was a note with 'Styrax' written on it in felt tip. He went inside.

It was the freezer locker. Nothing more than a windowless room about five metres square. Metal trolleys stood along the walls crammed with boxes of ice creams, frozen curries and pizzas. The trolleys looked like evil robots themselves, dormant, silent. Waiting to come to life and deliver death to all mankind using saturated fats.

But in the middle of the room was the new Styrax. It was slightly larger, fatter with a dark grey finish. Mervyn was impressed. It actually looked like a piece of space-age transportation that had evolved into an evil robot race, rather than the 'bubble car with attitude' the original series budget had conjured up. It had that gritty sturdiness that the original lacked.

Then there was a rumble and a clang, and Mervyn was left in darkness.

CHAPTER TWENTY

The door had just closed on him.

Surely that wasn't supposed to happen? He started to panic.

Don't panic, Mervyn told himself. *You'll achieve nothing by panicking.*

I'm a writer, Mervyn replied to himself tartly. *Most of the things I do achieve nothing. Why should I start avoiding things that achieve nothing now? Don't tell me not to panic!* He did some more panicking.

All right. Mervyn took a new tack with himself. *Let's look at this logically. There is no point having a freezer locker that cannot be opened from the inside; people would get trapped in them all the time and die cold and horrible deaths...* He had another quick panic. *Are you listening Mervyn? Forget the cold and horrible death bit. I'm making a important point here. To avoid such a tragic occurrence, there HAS to be a handle on the inside of the door.*

Good thinking, Mervyn. He scrabbled along the walls of the locker, hands sticking on the cold metal of the trolleys, until he felt the wonderful shape of a handle.

He pulled it. The lever came away in his hand. The shock caused him to drop the handle, which jangled to the ground. It was too loud in such a small space.

So he was going to die. The production team had had enough of him, and locked him in here to die.

He was going to die.

It didn't make as much of an impact on his brain as he thought. Perhaps he'd worn himself out with all the panicking. Perhaps he was too frozen stiff to worry about it any more. God, he was so very, very cold. Perhaps this was revenge from the patron saint of Cornwall, St Piran, for his rude thoughts about Cornish hospitality. He offered up a silent prayer, promising never to be rude about the Black Prince Tavern's central heating ever again.

He was still too detached from the whole dying thing. He had to focus, create a sense of urgency about the situation so he could think of a way out.

He was going to die.

He. Was. Going. To. Die.

He was never going to finish his novel.

So what else is new? You think I'm going to finish the bloody thing if I live?

Okay... He was going to die.

He was never ever ever going to have sex again.

I don't think my penis cares at this precise point about never having sex again. It's about the size of a jelly bean as it is. Even if I ever live, I don't think I'll ever extract it from inside my scrotum and grow it back to normal size.

So he was going to die.

Oh my God, he was going to die!

And my underpants are disgusting!

How bloody ironic, he thought. All those jokes about always wearing clean underwear in case you get run over – well the joke was on him. Very bloody funny. His icy body would get carted out of here to meet doctors, pathologists, mortuary attendants and embalmers wearing his emergency pair; underpants that had now reached the age at which they could legally vote and drive a car.

Mervyn's survival instinct rebooted. Like many cringing Englishmen, he stoked it up with quiet indignation. He fantasised about to whom he was going to complain about the faulty door, the phone calls he would make, the letters he would write. The vouchers he would get in compensation. He mentally steeled himself for a long grim fight, tedious phone calls to mystified, slow-witted people in customer services, indifferent letters from assistants of assistant branch managers, but finally there would be the grovelling apology from the head of the supermarket and an ironic trolley full of frozen meat as reward for his two ordeals; first his ordeal trapped in a freezer, then his ordeal trapped on an 0845 number listening to Bach.

But he would only collect that prize on the other side of this bloody door.

Mervyn practised a few screams; quiet, polite ones to begin with. Even in mortal danger, Mervyn didn't like to make a fuss. He soon managed to lose his inhibitions, but five minutes of yelling at the top of his lungs brought no response.

He tried long screams. He experimented with a series of short, sharp 'hey!'s. He had a go at alternating between the two. 'Heeeeeyyy! Hey! Heeeeeeyyy! Hey! Heeeeeeyyy!'

Nothing still.

Mervyn felt wretched. Not only was he going to die, there was also nowhere to sit. He'd reached the age where a Nice Sit Down was important. Thank heavens it was an early-morning location shoot, because he'd already dressed to keep warm, putting on a jersey underneath his jacket. Pulling his hands inside the sleeves to make crude mittens, he groped around in the darkness and pulled out a box of something to sit on. By the feeling of it on his bottom, it was a box full of frozen chips.

Then there was a rattle. A scrape. Rescue!

'Hey,' croaked Mervyn. 'I'm in here!'

The door opened, light flooded into Mervyn's eyes.

'Mervyn?'

It was Randall. His green customised tie was swinging from side to side as he hauled the door open.

'Close that door,' said Mervyn, 'there's a hell of a draught.'

'What?'

Mervyn rushed out of the freezer, standing as far away from the open door as possible, frightened that it would reach out and swallow him up. 'Sorry, I always make stupid jokes when I'm terrified.'

'What are you doing in there?'

'I'm a writer. Isn't that where you keep the writers?'

'What are you doing inside the refrigerator?'

'I wanted to see if the light went off when you shut the door.'

'What?'

'Okay, I'm calming down now. I'm calming down. I'm calm. The heart rate is falling.'

'Do you need anything? Brandy?'

'No. Coffee. Lots and lots of coffee. I am so desperate for coffee. You know those cups you get in your country? The ones you call "tall"?'

'Yeah?'

'I could drink one of those.'

They walked out of the back and into the aisles.

'Thank you for letting me out. I was worried that no one would hear me.'

'I didn't hear you. I was looking for the Styrax prop. It wasn't where it's supposed to be.'

'It was in the freezer with me.'

'It's what?'

'It's back in there.'

Randall gave Mervyn an odd look, then called over a props man. 'I've just been told the Styrax is inside the meat locker. Don't ask us why. We don't know. Just get it out.'

The props man looked at Mervyn with deep suspicion, then ran off to the locker.

Randall gripped Mervyn's shoulder with friendly force. 'Mervyn. We don't know why it's in there, right?' he said lightly.

'No.'

'Because you didn't put it in there, right?'

'Of course not. I was told that the Styrax was in there and you'd invited me to have a look at it.'

'In there? Why would we want to put it in there?'

'Well I just assumed you needed to...' muttered Mervyn lamely. 'Keep the paint fresh or something.' Then Mervyn remembered. 'There was a note on the door. It said "Styrax".'

They went back and looked at the door. The note had gone. Of course it had.

They tracked down the runner who delivered the message. She was swanning around, blatantly giving coffee to other people who weren't Mervyn. That's what annoyed him the most; not the whole her-sending-him-to-his-almost-death business, it was the her-getting-everyone-else-a-coffee-but-him business that really wounded.

She saw Randall and Mervyn coming towards her. 'Hi. Do you want a coffee, Randall?'

Oh, the bitch knew how to twist the knife. She so knew.

'No thanks. Mervyn would quite like one.'

She looked at Mervyn dubiously. 'Sorry, do you drink coffee?'

'Yes. I do. On occasions.'

Whenever I'm awake.

'Sorry, I thought you didn't.'

'Forget the coffee. Did I just call you from the OB van and ask you to ask Mervyn to go to the meat locker?'

'Behind the delicatessen? Er...Yes.'

'To see the Styrax?'

'Yes.'

'But I didn't do anything of the sort.'

The runner blinked, confused. 'It sounded like you. It was American. I'm sure it was you.'

Randall's eyes narrowed. 'This is very concerning.'

'It must have been a mix-up. Just a communications cock-up,' said Mervyn, in his best let's-not-make-a-scene-and-just-go-and-get-coffee voice.

Randall didn't look convinced.

CHAPTER TWENTY-ONE

>CLICK<

[SIGH]

This is, without doubt, the shittiest point in my life.

My life resembles the shittiest public toilet in the shittiest train station in the shittiest town in this shitty country. My life is wet toilet rolls sitting in the bowl, clogging up the U-bend and swilling urine-coloured water onto the floor.

My life is excrement smeared on the edge of the bog.

That's what this fucking location shoot is.

And yet, and yet, this fucking lousy trip to the middle of Dreary in the county of Fuckall is just about bearable. I thought I could get through it. I'd placed tissue paper on the door handles, wiped the shit off the seat, and avoided the puddles of metaphorical piss on the floor.

And then guess what? Someone's put shit in the soap dispenser, and wiped their shitty arse with the towel on the wall. Because Mervyn Stone is still here.

The turd which, no matter how much you flush, keeps bobbing up again, the same shit-eating grin on his shitty face.

I tried to kill Mervyn yesterday. Just an innocent accident on set, I thought, nothing too dramatic. Nothing, which screams 'murder'. Don't want to get the police running around, searching my stuff.

I know I didn't try very hard to kill him yesterday. Don't you think I don't know that, okay? Of course I know it. I thought; just do a quick pull on the chain, and that would be it, he would disappear down the U-bend. Flush him into the sea. But no, not him. Not the floater from hell.

Just goes to show, I'm going to have to try a bit harder. Proper planning next time. I'm also going to have to be clever, and careful. I saw Nick...

[SIGH]

... looking at me in a funny way when I walked off the set. Can't let anyone get suspicious. Not good.

I'll set him a little trap tomorrow. And the beauty of it is, I'll be nowhere near when it happens.

[SIGH]

Tomorrow, Mervyn fucking Stone dies.

No mistakes this time.

CHAPTER TWENTY-TWO

The next morning Mervyn woke up surprisingly refreshed, considering all that had happened. He guessed the lungfuls of fresh country supermarket air had done him the power of good.

He removed the badger from his crotch and started to dress hurriedly – the room was freezing. He couldn't wait to tell Maggie all the things that had been happening to him. There had been an attempt on his life! He felt like a really interesting person, for once. He hadn't told her that he was working with the Stepford Wagz; she was bound to be impressed. Perhaps she would be so captivated by his exploits she would replace the badger in his bed.

First things first. He had to deal with the increasingly desperate problem of his lack of underpants. He had still failed to get to Marks & Spencer, the village didn't have a laundrette, and he lacked the courage to ask the barmaid if she minded washing his smalls for him. All his pants had now been worn far more times than was healthy – and that included wearing them inside-out. They were very ripe. He swore he could hear them plotting inside his suitcase, planning on stealing a car and driving to the coast where they could park on the cliffs and make out with dirty knickers. The incident in the freezer was an important lesson as well. He couldn't get caught out like that again.

So this morning, he had to make a choice. Desperate times called for desperate measures. He put on his shiny old swimming trunks, which were too tight and itchy but at least it gave him some support. They might make him walk a bit funny but they wouldn't try to growl at him at an inappropriate moment.

He was passing through the bar, having nodded self-consciously at the drunk, when he heard Maggie; her big man-like laugh erupted in the lounge.

That couldn't be her. How could that be? How could that laugh exist without him there to make it happen?

Of course. It couldn't be her. It had to be another woman with a big manly laugh, or a burly man with a slightly feminine giggle.

But it was her.

She was sitting with someone. A man. His back was to Mervyn, so he couldn't see who it was; but the man spoke, and Mervyn instantly recognised those languid tones.

Roger Barker.

Mervyn went up to the table and stood there over him, in an 'Excuse me you're sitting in my seat' fashion.

'Hello Mervyn' said Maggie.

'Mervyn!' exclaimed Roger. 'Are you staying here too?'

'Hello Roger. Yes. Yes I am.'

'What fun! Pillow fights and pyjama parties all round!'

Maggie laughed. Mervyn seethed.

Roger was dressed in a very typical Rogery way. He wore a cricket jumper (even though it was nearly October) just to remind everyone how athletic he was, designer jeans and expensive trainers. He had a fountain of charity badges pinned self-consciously to his jumper; the Lord's Taverners, the Grand Order of Water Rats and the Sons of the Severed Ankle were just a few. He had a huge expensive watch round his wrist. It must have been incredibly heavy, it certainly seemed to drag his hand down – it usually needed to be rested on the nearest female knee.

His hair, once blond, was now grey and, even though there was much less of it it, still flopped into his face in a self-effacing college-boy look that helped him charm his way into jeans, up skirts and into boiler suits. His face was a deep scary orange, as though he'd stood too close to a fence while it had been weatherproofed.

Roger was an actor who had worked on the original series. He played a dashing advisor to the court of Prime Mistress Magaroth, who had tried to sleep with most of the major characters – both on-screen and off – during the seven years the show was on air. He had had three high-profile marriages to famous and beautiful actresses that each failed spectacularly after about 18 months, because – not to put too fine a point on it – no one was able to love Roger as much as Roger did.

Even though he disliked Roger intensely, Mervyn tried to sound delighted to see him. He had watched other people do it really well, but hadn't quite mastered the art himself.

'So, Roger. Good to see you, of course. What are you doing here?'

'Same as you, Merv. Same as you. I've been roped in for this new *Vixens* telly thing they're doing. I've got a cough-and-a-spit cameo as Magaroth the Prime Mistress.'

'But Magaroth the Prime Mistress was a mad old woman.'

'You don't need to tell me that! Apparently I'm going to be dragged up. Very Quentin Crisp. Very subversive. I've worn a few dresses in my time in panto – you should have seen my Widow Twanky, Maggie, it was a scream. I had everyone in fits – but I've never trannied up for the telly. Sounds fun. Anyway, a thousand quid is a thousand quid and all that. And I love the West Country, don't you, Mervy?' Roger put his hand to his mouth, in an overstated 'What have I said?' manner. 'Oh, you probably don't, do you? After what happened last time.'

'Roger's been telling me all the stories about the last time you filmed down here,' said Maggie.

Of course he would, thought Merv. *First rule of Roger when chatting to a lady – ridicule, marginalise and eliminate any male competition in the vicinity, and then dive in for the kill.*

'Oh yes, wasn't it dreadful, Merv?' chortled Roger. 'Remember when that arc light nearly fell on you and you squealed really oddly, like a cartoon chipmunk?' He dissolved into giggles. 'Oh my, Maggie, it was utterly hilarious. All the runners and the production staff copied him for weeks, and they actually got it on film! They put it on the end of a blooper tape with "That's all, folks!" written under it!'

He giggled and placed his hand on her arm. Mervyn noted with icy fury that Maggie didn't bother to remove it.

'And then, there was that time when Mervyn crashed his car at about two miles an hour! That was a scream!'

'I did explain what happened, I was in a hurry –'

'What happened was, it was an absolutely filthy day, weatherwise, great muddy raindrops, filth everywhere, and Mervyn's windscreen was utterly caked in mud. Couldn't see a thing out of it. And guess what he did? He just got in his car and drove it, and didn't think to clear the mud off.'

'My windscreen washers had stopped working. The wipers couldn't move the mud. They just smudged it and made it worse.'

'That's his story, washers broken, wipers couldn't clear the mud, just smudged it, exactly. BUT! He didn't think to put on the brakes, did old Mervyn, oh no...'

Old Mervyn. You slimy bastard. You're five years older than me if you're a day.

'... No, not old Mervyn, he just gently rolled his car down a slope and crashed it, very slowly, into a tree! It was the slowest of slow-motion crashes, you had to see it.'

'Yes, well no one found it very funny at the time –'

'And here's the really funny part of it. He tried to get it out of the mud, we all did, we couldn't shift it, and he just gave up! Just left it there! Two weeks later, after he'd gone back to London, he rang up a garage and got them to take it off to the nearest junkyard... And he never drove again!'

'I'd had enough of cars, Roger.'

'You can never have enough cars, Maggie,' said Roger, deliberately mishearing Mervyn. 'I've got a Range Rover for towing the yacht, an old Bentley for turning up to charity bashes, and a Merc which I use for pootling up and down the country. It's the one outside with KI55

ROG3R on the plates. The women all say "Kiss Roger?" and I say "Yes please!".'

'Anyway, I didn't like the car very much...'

'Oh God! And then poor Nicholas fell off that bloody boat and nearly died of 'flu!' Roger cackled. 'I shouldn't laugh. Something like that very nearly happened to me the last time I was on my yacht...'

Roger was never more than 30 seconds away from the words 'my yacht', especially when talking to a woman, just as he was never more than 30 seconds from the phrase that came next.

'You must come on my yacht, Maggie...' He put his hand over his mouth, in another 'What did I just say?' gesture, and sniggered. 'I've got a 30-footer. The yacht, I mean.' He yukked with laughter, and Maggie joined in.

'Sit down Mervyn, please. Join us,' Maggie said.

'No-no. I don't want to intrude.'

Roger slapped the table vigorously. 'Rubbish, come on. Pull up a seat Merv, join the party.'

Mervyn sat down stiffly. His hands immediately started fiddling with things on the table. After listening to Roger's ragged laughter for a while, he noticed that his right hand had found a butter knife and was gripping the handle very tightly.

Roger edged closer to Maggie and whispered unnecessarily into her ear. 'But that's not the end of it. Did you know old Merv became a producer?'

'Really?' said Maggie, impressed.

'Oh yes. For all of two hours! Because Nicholas caught a massive chill, so Merv had to fill in. And Ken didn't like that one little bit, oh no!' Roger tapped the side of his nose knowingly. Then he tapped the side of Maggie's nose, and she laughed. Again.

That was my nose, Mervyn thought. *I saw it first.*

'Well, the director couldn't stand Merv – can't think why – and after an hour of getting bossed around by old Merv he snapped and punched Merv on the nose! Just like that!'

Mervyn stood up. 'Right, I think I'll go and get my breakfast.'

'Are you going to join us?' said Roger.

'Yes,' said Maggie. 'I'm sure they'll set another place for you.'

'No, I'll just be over there. Got more space to read my paper.'

Mervyn was crushed. He sat on his own in the corner. Then, after embedding his nose in the newspaper and trying not to listen to the explosions of laugher from their table, he decided on a perilous expedition to the breakfast buffet, circumventing Roger's ego on the way.

Maggie stood beside him. She lay her napkin out on the table. The word 'HELP!' was written on it in eyeliner.

Mervyn's heart bounded back into his ribcage. He looked at Maggie, who twitched her eyes in the direction of Roger, rolled them in an exasperated fashion, and shaped her eyebrows in the universal sign of distress.

And then she was snatching up a piece of fruit and disappearing towards the fruit juices.

'Lovely lady,' said Roger, appearing beside Mervyn at the buffet table.

'She is,' agreed Mervyn.

'Okay Merv, I'll cut to the chase. All's fair in love and war and all that, but I think I've got a chance here. So if you could back away a bit, that would be great. You're cramping my style.'

'I'm cramping your style?'

'Yeah, we were having a lovely breakfast together and then you come and sit with us. Couldn't you see we were together?'

'If you recall, she asked me to sit down.'

'She was just being polite. You know women. They humour even the worst kind of bloke...'

The corner of Mervyn's mouth twitched, a sure sign that his irony detector had just exploded.

'... So, to cut a long story short, I was first, I've put my towel down, I've pitched my tent. You go try out someone else.'

'Maggie and I breakfasted together before you got here.'

'Come off it. I was here with her yesterday morning and you were nowhere to be seen.'

'That's because I was out on location. We had an early shoot.'

'Yeah, yeah. Nice try, good story. Fact is I got to her first.'

'Well I know that, Roger. You did get to her first.'

'Good, glad you admit it.'

'You most definitely did, as you say, get to her first.'

He said it in such an odd way that Roger looked at him. 'What?'

'Don't you recognise her, Roger? Surely you do.'

'No.'

'Seriously? You don't recognise her?'

'No I don't. I've not met her before.'

'Oh, I beg to differ.'

'No, I haven't. I'd remember a hot filly like her.'

'Do you remember what you used to do on location, Roger? When you used to turn up unannounced at houses in the locality, knock on the doors and ask to watch that week's episode with the family?'

'Of course. Great publicity, Mervy. Everyone thought so.'

'Well, not everyone. Do you remember those times when it wasn't great publicity? Do you remember the last time we were in this neck of the woods? Do you remember when the BBC had to pay hush money to the parents of that 15-year-old girl, who just happened to open the door to you when you'd "come to watch the episode" one evening?'

'Keep your voice down,' Roger glared at him. 'What's that got to do with the price of fish? She said she was 16. Anyway, she didn't complain at the time.'

'Of course she didn't. She was the only one who was completely happy about it. She never forgot you either.' Mervyn turned his eyes back to Maggie. Roger followed his gaze disbelievingly.

Maggie waved cheerily at them both.

'She's been waiting to catch up with you for years, Roger.' Roger's face was as white as his cricket jumper. 'So I'll leave you to chat about old times. As you said, you got to her first.'

Roger ate extremely quickly, his fork plucking at bits of sausage and mushroom so busily that his expensive watch was a blur. Then he disappeared, swigging his tea and wiping his mouth on his napkin as he went, leaving vapour trails of choking aftershave behind him.

Mervyn waited a few seconds then went over to Maggie. Her look of immense relief made him grin so much his face hurt.

'How on Earth did you get rid of that man so quickly? It was like he hadn't eaten for days.'

'Oh, you know these men of action. Always in a hurry to get back to their yachts.'

'Oh God. He was such a bore yesterday morning. I was praying you'd show up. It was all "my boat" this, and "my little dinghy" that. You'd think he was Christopher Columbus the way he talked about his adventures on the sea.'

Mervyn glowed with pleasure.

'He's invited me on his yacht, of course. I couldn't think of anything more boring than being trapped on a floating bit of wood with him. He probably wears a jumper with an anchor on it, and a sailor's hat.'

'I don't think he'll make the offer again.'

'You said something naughty to him. Admit it.'

'Let's just say, if he comes up to you later and offers you money to keep quiet...'

'Yeah?'

'Just take it.'

CHAPTER TWENTY-THREE

They had a brief, contented chat about types of annoying people they had experienced over the years. Maggie hated men who ordered for her in restaurants without asking what she wanted; Mervyn hated women who, on finding out he worked in television, wanted him to list all the famous people he'd met.

... And soon it was time to part. Maggie hugged him, and offered him a lift, but he regretfully declined. It was only after Maggie left that Mervyn realised he hadn't even mentioned someone was trying to kill him.

He wondered why that was.

He slowly worked out what his subconscious already knew; that the attempt on his life was a bit rubbish. Surely, he realised, someone would have found him long before he froze to death? If not the film crew then the supermarket staff opening up the store a bare hour after he got locked in. It was so pathetic, so half-hearted, the danger barely registered, and he didn't want anybody to spoil his holiday.

It was such an odd, unusual sensation for Mervyn, to be in the sights of a murderer.

No, that wasn't it. It wasn't odd. It wasn't odd at all. It was a very usual sensation for Mervyn to be in the sights of a murderer. This was the second time in two years a homicidal lunatic had attempted to do away with him. That wasn't the unusual sensation he was feeling.

It was such an odd, unusual sensation for Mervyn to be happy.

CHAPTER TWENTY-FOUR

Randall insisted he give Mervyn a lift to that day's location shoot. To quote him exactly: 'I'm taking no chances. You're very precious. The *Vixens* fans would never forgive me if you got killed on my watch.'

Mervyn thought the sentiment was ghoulish, but even so he was glad when Randall's 4x4 roared up outside the Black Prince. Mervyn opened the passenger door and was enveloped by a welcoming blast of hot air.

In the back was a rather thin girl with lank hair.

'This is Penny,' said Randall. 'She's staying at your hotel. She doesn't drive either.'

''Lo,' said Penny, in a dull voice.

'She's the script editor for *Vixens* – hey, your old job!'

'Oh really? Perhaps we can compare notes,' said Mervyn brightly. But Penny wasn't listening. She was staring out of the window, twirling a lock of her hair round her little finger. That was the end of that conversation.

'Well I made a few enquiries, Merv. The Styrax was left out the back as the warehouse was the designated space for the larger props. Some joker just wheeled it a few feet inside the meat locker, then got you to go inside.'

'Perhaps they're not just after me. Perhaps someone's trying to sabotage the production.'

'That's not beyond the bounds of possibility. The letters I've had. God, and I thought *Buggins the Bucket Bear* fans were screwy. But ours is a closed set, maximum security. No one gets in and out without a pass.'

'So we're pretty sure it was foul play.'

'Not nervous are you, Merv? Want to hightail it back to London?'

'Well...'

'I'll double your retainer.'

'... I'm definitely staying.'

'Good man.'

'You didn't have to bribe me, Randall. I wasn't going anyway. As murder attempts go it was pretty pathetic. I'm going to be on my guard today.'

'Hey, is this the old Brit stiff upper blitz spirit I keep hearing about?'

'Definitely.' Mervyn grinned widely. It felt odd on his face, like a pimple that had grown overnight.

They fell silent. Mervyn felt he had to say something about

yesterday.

'So how much footage did we get, in the end?'

'Oh, about eight minutes.'

'I'm sorry about what happened. I feel it was all my fault.'

Randall's face did a shrug. 'Well you meant well, but... Yeah, you were a jerk for rewriting that scene without clearance. That's what read-throughs and shit like that are for.'

'Glyn doesn't seem to invite rewrites in read-throughs.'

'That's true. But that's my problem, not yours. It wasn't for you to do it on set. It wasn't your job.'

'I know. I'm sorry.'

'But, as I pointed out to Louise – who was cursing your name and demanding you be deported from Cornwall forthwith – you were just trying to save a situation that Ken created. Ken just wanted to get rid of a problem and offloaded it on you. He should have sent out for Glyn. Or Penny here.'

Mervyn glanced in his mirror. Penny hadn't bothered acknowledging the mention of her name; she just kept on staring out of the window. He couldn't imagine Penny dealing with an angry Wag.

'It's Ken that's at fault here,' muttered Randall. Mervyn didn't argue. 'And if Glyn hadn't been quite such a dick about your changes, we could have got a whole day's filming in the can by now. He should have done what any sane writer would do. He should have offered to tweak the new lines a little, praise the actress for her cleverness, praise you to the skies for your initiative, and then quietly snip the sequence out in the edit. As it is, the whole thing is gonna be a cause célèbre for the dark-haired one, and now she's gonna be watching the edit like a hawk to make sure it all stays in. His stupid fault. I thought he'd know better. He doesn't act like a professional TV writer, but then, no one acts like a professional TV anything in this damn country.'

Something told Mervyn that the triumvirate of Louise, Ken and Glyn was starting to wear Randall down.

The car surged through the landscape, as big and strange as a flying saucer. The Cornish roads were very narrow and in places only grudgingly let them through, overhanging branches knocking angrily on the roof and windows. There were times when they'd whiz round a corner and have to brake sharply as they'd be bumper-to-bumper with a car coming the other way.

'My, we're going very fast,' said Mervyn brightly, hoping Randall would take the hint.

'No worries. I'm a very careful driver. I've always been a very careful driver. Where I come from, you have to be.'

'So you said.'

'I'm very good at anticipating trouble spots.'

'Glad to hear it.'

'That's why I've got to thinking that employing Ken was a bad move.'

'Really?' said Mervyn, innocently. He glanced in the mirror to see if Penny was listening, but she was in a world of her own.

'He doesn't seem that stable to me.'

'Well I did say.'

'Yeah, you did. And you were right. Others have been complaining. Nick in particular.'

'Nick doesn't seem the type to complain about anything.' Randall said nothing. He kept his eyes on the road. 'It seems to me that Nick and Ken have much the same way of working,' Mervyn continued. 'If it's going to be too expensive, tricky or time-consuming, then let's cut it.'

'Oh Merv, you have got a naïve outlook on things. Yes, that's Nick's way of working. He's a cautious man, feels slightly out of his depth. It's only natural he doesn't want to go anywhere where there's a possibility of a huge fuck-up. But he also owes his position to Glyn. He produced *Dog the Wagz*, and came across with Glyn, part of the Glyn Trelawney package. If Glyn's not happy then Nick's not happy. Nick's very anxious about staying useful, and that means causing a stink on Glyn's behalf at all times. And I mean... at all times.'

As if on cue, there was a ringing noise from a device fixed above the windscreen.

'Excuse me, I need to take this in private,' said Randall. He switched off the hands-free and pulled a mobile out of his shirt pocket.

'Nick,' he said with weary resignation. 'How are you?'

Randall listened for a very long time, saying the odd 'yeah' and 'ahh-ha' and then 'I'm sure he didn't mean to' and then 'I'm sure that was an honest mistake on his part'. Mervyn couldn't hear anything, but he guessed there was a long shopping list of Ken-related complaints coming from Nick.

Mervyn was also aware that the 4x4 hadn't slowed down at all. Randall was conducting what was obviously a tiresome conversation while still driving his car at a dizzying speed down an anaemic little country road. Mervyn's knuckles were hurting; he realised he was gripping the sides of his seat so hard he was leaving finger marks on the upholstery.

CHAPTER TWENTY-FIVE

Today they were in Trebah Gardens near Falmouth. It was a lush stretch of land on the banks of the Helford stuffed with an amazing array of subtropical plants, a perfect location for an alien jungle.

Mervyn hopped down from the 4x4. There was no one about, very few cars and no catering van.

'It's quiet,' Mervyn said.

'It would be,' said Randall, dragging out a large refrigerator box from his boot. 'That's why I've got this. Most of the cast are back at the supermarket, recording the footage we should have got yesterday.'

'Oh. Sorry.'

'Stop apologising already, Merv. Shit happens. It's all part of the rough and tumble of TV production. Bryony the location manager – she's become second unit director for a day. She's playing catch-up while we're here to try and keep to schedule. We're shooting all the scenes we can here with Roger and Holly.'

'Holly?'

Randall narrowed his eyes. 'I gather that most of the internet refers to her as "the ugly one".'

Mervyn felt slightly ashamed. He must make an effort to learn the Wagz's proper names. Chrissie was the dark-haired one, Gemma was the blonde, Holly was the ugly one. Chrissie dark-haired, Gemma blonde, Holly ugly... It wasn't fair, because Holly wasn't ugly at all; a bit pudgy with a flat nose and a heavy jaw, but far from being ugly. Unfortunately, circumstances conspired against her. She was forced to spend most of her days getting photographed standing next to two stunningly attractive females with incredible bodies. It was inevitable that she looked like the 'ugly one'. He resolved to call her 'Holly' the very next time he met her. That would be the nice thing to do. The right thing to do.

The weather wasn't good. It was cold, and the wind was being very cheeky, lifting up the hood of the gaffer's cagoule and trying to snatch the tablecloth from the buffet table. But despite the blustery weather, and even though they had no hot food, one urn of water, a jar of coffee and a box of tea bags between them all, without Glyn and the screaming actresses it felt blissful.

Unfortunately, they still had Ken.

They walked into the gardens, and could hear him before they could see him.

'Okaay... You've been separated from the other Gonks...'

'I'm a Gorg,' said the Gorg.

'Yeah, whatever. You've been separated from the other Gonks and you hear a ship landing over there somewhere, and you go and hide behind the tree.'

'What tree?'

'The cross on the ground. There's going to be a tree there. We're going to put it in later...' Ken added 'apparently' under his breath.

'Well... Can't I hide behind a tree that's actually here?'

Ken, sighed, looked at the Gorg in weary disgust, then realised he didn't know the answer. He pressed his mike. 'Can the Gonk hide behind a tree that's actually here?'

He listened.

'No' he said, finally. 'We're putting in another tree using computers, because none of the trees here look alien enough.'

'Can't I hide behind a real tree, and then you put a CGI tree over the tree I'm hiding behind?'

Ken touched his microphone again. 'Can the Gonk hide –'

He stopped because there was a tinny noise flooding his earpiece. It sounded very angry, it sounded like a woman's voice, and it lasted a very long time. Ken closed his eyes as his headache grew and festered. 'No,' he told the Gorg, 'cos it's going to fall over when Elysia blasts it with her ray gun, and we'll need to see you after it falls.'

'But if...'

'Shut up!' said Ken. 'Just do it, okay. Tree, there. You, there.' He blundered out of shot. Someone else shouted 'Action!'

The Gorg said his line into his wrist radio, then he jumped behind back on his mark. Holly stepped into the clearing, looking this way and that, using all her acting skills to pretend she couldn't see the Gorg, who was hiding behind the invisible tree.

She pretended to hear an imaginary noise.

'I see you, hairy guy.' She fired her plastic gun at the imaginary tree. 'Come on out with your paws where I can see them.' The Gorg surrendered. 'Fine. There's a good boy. Now are there others of your kind round here?'

'Cut. Great. Now, move to scene 52.'

The location team shunted awkwardly about three yards to the left. They did another tiny scene, and another, and another. Ken was charging through the script, putting lines though pages at a furious rate. There were no retakes, even though it seemed very rough and ready.

'I wasn't sure about that one,' said Holly, after a particularly brutally shot scene, 'I think I said the line wrong. Can I do it again?'

'It was fine, trust me,' snapped Ken, and marched his team to another part of the gardens before she could open her mouth again.

Same old Ken, thought Mervyn. *I wonder if he makes love like he makes his shows? Three seconds of furious activity and then on to the next position, trying not to notice how unsatisfied everyone else looks.*

Holly was obviously not at her best. She looked upset and distracted between takes. It was as if she was part of a gestalt entity and couldn't function without the other two girls present. Everyone could see she was ready to collapse like a Yorkshire pudding. Everyone but Ken.

'Okay, this is scene 64. Can we go for a take?'

Holly bit her lip. 'Ummm... Couldn't we do a bit of rehearsal first? Go through the lines a couple of times?'

Ken flicked through the script, as if it was something he hadn't read yet. 'It's just six lines. You'll be fine.'

'Aaand... Rolling... Action!'

Holly stood there, not moving, not doing anything, trapped by powerful lights like a petrified rabbit on a motorway.

'Cut!'

Ken lumbered back into the clearing. 'I've told you, you'll be fine. You can do it.'

'But... I can't.'

But Ken had gone again.

'Rolling... Action!'

Holly flapped her hands helplessly. A tear trickled down her cheek.

Ken came back, sighing loudly, his hands balling into fists. He looked like he was pretending to be a steam engine. 'Okaay. What's up? It's just six lines. One scene. Just say the lines.'

'But... I should be talking to someone else? Doesn't someone else have to do the other lines?'

Ken glanced at his script again. 'Oh,' he muttered. 'I see.'

'I'm sure there's someone who's got to stand here with me –'

Ken shushed her, flapping his script angrily. He was conducting a conversation with his own imaginary friend. 'I thought she was talking to a CGI thing or something,' he said. 'Oh. Well where is he?' He looked up and shouted. 'Is Roger Barker here? Is he here? Where is the old... Where is he?'

'Hes wasn't called till 11.30. He's in make-up and costume. He should be ready in half an hour.'

Louise strode up to them; it was she who was supplying the voice on the other end of Ken's earphones.

Ken looked at his watch. 'So I'm stuck here doing nothing.'

'Well Ken, we didn't realise how efficient you'd be. There's not many directors who can keep the same pace as you.'

Ken didn't notice the shovelfuls of sarcasm in her voice. He was too busy looking around, trying to think of things he could shoot without Roger. He finally gave up. 'Okaaay everyone. Let's be back for 12. Sharp.' He walked away without acknowledging Holly, and stalked off to harangue costume and make-up.

Holly stood there while everyone raced to find the catering van. She still looked bereft and was teetering on the edge of tears.

'I was terrible wasn't I? I was so crap.'

'Nah, not a bit of it! You were hot, sister! Really on the mark! You go girl.' Randall was playing the pompom-wielding cheerleader to the hilt.

Her eyes swivelled pleadingly to Mervyn. 'Is that true? Was I really okay?'

'I thought you were marvellous, Ugly.'

The world screeched to a halt on its axis as everyone's brains struggled to compute what Mervyn had just said.

'Holly,' said Mervyn quickly. 'Marvellous, Holly. You were marvellous Holly. Holly. Yes.'

Every word he said plunged him deeper into the abyss.

Then the world started moving again. Holly's eyes flooded over and she ran from the clearing.

Randall's eyebrows tickled his hairline. He turned slowly and, without looking directly at Mervyn, patted his shoulder.

'Good work, Mervyn,' he said, echoing Glyn.

And then he walked wearily away in the direction of Holly's car.

CHAPTER TWENTY-SIX

When the *Vixens* crew raced to the catering van and found it wasn't there yet, they grumbled darkly and raced for the location bus to get the few up-to-date newspapers lying around inside.

Mervyn noticed that the rest of the production team was joining them. The roped-off area of the car park with 'LOC' hanging on it was now full of familiar cars. He got himself a tea and watched everyone arrive.

Ken barged out of the costume van in impotent fury. Mervyn knew that he'd been sent away with a flea in his ear and had been told in no uncertain terms that they couldn't be rushed.

'For a man who hasn't worked in proper telly for over a decade, he doesn't look very happy.' It was Steve O'Brien who spoke. He was suddenly at Mervyn's side, tapping his fag into the bushes with one hand and carrying a polystyrene cup in the other. 'Hi Mervyn,' he said, 'how goes the heady world of *Vixens from the Void*?'

'Oh, as well as can be expected,' Mervyn said neutrally. 'How's life in the even headier world of the making of the making of *Vixens from the Void*?'

'It's a complete madhouse. Oh, no, not a madhouse, what are those things that aren't madhouses? Funhouses. It's a complete funhouse. Bendy mirrors, air jets up the knickers, silly sirens, the works. I'm getting lots of stuff that is very entertaining, but I can't use any of it. The "making of" doco team aren't happy either. Every time they point their cameras there's some disaster, usually involving Ken.'

'And that's bad, is it?' Mervyn still didn't quite believe this strange corner of journalism where Bad News was No News. He still had a lingering suspicion that it was some elaborate trap designed by Steve to get him to start dishing the dirt.

'They can't use it either. Oh yeah, they can show a few tense faces and the odd star kicking a litter bin to let the great unwashed know that, contrary to their suspicions, making television is quite hard work. But this is in a different league. Their brief and my brief is to cover the making of a television programme. There's not much they can do if the television programme isn't actually getting made.' He blew some smoke out, which was instantly snatched away by the wind. 'Unless Product Lazarus tells me to write the story of a television disaster, we can't use any of it.'

'Well I suppose they have a right to decide what the public should know and what they shouldn't know, and if they don't want anyone to hear about it, then you'll just have to toe the party line...'

'Yeah, I suppose that's what we'll have to do, if they want to keep it quiet,' grinned Steve.

'It's the price you pay,' grinned Mervyn back.

'If you want to keep it quiet, then that's what you do,' smirked Steve.

'Well, if news management is your priority, then those are the rules you have to live with.'

'Yeah, keep it hush-hush.'

There was a long silence before Mervyn spoke again.

'Sorry, is this another one of those conversations when you think I'm joking, but I'm really not?'

'Oh, you're not joking?'

'No, I'm really not joking!'

It was an odd sensation for Mervyn; he *liked* Steve, but he didn't *like talking* to him. It seemed that when he was with Steve, everything Mervyn uttered was either foolish, or naïve, or both.

'Oh. Well, it's the same with any press office of any media company laying down the law with us. It's not about keeping it secret at all; they clamp down on us because they're pissed off – because they know *everyone's* going to hear about it anyway. It's your classic over-compensation. Like your impotent man trying to chat up every woman in the room.' He pulled out his Blackberry and slid his finger over the screen. 'Here's a typical fan site from this morning.'

It read: 'VOICES FROM THE VOID DISCUSSION FORUM', and a list of subject headings, 'Gemma to walk?', 'Will it get finished?', 'Footage of THAT row (spoilers)', and 'sign my pertition glin trelorny must go now!!!'

'And that's just a tip of a very large iceberg,' Steve continued. 'Funny isn't it? Back in your day *Vixens* barely had a press office; you had an alcoholic producer, a shag-happy star and directors going berserk on set and no one knew anything. Now you've got press officers by the bucketful trying to deny everything – and no one believes them.'

Mervyn drained his coffee cup. 'Well, "back in my day" there were still press officers, and things did end up in the papers. We were hounded on location. I could tell you some stories...'

'But I'm not talking about the papers. That's my point. The papers used to manage the news and decide what became a national scandal and what didn't. I'm sure there were deals struck between *Vixens* and the tabloids all the time.'

'Well of course there was. If they found out anything juicy that would really hurt us, like a happily married actor being gay...'

'Like Tara Miles.'

'Um. Yes. Tara being a case in point. Ah... I think she's still officially "straight" by the way...'

'Mum's the word, Mervyn. I'll never tell. Well, I won't tell anyone who doesn't already know, anyway.'

'Well Tara's secret was a very good example. The tabloids knew, but they were always willing to do a deal. "Give us an exclusive photo shoot," they'd say. "Put the Vixens in teddies and pyjama tops for our Naughty Nightwear week and we'll 'forget' we found out about it." It just becomes one of a thousand stories that nobody is aware of apart from a select few... And if it comes out now, who's going to be interested?'

Steve smiled. 'But that's the thing. Nowadays, gossip has become democratised. You'll always be able to find one person in the country who wants to know about *something*, even if it's the colour of Mervyn Stone's underpants.'

Mervyn shifted uncomfortably in his seat. At that moment, his 'underpants' were bright orange with palm trees running along the hem and pineapples dancing round his crotch. He wouldn't want anyone to know that.

Steve continued. 'The tabloids aren't in control any more, and they can't dictate what gets an airing and what doesn't. There's a 24-hour gossip machine out there and it's called the British public, with the latest snoop technology at its disposal. The internet's already in meltdown, there's videos posted on fan sites of screaming matches between Glyn and Chrissie and first-hand accounts of the whole thing grinding to a halt with barely any footage shot.'

Mervyn felt an icy coldness squeezing his heart. 'Was there anything about me?'

'Not that I'm aware of. There's great phone-cam footage of Chrissie calling Glyn a patronising bastard,' Steve chuckled. 'The only people who won't be reporting this debacle is the DVD doco boys and me.'

'But who would leak this stuff? Who's trying to sabotage the production?'

'No one's trying to do anything like that. It's the public again; probably just a fan who's conned their way on to the set, or a scene-shifter who wants to earn a few bob from the tabloids or just someone who likes to go on forums and say they know something that everyone else doesn't. It's the bloody public, Mervyn – they spoil the information machine for everyone. The stars, the press, the PR people...'

The roar of an expensive engine stomped on their conversation. Chrissie the dark-haired one hurtled into the car park in her black Audi R8. The car door opened, and needle-sharp stilettos stabbed the gravel.

Mervyn raised his hand and smiled feebly, but she looked right through him – or he presumed she looked right through him, it was difficult to tell what was happening behind her sunglasses. Anyway, whether she saw him or not she didn't wave back. Mervyn guessed he'd already been submerged in her memory, placed in the file marked 'Someone who was useful to me yesterday but not right now'.

Her phone exploded into life; a raucous metallic theme that Mervyn guessed was one of her old hits. She looked surprised. Mervyn looked at his own phone and realised there was the tiniest ghost of a signal floating in the area. Chrissie pressed a button and listened – her hard face becoming harder as she listened to a very long message.

'There's a good example of the way news management is messed up now,' said Steve. 'Take Chrissie. Her footballing grunt of a husband had an affair with a lingerie model six months ago. Not that Chrissie cared much – celebrity marriage of convenience and all that. A trashy newspaper found out about the affair, but the story got spiked because they agreed to do a big exclusive feature in the trashy newspaper's even trashier sister magazine.'

'How do you know all this?' asked Mervyn.

'Shhh!' Steve waved him quiet. 'Unfortunately, the story's well and truly out...'

Chrissie's red thumbnail played a random tune on the keypad and she was soon talking loudly into the phone. 'Michelle it's me. What's going on? Well, have you talked to him? I'm sure he says it's not down to him, what do you think? Well "Probably" ain't good enough, Michelle – can't he do something about it?'

Steve winked at Mervyn. 'She's talking to her PR person-stroke-manager, asking her if she's talked to the tabloid editor who's responsible for keeping the story under wraps. She's asking her manager if she thinks the editor is responsible for the leak and perhaps, if so, they can buy the editor off again. Unfortunately the answer's "no" and "no".'

Chrissie continued a one-sided conversation, in which she listened, said the word 'bitch', listened, said the word 'bitch' again, listened, and said the words 'fucking bitch'.

Steve continued: 'You see, the story is down to a hairdresser who got phone-cam footage of Chrissie's husband and aforesaid model having a pre-shag dinner in a Beefeater, and it's taken the hairdresser six months to work out how to upload it on YouTube. Now it's a free-for-all in the press and they all have to cover it. The only thing that's left to do is damage control.'

Chrissie frowned. 'Why should I talk to him? I'm busy.'

Steve grinned. 'Her manager's suggested that she actually talk to her husband about it and work on a plan of action.'

Chrissie listened for about 20 seconds, and sighed. 'All right. Christ...' She redialled, listened to a recorded message and said 'Vince. It's me. Don't talk to anyone but Max, not even your mum. Especially not that cow. Talk to Max, then ring me. If you can. I might as well be on the moon for all the fucking signal I have.' She tottered away.

'How do you know all this?' said Mervyn again.

Steve shrugged. 'I'm on Twitter.' He waved his Blackberry. 'And I've got a mate who supports Vince's football team. You think *Vixens* fans know too much about everybody's business? You should meet your dedicated footie fan.'

The female runner with the purple hair was going round with a pen and paper, talking to the crew. She scuttled up to Mervyn.

'Hi. Sorry about the coffee mix-up yesterday.'

'That's quite all right, no harm done,' Mervyn lied.

'As we won't get the catering van until the afternoon, I'm taking orders from the gardens' restaurant. What would you like? They do a good selection.'

She handed the menu and the pen to Mervyn. The food looked splendid; all locally sourced, of course. He ticked the gammon and mustard sandwich. The runner went on her way, ignoring Steve. Steve barely noticed, he was examining his Blackberry like a starship captain who'd just beamed down onto a hostile planet. When he eventually looked up, Mervyn pointed to the runner. 'She's taking orders for food. You can catch her if you hurry.'

'Sadly not for me,' Steve shrugged. 'I'm not official enough.'

'I'm sorry to hear that. You can have a bite of mine.'

'No thanks. I'm a vegetarian.'

'You don't even know what I picked.'

'You picked gammon and mustard.'

Mervyn's mind gaped. 'How did you *know that*?'

'Like I said, I'm on Twitter.' He waved the Blackberry again. 'That runner who just took your order is doing a sandwich sweepstake. I think I'm ahead with chicken salad now, but Lucy in costumes is catching up with hummus and mushroom.'

Mervyn felt unnerved. He thought it would only be a matter of time before Steve came up to him, slapped him on the back and said 'Sorry about your underpants, Mervyn. I hear they could stop a cow dead in its tracks.'

CHAPTER TWENTY-SEVEN

A car arrived, vibrating madly. It was thudding with the beat of what might have been a familiar tune, but the song was distorted beyond recognition. Mervyn and the rest of the crew instinctively covered their ears, bracing for the moment the car doors opened.

'Jesus,' said Steve. 'I saw Coldplay last year and they didn't play their own songs as loud as that.' Mervyn couldn't even begin to imagine what the noise was like inside the car.

Glyn was in the passenger seat. Nick must have made a special journey back to the hotel to fetch him. *That's a great use of a producer's time,* thought Mervyn.

The music was shut off. Then it started again, even louder. Then it went off again. Then on again. They seemed to be wrestling over the knobs on the dashboard, a heated argument dribbling away into a petty squabble over the car stereo.

Glyn emerged, and the music emerged with him, unbelievably loud, thudding across the car park like a dancing giant. He left the car without a backward glance or a 'Thanks' to Nick.

Mervyn could see Nick inside, his head resting on the steering wheel. Nick turned off the car engine, and there was blessed silence. He finally raised his head and wearily dragged himself out of the car, staggering to the production van.

Mervyn didn't need to ask Steve about the story behind *that* little show.

Glyn didn't go anywhere immediately. He mooched around the car park, pacing backwards and forwards, trying to calm down and get into his current role of pound-shop Russell T. Davies. He switched his grin on like a light-bulb, aimed it at Mervyn and slapped him on both shoulders with his open palms.

'Mervyn, Mervyn, Mervyn! Good to see you're still surviving, my lovely! Day two of school, eh? Still don't know where to hang my coat and I don't know the teachers' names yet, but I'm very keen on Miss Baudelaire who teaches French.' Then Glyn jogged away to the location area, passing a particularly delicious make-up girl running back to the van with a heavy make-up bag on her shoulder. She was in a hurry, her unfettered breasts fighting each other under her cotton shirt.

Incredibly, Glyn did a complete double-take, staring at them wolfishly as they jiggled before disappearing into the foliage.

'Now there's a queen who needs to come to terms with who he really is.'

Mervyn glanced at Steve. He wasn't talking about Glyn; he was looking at Roger Barker.

Roger had emerged from the make-up trailer, painted and rouged, enormous eyelashes flapping against his eyebrows. He had squeezed his huge bustle dress through the door and it was buzzing with swarms of costume girls holding pins in their mouths. An elaborate wig in the style of an 18th century aristocrat was piled on top of his head. 'I'm ready for my close-up, Mr DeMille,' he said to no one in particular, then laughed very heartily because no one else did.

One of the costume girls disappeared completely inside the bottom of the dress and Roger played it for all he was worth, squealing and pretending he was being interfered with. 'Steady on with those pins, Lucy, I may be the queen, but I'm nothing without my crown jewels!' The costume girls didn't respond. 'It's okay, they don't hate me. They're not talking to me because they've got pins in their mouths,' shouted Roger, again to no one in particular.

'The whole world can't have pins in its mouth,' Mervyn hissed under his breath. Steve spluttered with laughter.

The runner scurried up to Roger, waving her menu. Roger took a long time to decide. Mervyn wondered if he was genuinely indecisive or was he deliberately making the runner wait. There were all sorts of tricks 'stars' got up to on set to reinforce their power; none of them *ever* turned up on time for anything, but there were many interpretations of how late they should be. Some, like Vanity Mycroft, took it to extremes, barely being seen in the mornings. When she didn't sign up for season three of *Vixens* he was annoyed, but also relieved. It meant they were actually able to get some work done.

Roger finally made his choice, noticed Mervyn, and sashayed up to him, holding his dress high to avoid the puddles.

'What's your name again? I'm sure we've met before!' chortled Roger.

'Hello Roger.'

'Mervyn isn't it? It must be ages since we last saw each other.'

'Yes.'

'Must have been ooh, four hours since we last met,' he said, driving his joke into the ground and burying it with a shovel. 'You haven't changed a bit.'

'Really? I feel like I've aged years since I had breakfast with you.'

Roger ignored that. He was the type of bloke who made his little jokes, laughed at them, and moved on; he wasn't interested in sparring with Mervyn. 'It's weird being a woman for the day, all these straps and bits of elastic. I'm used to taking them off girls, not putting them on me.'

Steve winked at Mervyn, then disappeared.

'I thought about having a shave for this, get rid of the overnight stubble, and then I thought "Sod it! – Emilia Green never did when she played the part, so why should I?"' He nudged Mervyn in the ribs. Mervyn thought that people only did that on adverts and comedy sketches. 'So, have you written this?'

'I'm a consultant. The writer's going to be here any moment. He's also an executive producer, and, if it gets a series, the show-runner.'

'Oh right. A big cheese. What's he like then, this bloke?'

'Oh he's very nice. Very friendly. Lots of jokes. He's very collaborative. He loves actors to just change the script when they can,' said Mervyn naughtily. 'He's a big fan of the organic acting process.'

'Sort of like a Mike Leigh type?'

'Yes, I think you could say that.'

'Oh. So he's in charge of everything? Should I talk to him about changing digs?'

'Well...'

'No offence, but the place I'm in now is completely unacceptable.'

Of course it is, thought Mervyn wryly. *Completely unacceptable. NOW it's completely unacceptable.*

'Do you know where the pop star girls are staying? Do you think they've got rooms free there?'

'I'm not sure.'

'If it's more expensive I'd be willing to pay the difference.'

Of course you would. 'I think they've rented their own cottages.'

'Oh.' Roger deflated. 'Perhaps they've got room for a small one, if you know what I mean. Not that I am small.' Roger hopped to the other of his obsessions. 'Have you heard? There's no catering van.'

'Ah, well there's a reason for that –'

'No catering van and I've had to order a sandwich. I'm starting a full day on location and I've been offered a bloody sandwich!'

Mervyn looked at the berouged Roger with a tiny grin.

'No!'

'A bloody sandwich!'

'Disgraceful. Don't they know who you are?'

'I know.'

'They should have at least let you eat cake.'

Ken appeared, jumping from foot to foot with impatience.

'Ken! Great to see you mate! How are you doing?' Roger pushed out a hand to shake, but Ken ignored it. 'We were just talking about you, weren't we Merv?'

Ken's eyes narrowed. He glared at Mervyn with angry bloodshot eyes. 'Oh yes?'

'Just this morning over breakfast. What're your digs like by the way? I'm wondering if I can get moved to another B&B and I need to know who I can speak to round here.'

'Yeah, whatever. Just get on set.' Ken walked away, and Roger's grin switched off.

'What's Ken doing here?' he asked Mervyn.

'He's the director.'

'Yeah, right,' Roger sighed. 'Always the funny guy. What's he really doing here?'

'He's in charge of catering.'

'Thank you, Mervy. A straight answer. Much appreciated. Let's leave the jokes at the door. We're working now.' Roger shook his head. 'In charge of food. Of course he is. Figures. That's why there's no catering van.'

Roger wandered off after Ken, forgetting to hitch his skirts up and eliciting cries of anguish from Valerie in the costume van. He could hear Roger's voice as it drifted away. 'Ken, I can't go a day without red meat. Do you think you can send out for steak and chips...?'

CHAPTER TWENTY-EIGHT

Mervyn noticed that the sandwiches had arrived. There was a big pile of paper-wrapped bundles in a box, plonked on a picnic table. He rummaged through the box, found the one marked 'M. Stone', stuffed it in his satchel and wandered down to the shoot.

Roger was in the middle of a clearing, standing to one side of a pole with a sock tied to it, presumably another substitute for some CGI.

Roger saw Mervyn and sidled up to him, a big false grin on his face.

'He wasn't in charge of catering at all,' he hissed.

'Oh really?'

'I'll get you for that.' Roger was trying to sound jovial, which was difficult for a man with no sense of humour. 'I'm going to make your life hell on this shoot.'

Mervyn looked at him and gave a sardonic smile. 'Sorry Roger, I'm afraid Ken has beaten you to it.'

Roger was aghast. 'Ken bloody Roche! Directing this thing? Do they have April Fool's on a different day in Cornwall?' He looked at his expensive chunky watch to check the date. 'I mean, is it on October the first down here?'

'They want it to have the feel of the old series.'

'Fuck that! We want it to be good!'

Bryony piped up 'Roger, you've left your mark. Please. You need to stay exactly there.'

'Fine, sweetheart.'

'No... *Exactly* there. Otherwise Clockworks can't get your crashed spaceship in behind you.'

'Oh,' said Roger, pointing at the stick with the sock on it. 'I thought that *was* the crashed spaceship. I was going to congratulate you for having better special effects than the old show.'

Bryony smiled, humouring him.

Ken slumped into view.

'Okaay, Roger. This bit of Cornwall is pretending it's a hostile alien planet.'

'Ken, Cornwall doesn't have to pretend. It *is* a hostile alien planet,' Roger cackled, and elbowed a nearby Gorg in the ribs.

'Can we just get on?'

'Ready when you are, Kenny boy.'

'Okaay, you've been captured by the gonks...'

'I think they're Gorgs, Ken.'

'I *am* a Gorg,' said the Gorg.

131

'Just do the scene, Roger, we've wasted enough time...'

Roger wasn't an actor. He *looked* like an actor; he had an actor's big lustrous hair, he had an actor's big lustrous laugh, and an actor's nose. He stood next to actors on occasion and attended their parties, their charity bashes and their funerals. He was shallow, he loved talking about himself, he'd played 13 parts on television since 1968... But he wasn't an actor. Because he didn't act. All he did when asked to act was raise his voice and waggle his eyebrows.

Fortunately that was what was usually required, and this morning was no exception. Roger played up his part like a pantomime dame, showing his knickers, fluttering his fan and coming out with a high-pitched falsetto squawk, which was an old man's idea of how an old woman sounded. It was going to liven up a rather young and bland cast, Mervyn had to admit.

He continued in that vein for an hour. Bryony returned from the OB van having looked at the footage she'd shot that morning, and everything was going well.

But then she went pale. She whispered in Ken's ear. He went pale too. 'Okaay everyone, let's do scene 71.'

The crew looked bewildered. They'd just done scenes 71 to 76.

'Scene 71, everybody.'

Roger looked around, waiting for someone to say something.

Ken wiped his forehead with the back of his hand. 'Roger?'

'Yes?'

'That was good, but next time...'

'Yes?'

'Take your watch off.'

'Six scenes? We went through six scenes with him wearing a bloody watch?'

Nick shrugged at Louise. 'Apparently.'

She walked around the car park in a wide circle, trying to calm down. Eventually she came back to Nick, who was standing with his arms tightly folded. 'So... has anyone asked Ken as to how he managed to miss the watch?'

'Apparently he was relying on Bryony to notice that sort of stuff and she wasn't there...'

'Okay, he let someone else do his job. No surprise. What about costume? What has Valerie got to say for herself?'

'She said Roger wanted to keep the watch with him. He insisted. He promised he'd take it off for takes.'

'Well he didn't, did he?'

'No he didn't.'

'And everyone else? The camera guys?'

'They assumed it was some kind of space bracelet.'

'A space bracelet? A fucking Rolex space bracelet?'

Nick shrugged again. 'Perhaps we can cut a few of the scenes for reasons of time...'

'No fucking way. I'm not losing a second because of those two arseholes. We're going back into the forest and we're going to finish them, even if we do it in the dark.'

The light was fading. Arc lights were cranked up. Ken was flailing, a man slowly sinking into a swamp.

'Okaay, scene 74, take two,' he gabbled. Roger and the blonde one scrambled for their marks. 'Okaay, hold the gun steady... rolling... action!'

Roger adopted his falsetto voice. 'Arkadia, my dear, why are you pointing that at me? Try aiming it at the nasty robot people. They're surrounding us as we posture.'

'So we'd better do this quickly,' snarled the blonde one. 'Then I can get back and tell the Council of Mistresses that you were killed by the Styrax.'

'Treachery!' spat Roger.

'It's for the good of us all. With you gone we can finally...' she drifted to a halt, confused.

There was a strange noise. A rhythmic bleep-bleebity-bleep noise that got steadily louder. It certainly wasn't anything to do with the shot.

'CUT!' shouted Bryony.

The bleep-bleebity-bleep sound carried on. Everyone was looking puzzled, then one by one, they all started looking in Mervyn's direction.

Mervyn realised with a shock it was his own phone. He'd forgotten what it sounded like; it hadn't rung for days because of the appalling signal coverage. Ever since he'd arrived, his phone had been like a regular at the bar of the Black Prince: sullen and silent, only making a noise when it needed juicing up.

Mervyn wrestled with his coat, desperate to retrieve the phone and stop the noise. 'Sorry, sorry, didn't realise I actually had a signal.'

Mervyn stumbled off into the woods, Ken's glare scorching his back.

'Hello?'

'Hi. It's Dominic.'

'Dominic?'

'Dominic Stone.'

Oh. *That* Dominic. Mervyn's son.

Ten years ago, he'd found a scruffy kid on his doorstep asking to talk to Mervyn about his life. What Mervyn expected to be the usual yawn-stifling fanzine interview turned into something quite mind-boggling.

Mervyn didn't like uncomfortable situations, and this one had seemed like the ultimate. When it came to meeting a long-lost son, it ranked even above being forced to make a best man's speech. But to his initial relief, his son contained the same confrontation-avoidance gene that had sent his father scurrying under tables the moment people started raising their voices in his vicinity. Dominic didn't demand vengeance for the years he never had with his father, or monies for the years of counselling that he thought he deserved. He simply shook Mervyn's hand affably and bought him a latte from Costa. They were there for half an hour. Ten minutes was taken up with the father/son stuff, 20 minutes was spent with Dominic demonstrating to Mervyn all the ring tones on his mobile phone.

Over the years, through phone calls and the occasional e-mail, they kept up a friendly but rather shallow relationship. Mervyn had started to regret the lack of shouting and tears that marked their first meeting. If there had been some emotion to begin with, perhaps he might have got some emotional traction with him now. As it was, Dominic demanded nothing of him, expected nothing from him. Which meant Mervyn felt he had to do something for him.

'Sorry Dominic. I didn't recognise your voice.'

'Hey Dad. No worries. My bad. No talkie long time. Totally my fault. Rush rush.' Dominic talked in sentences of two, three or, if he was feeling particularly expressive, four or five words. He was the only person whose phone calls were more abbreviated than his texts. Mervyn remembered that his son broke the earth-shattering news of his parentage with the words: 'Thing is. My mum. Did the dirty with you. Apparently. So you daddy, me Dominic. Do we hug? Let's not.'

It all set Mervyn's teeth grinding. Mainly because after a minute of listening to it he ended up imitating it himself.

'So how are you Dominic? What job are you orbiting this week?'

Every time they spoke, Dominic was doing something new. He stored up life experiences like his mother, but not with any particular goal. He was the ultimate ambition-free drifter; picking up a job like it was a shiny toy, getting bored and finding another.

'Great job, Dad. Underground driver. Circle Line. Incredibly cool. Nice and warm. Place to sit. Pay you shed loads. Only two potential bummers. First bummer: the suicides. They jump off platforms. Under trains. V. v. messy.'

'I can imagine that's a downside.'

'Bummer is. Poor suicide types. Problem solved, they think. Trouble is, platforms not good places. Train slows down. Most of them live. A bit splattery. But no die.'

'Seems a pity.'

'Yeah. They should try bridges. Jump off them instead. Deffo mortality potential.'

'Thanks Dominic. I'll definitely take that advice on board when the black despair finally takes hold.'

'Write it down. V. useful.'

'So what can I do for you, Dominic?'

'Weird thing happened. Thing is, man rang me up. V. mysterious. No name. Asked about your monsters. The Styrax.'

'Oh yes?'

'Wants the rights. So asks me! "Name your price." "What?" I say. "Monsters not mine. Deffo not. Talk to Dad – Dad's the monster man. Big bad alien king." Then man says. "Not to worry. Just asking. Hypothetical stuff. If you owned rights. Would you? In principle."'

'I see. V. odd. And you said? I mean, that's very strange, and what did you say to that?'

'The amount he said? Deffo. Could go round world. Several times! Well up for that. Hope you don't mind.'

'Of course not, Dominic. You're my closest relative. Once I'm gone, everything I've got is yours.'

'Thought so. Love you Dad. Have to go. Duty calls. Everyone not pleased. Looking at me funny. Better get off platform. Back into train. Passengers might sue.'

'You stopped your train to make a phone call to me?'

'Yeah. Off at Earl's Court. Had to really. No signal underground. That's the big second bummer. Bye, Dad. Love you and stuff.'

Mervyn tucked his mobile away thoughtfully. There was only one reason why his son would get a phone call like that. Someone expected Dominic to inherit the rights to the Styrax, and there was only one way that could happen.

Deffo mortality potential.

CHAPTER TWENTY-NINE

Mervyn went for a walk in the gardens. He needed to be alone to think. The sky was starting to glow with sunset colours, and the faint cry of the seagulls mingled with Ken's distant screams as he tried to get his scenes in the can before darkness engulfed them all.

Mervyn sat near the restaurant to take advantage of the artificial light. He bought a coffee and a postcard and tried to compose a few paragraphs of his book. Five minutes later he gave up on the book and took advantage of his newly-found mobile phone signal to make some calls. He phoned his agent and told her about the extra money he'd been promised. He was thinking very hard about phoning his solicitor and changing his will to cut out Dominic, but decided against it. Why deny his only child an inheritance just to piss off some nutcase? No, he had to find and expose this person, whoever he or she was. That was the only way to end it... This person was annoying him now. Without the tiresome trying-to-kill-him nonsense, he would be really content right now.

If only this potential murderer would go away and leave him to enjoy his time with...

Maggie?

Mervyn blinked.

Maggie was sitting at the next table. She was like a genie; it was as if the act of thinking about her had conjured her into existence. She was reading a book on the gardens, flipping the pages with long delicate fingers. He watched the muscles in her jaw twitch and flex as she munched on a biscuit. He watched her foot stretch leisurely, allowing her shoe to slip off and flap against the heel of her foot.

He leaned across, trying to move into the edge of her peripheral vision. She wasn't noticing him. He bent lower and lower, scraping the floor with his shoulder and feeling rather foolish. He waggled his fingers.

Her eyes flicked across to him, just for a split second, and she realised she was being watched. Her cup clattered against her saucer, and she started to choke. And kept choking. Alarmed, Mervyn sprang up and started slapping her hard on the back.

'What are you doing here?' she spluttered.

'We're filming in the gardens today. We're just over there.'

'Really? Ooh! Exciting!' She stretched her neck to catch a glimpse of the cameras, but could see nothing.

'What are you doing here?'

'I come here when my mum's pretty bad and doesn't want me in the room. This afternoon she thought I was Adolf Hitler come to interrogate her.'

'Oh. I'm sorry.'

'Don't be. It's just a small setback in my plans for the Fourth Reich. I don't know how she saw through my disguise.'

Mervyn was never ready for Maggie's flippancy, he always took a second to be shocked before feeling delighted at finding a woman with such a darkly humorous streak within her.

'Do you want something?' she asked. 'I'll get you a coffee.'

Mervyn bit his lip, his writer's instinct for scavenging struggling to break free. 'I couldn't.'

'Oh go on. I can see you want another.'

'I've got a busload of free coffee just over that hedge.'

'Yes, and that's why you bought one over here, is it?'

'Well...'

'And they won't let you drink your telly coffee over here and you want to sit with me, don't you?'

'Your logic is good... But you've already given me a lift in your car – if you buy me a drink then I'll officially be the woman in this relationship.'

'You're right. Tell you what. I'll get you a coffee, and you can lend me your jacket if it gets chilly.'

'That sounds like a deal.'

'Do you want food?'

Mervyn patted his bag. 'All sorted. Sandwich courtesy of the magic of television. And they bought it at this restaurant, so I don't think they'll move me on for eating it.'

Maggie disappeared inside and returned with two coffees. They drank them, sitting companionably side by side, not talking.

This is what a good marriage probably feels like, thought Mervyn. *You're not talking to each other, but it's not because you don't want to. It's because you don't have to; you're just aware of the other person and enjoying the fact you're together.*

Mervyn eventually broke the silence. 'If you want I could introduce you to the Stepford Wagz. They're all here this afternoon.'

'Oh no. I couldn't!'

'Why not? Come on!'

She shook her head, laughing. Her ringlets slapped against the side of her head and continued bouncing long after she stopped. 'Have you never heard of the old saying, "Never meet your heroes"?'

'I prefer my old saying: "Never meet your fans."'

She laughed again. All of a sudden, Mervyn knew it was his sole life ambition to make that woman do her giggle and cause all the hair-bouncy action that went with it.

'Come on, I'll take you to meet them.'

'Absolutely not Mervyn. Anyway...' she looped her arm in his. 'Why would I waste my time in this garden meeting pop stars when I could spend it walking round this garden with you?'

She took him into the undergrowth.

'It's very peaceful here.'

'Yes, it is.'

They walked through the gardens, stopping and looking at the plants. 'Oh, look at the fuchsias!' she said, gasping with delight. 'Aren't they beautiful?'

'Oh yes,' said Mervyn, hoping that he was looking at the right thing. She was pointing at a huge blanket of bluebell-type things (only they were red), trailing down a wall. 'Very lovely.'

'I knew you'd like them. I have an amazing skill – just by talking to people I can guess what type of flowers they're into.'

'Really?'

'I thought you'd be a fuchsia person.'

'Absolutely. Yes. I like them very much,' said Mervyn uncertainly.

What he knew about plants he could write on the tiny withered leaves of the thing that had died on his bathroom window sill, but he was damned if he was going to admit that.

She gave another gasp; she had seen something else. 'Agapanthus!' she exclaimed, running ahead. 'These are *my* favourites.' She was standing by a large flower with a round blue head, like an enormous dandelion clock. 'What I like about them is – they look like a lovely big flower when you're quite a distance away. But when you get closer, you can see what it really is. Lots of little flowers.'

Mervyn looked closer, and sure enough the big blue flower was lots of little blue flowers clustered together.

'So it is. It's very pretty.'

She laughed at him. 'You're not impressed.'

Mervyn tried being direct. 'I prefer lilies,' he said simply, staring into her eyes. 'They're pretty, they smell nice, and they leave their mark on you if you're not careful.'

Maggie smiled bashfully and looked away. 'It really is very peaceful here... How's your filming going? Is that peaceful?'

'Oh, not peaceful at all. It's been a terrible shoot. Lots of problems, stuff going wrong, creative differences, someone's been trying to kill me...'

She laughed, and her hair did the bouncy thing again. Then she caught his expression. 'Seriously?'

'Oh yes, it's been a nightmare, retakes, fighting over the script...'

'I mean, seriously as in someone's seriously trying to kill you?'

Mervyn told her about the incident at the supermarket. Her eyes widened in a wonderful, innocent way.

'It could have been an accident, but then my son got this phone call...'

'Son? You're married?' she said, a little too quickly.

'No,' he said, even quicker. 'Dominic's the product of an unwise dalliance with a completely loopy actress when I was at university.'

'Ah.'

'She was always seeking out life experiences to enrich herself as an actress, which usually meant sleeping around behind my back and taking huge quantities of drugs. Neither made her any better as an actress, but at least they had the advantage of keeping her quiet for a few blissful hours.'

'Ah.'

'One day she decided – without telling me – that the act of childbirth was an essential part of an actor's "experience palette" and flushed her contraceptive pills down the faculty toilet. Take it from me, Maggie, actresses can be a bit batty. You wouldn't believe the things they're prepared to do in the interests of their career.' He put air-quotes around the word 'career'.

'I'm sorry,' Maggie said, blushing. 'You were telling me about this phone call from your son. Please continue.'

'Well, I got a phone call from him just now. He'd been contacted anonymously and asked what he'd do with the Styrax in the unlikely event I dropped down dead tomorrow and he inherited the rights.'

Her jaw dropped. 'No!

'Oh yes.'

'That's just weird. And creepy.'

'I'm not arguing.'

'You're taking this all very calmly.'

'Well, my mysterious assailant hasn't done a very good job so far. He or she didn't even manage to give me frostbite.'

They'd walked round in a wide circuit and found themselves heading back to the spot where they'd met. He could see their table, which was still vacant. Mervyn had placed his bag on his chair and looped his jacket over the back – a typical Londoner's way of claiming ownership of the spot. There was nothing remotely valuable in either his jacket or his bag, so Mervyn was quite relaxed – if a little annoyed – to see his bag had been tampered with. It was lying on the ground, its contents strewn around his chair. His *Vixens* script was flapping around like a wounded bird.

It was only as they got closer that they noticed something white by the bag. At first Mervyn assumed it was a plastic bag, but then he saw it had feathers.

'What's that?' Maggie was concerned.

'Is that a seagull?' said Mervyn.

It was a seagull. It was splayed out under his chair, beak open, eyes staring, wings spread at an awkward angle. Crumbs and bits of crust were scattered around its body. Mervyn tapped the bird with his foot. It was quite dead.

'It must have hit the window of the café and been killed instantly,' said Maggie. 'I've seen birds do that.'

'I don't think it could have bounced all the way back to our table, no matter how hard it hit the window. I could be wrong, but my guess is that it went in my bag and ate my sandwich.'

Maggie gaped at him. 'Your sandwich!'

'Yes. The one that was sitting in a big box with my name written on it.'

There was nothing left of the sandwich but crumbs. Mervyn gingerly took the dead seagull by the foot and held it above the bin.

Maggie was astonished. 'What are you doing?'

'I'm dumping it.'

'I bet you do that to all the gulls.'

Mervyn laughed, and dropped the seagull.

'Shouldn't you take it away to be examined?'

'I don't think the police round here have the time – or the resources – to do autopsies on seagulls. It might have had a heart attack, but I think, given what we know, we can guess it was poisoned.'

'Well okay, Sherlock, but what are you going to do now?'

Once again, Mervyn couldn't answer. Once again, he hadn't the faintest idea.

CHAPTER THIRTY

>CLICK<

[SIGH]

Same shit, different day.

Once again, Mervyn Stone stays wedged in my U-bend, no matter how hard I yank the chain. Jesus. What went wrong? I tried very hard this time. I made a plan.

[SIGH]

How he can be better than me? He's got 'loser' written all over his shitty face. Why won't he flush?

Talking of shits, Roger Barker was being his usual twatty self. Shitty actor, shitty personality, arrogant shit. I'll give him jokes. I'll laugh his head off for him, with a fucking chainsaw.

If I'd thought it through, I could have killed Roger first, murdered HIM as a rehearsal to kill Mervyn, but I've done that now. No regrets.

God knows how I could have knocked Roger off though; maybe I could have got some cyanide and put it in that bottle of amyl nitrate he keeps in his briefcase on the off chance he gets lucky. The nitrate will probably kill him anyway. He'll end up dead meat, collapsed over some poor flabby make-up girl.

God, Roger really is an old woman this time round. You would not believe how much of an old woman he was today.

But no. Roger's a dick, and everybody knows it. That's his crime, and that's his punishment. But Mervyn... No, Mervyn is in a class of his own.

So I didn't get you this time, Mervyn. Never mind. There's more than one way to skin a twat. The clock is ticking, Mervyn fucking Stone. And it ticks for thee.

CHAPTER THIRTY-ONE

The moment Mervyn sat down for breakfast, Maggie bent low over the teapots and whispered: 'So, have you decided what you're going to do yet?'

'I'm going to set a trap,' said Mervyn. 'And if you want to, I could use your help.'

The journey to the shoot was tense. Randall was uncommunicative; his eyes were trained on the road and his tie had ended up resting on his right shoulder, but he didn't even notice. He looked like he had things on his mind. Mervyn decided not to mention the dead seagull.

Penny something-or-other was also silent, lounging in the back, reading a script and making little doodles in the margin.

'Everything all right, Randall?'

Randall flashed his teeth. 'Sure it is. All hunky-dory. We've hit a few potholes on the freeway, but we're on schedule.'

'You seem preoccupied.'

'Can't get anything past you, Merv. I've just had some good news from the US... and some bad news. Nothing the gang can't handle.'

'Oh, anything you can tell me?'

'I'm gonna tell everybody, but I prefer to tell everyone in one go. I'm sure you'll understand.'

'Definitely.'

And that was their conversation for the whole journey.

It was day two in Trebah Gardens, and Ken was instantly in trouble. Cameramen and lighting riggers were carrying equipment back to the spot where they were yesterday.

Louise was shouting at Ken. Nick was standing to one side, arms folded. Louise was furious and she wasn't worried about hiding it.

'There's barely enough time to do this again, what were you thinking? We need that shot!'

Ken glared at her, but said nothing.

'We could just make it a smaller shot. I mean, we could cut the tree for reasons of time...' said Nick hopefully.

'No, we are not doing that. Clockworks spent a week designing that damn tree and we're not losing it because we haven't got a ten-second shot. Okay?'

'If you'll excuse me, I've got a job to do,' snapped Ken.

'Good,' said Louise. 'It's about time you fucking started.'

Ken marched away, flipping a lit cigarette into the grass.

Mervyn watched all this from Randall's 4x4. The American switched the car off and blew out a big sigh. 'What now?'

Mervyn left the car and approached Louise, who was kicking the gravel angrily with her foot. 'What's going on?' asked Mervyn.

'It's a production matter.'

'I am on the production team, as it happens.'

'Oh yes, I remember your contribution as a member of the production team the day before yesterday, when you ground filming to a halt. And yesterday, when you insulted one of our leading ladies and she wouldn't come out of her trailer for three hours. You're a cog in a well-oiled machine, Mervyn.'

Randall joined them, twirling his car keys in his hand. 'What's going on now?'

Louise didn't answer, she just leaned against her car, pushing a cigarette between her lips with shaking fingers.

Nick eventually spoke. 'Ken filmed yesterday morning's tree sequence with no prep, and didn't allow enough space in the shot for the CGI. Not only that, he didn't time the CG animation, so the actors moved too quickly. And he didn't allow for the noise of the tree falling, so the actors were speaking too softly.'

'Well you can't blame Ken for not allowing for the noise,' said Mervyn. 'If an imaginary tree falls in a fake forest and there's no one to see it, does it really make a sound?'

'Ha bloody ha, Mervyn,' said Nick. 'You're such a tonic in these trying times.'

Louise folded her arms and stared at the gravel. 'I swear Ken's doing his level best to sabotage this project.'

Randall and Mervyn exchanged glances. Mervyn's own words came back to him. *Perhaps they're not just after me. Perhaps someone's trying to sabotage the production.*

'Well,' said Randall. 'He was a good idea at the time.'

'He was *your* idea at the time, Randall.'

Randall glared at Louise, and Louise glared at the wing mirror of her car. Mervyn felt very privileged; he'd never seen the ancient TV executives' ceremony of the Passing of the Buck before.

Randall threw his shoulders back and took charge. He patted Mervyn on the shoulder. 'Okay, I better go see if we can salvage anything. I'll talk to Bryony and the Clockworks boys, see if we can avoid a reshoot. Nick, make sure Ken doesn't make any more mistakes this morning. Lean on him very hard.'

Randall was leaving when Mervyn said; 'Randall, I don't suppose I could watch the television in your car? There's my episode of *Doctors* on today, and I'm curious to see how it turned out.'

'Sure Merv,' Randall tossed him the keys. 'Just don't watch it for more than a half-hour. You'll flatten the battery.' Randall jogged off, followed by Nick.

Mervyn and Louise were alone. Louise didn't acknowledge him, she just kept on smoking furiously, ash cascading on to the bonnet of her car. It looked like the stress of making a television programme was starting to get to her.

'Louise, I have a question to ask you.'

'What?'

'Have any members of the production team made any enquiries about who holds the rights to the Styrax in the event of my death?'

Louise shrugged. 'Not to my knowledge. Why do you ask?'

'Because I've been told someone did.'

'Not from my office they didn't. Why should they? Bloody Styrax. If I had my way, we wouldn't have the bloody things at all. They're just one more headache.' Her eyes fixed on a non-existent horizon. 'God, I hate this! I hate it all! When they showed me old tapes of *Vixens from the Void*, I thought, "God, what utter rubbish. What a cheesy load of crap. There's no way this can be remade in a way that won't get laughed off the screen."'

'No offence taken,' said Mervyn drily.

'Yes, Mervyn. Offence given. I mean it, if you're offended, I'm bloody glad. It was a shoddy awful piece of work, even for the 80s, and you all should be ashamed of it. What, were you all pissed or off on holiday or what when you planned it? When they put it out of its misery they were doing us all a favour; but of course, everything has to come back now, doesn't it? That's the fashion. Product Lazarus bought the rights – against my advice I might add... And Randall was so enthusiastic. I knew this was a mistake.' She wandered away gloomily, scuffing the gravel with her boots. Mervyn could hear her voice droning into the distance. 'I should have gone to the Shopping Channel when I had the chance. All they do hold jewellery up to the camera and talk about it. So much easier...'

Mervyn wasn't going to watch the television in the car. He'd never written an episode of *Doctors* in his life. He had other things to do.

He opened up the boot of Randall's car. His aged leather holdall was there. It had, until last night, contained his noxious underpants. He'd emptied the holdall (putting the pants in a very secure plastic bag) and marked it up prominently with 'M. Stone' on the handles, filling in the little plastic label on the side with his name and his address. He carried it out, plonked it on a picnic table and left it there, gaping open.

Mervyn leapt into the undergrowth, where Maggie was waiting.

'Time to go,' he said.

CHAPTER THIRTY-TWO

'This is quite some date,' said Maggie.

Mervyn raised his digital camera and looked at the viewscreen. They were crouched in Randall's car, slumped low in the back seat, peering cautiously through the boot. The tinted windows were perfect for hiding their presence.

'Are you expecting anything exciting to happen?' she asked.

'Not the first time a woman's said that to me in the back of a car.'

They grinned at each other, for slightly too long.

'As you can guess, I've thought about this a lot,' explained Mervyn. 'The poisoned sandwich seemed odd to me. My attacker couldn't have known whether I'd ask for a sandwich at all or even just buy a meal from the restaurant. It's almost like he or she was just wandering around the location with a pocketful of poison, waiting to put something in whatever food or drink I decided to have.'

'Sound thinking. I'm impressed.'

"From that conclusion, and assessing the incident at the supermarket, I'm thinking: if you were to give this murderer a one-word description, it would be "opportunistic".'

'I'd concur, Holmes.'

'There doesn't seem to be that much planning involved, more a spur-of-the-moment creativity that smacks of desperation. If that's the murderer's modus operandi, then how could he or she resist my bag just laying there, gaping open, its contents for all to see? Surely he or she would try and drop a bomb in it, or a poisonous spider, or something?'

'Look! There's someone at the bag!' hissed Maggie.

Mervyn looked. It was one of the runners, the female one with the purple hair. She looked at it, inspected the name tag on the handle and walked away.

'No,' he lowered the camera. 'False alarm.'

'Maybe she'll come back.'

'Maybe...' Mervyn was doubtful. 'Pity. She was near the top of my suspect list.'

'That little girl? Why?'

'She gave me the message to go to find the Styrax in the supermarket, and she got me my sandwich. The circumstantial evidence is quite strong.'

'What motive could she have?'

Mervyn shrugged. 'Well... it all depends what this mystery assailant wants to accomplish, really. Either he or she has a personal grudge against me...'

'Like Ken.'

'Yes, like Ken. Or perhaps there's a professional reason to get rid of me, like putting the rights of the Styrax into the hands of someone more malleable. Glyn would like that to happen. And if Glyn wanted it, then Nick would want it too. Or maybe there's a more general reason, to sabotage production so much it stops the filming. That could throw the suspects right open. Or, perhaps there's a mad fan on board, who thinks this whole project is a crime against all that is *Vixens* and wants to stop it at any cost.'

'The purple-haired girl could be a mad fan?'

'Perhaps. If there were an angry fan about on set, it might explain all the leaks on the internet.' Mervyn rolled on to his back and took a crafty photo of her.

'Mervyn no! Not from that angle! You'll get my double chin!'

'Don't be ridiculous. You haven't got a double chin.' He took another photo.

'Mervyn!'

She attempted to wrestle the camera off him, but he dodged her and opened the door. 'Right, it's lunchtime. They'll all be wandering around the gardens, stretching their legs and looking for places to eat. I'm going to sit by my bag and read my paper. Then I'm going to leave, come back, leave, come back, etc. etc., and see if anyone takes advantage of my absence.' He took another photo of her when she wasn't looking, saved it in his favourites and handed her the camera.

Mervyn went out and read his paper, pretending not to notice the production team arriving around him. He made a huge show of rooting around in his holdall, making clear to everyone it was his, then wandered off into the bushes.

Maggie watched the production crew sit at tables next to it, some glancing at it without interest. It began to get busy, and all the tables became occupied apart from the one with the bag; then that too was occupied.

Ken sat next to the bag, drinking tea. He seemed as though he was going to look inside, but thought better of it. He walked off.

The female runner inspected the bag again and put it tidily under a chair. Then everyone left for the afternoon's filming, and the bag was on its own again. Mervyn returned to the car, and opened the door.

'Hello down there.'

Maggie waved from her hiding place. 'Hello up there.'

Mervyn sighed. 'Okay, I'm officially starting to feel a little silly. And a bit bored.'

'I'm all of those, and I've got pins and needles as well.'

'I don't think anything's going to happen.'

'Merv!'

Randall was standing on the other side of the car park, arms folded. He looked tense.

'Merv, we got a top-level meeting in the location bus. Important business. I want you to attend.'

'Oh... ah, okay... in a minute.'

'Now, Merv, if you please. Everyone else is waiting.'

Mervyn slammed the car door and walked towards Randall. Randall pointed at the car.

'Wait!'

Mervyn stopped. Had Randall seen Maggie in the back seat?

'Merv, get the key out of the damn car. I have to lock up.'

Mervyn stopped, one foot in the air, paralysed by indecision. He turned round on the same foot, walked back, and opened the door. He leaned low and whispered in Maggie's ear.

'Sorry.'

'This is *so* not turning out to be a good date.'

Mervyn pulled the keys out and slammed the door. He tossed the key to Randall, who aimed it at the car like a miniature ray-gun.

There was chirp, and the car lights flashed. It was locked.

When Mervyn got to the bus, the senior production staff were all there; Ken was barely sitting; he was in a half-crouch, foot jiggling, tapping his cigarette lighter on the table surface. He was obviously frantic to get back to the cameras and crash through the afternoon's filming. Louise was sitting by him, arms tightly folded. She had assumed the crash position, ready for more bad news. Glyn was lounging on the back seat with his feet on a table. Nick was staring at Glyn, and Glyn was staring at his laptop, pecking at the keys, studiously ignoring the attention.

Mervyn picked a seat equidistant from everybody else.

Randall pulled the lever at the top of the bus doors. They closed with a sigh. Randall sighed too, and leaned against the door of the bus, loosening the knot on his fancy tie.

'We've got a problem.'

'Is this about the leaks?' said Mervyn.

'What leaks?' squeaked Nick.

'On the internet. The phone camera stuff.'

'This isn't about the leaks,' said Randall.

'It's nothing to do with our crew,' snapped Louise. 'It must be someone in the cast. I bet it's the Wagz playing games, building up publicity for themselves.'

Randall rapped impatiently against the bus window. 'Look, forget about the damn leaks. We'll investigate that later. That's hardly our most pressing problem right now. I've been sending some raw footage to the suits, and we have a problem.'

Mervyn wasn't surprised. He could conjure up an image of how hideous Ken's footage was and he suspected his imagination wasn't dark enough to do it justice.

'What's up with the footage?' Ken muttered. 'I'm very pleased with what we've got so far.'

'Oh, so are they. Don't get me wrong. They love it.'

There was a huge silence. Everyone looked at each other, stunned, like the survivors staggering out of a particularly nasty car accident.

'They... love it?' said Louise, cautiously.

'Yep. They think the girls are coming across real well on screen. The script is funny...'

Glyn doffed an imaginary hat.

'The sets look good. Mundane and low-tech, just like the original *Star Wars*. Their words...'

Louise harrumphed to herself.

'And they think the camera work is really interesting. Low shots, extreme close-ups, they think it's got a real *Battlestar Galactica* vibe.'

'What extreme close-ups?' said Ken indignantly.

Nick looked nervous. 'We've had to junk the mid-shots and keep the close-ups to hide things, watches, boom mikes... Clockworks had to crop a lot of shots digitally. Basically we had to make room to put a lot of their effects in the foreground instead of the background...'

'You've played with *my* footage?' Ken was outraged. 'I want to see it!'

'Shut up, Ken,' said Randall. 'You're lucky what you shot was usable.'

'So they've seen it and they like it. Then what's the problem?' asked Louise.

Mervyn was completely unprepared for what Randall said next.

'They got a problem with the Gorgs,' he said.

'What... kind of a problem?'

'It's been pointed out that they're actually naked.'

'What?'

'Now this is not my view but...'

'But they're huge hairy animals,' said Louise. 'I'm sure they don't have a problem with naked dogs. Or naked cats.'

'That's pretty much what I said, but the way they understand it, they're human life-forms who have regressed into primitive barbarism. So they're basically naked stupid guys. So we need to get them clothes.'

Louise stared disbelievingly at her coffee cup. 'You've got to be kidding. This is a joke, right?'

'Anything but. Hey, I don't make the rules, but that's the way it is. Product Lazarus is used to making kids TV, and they're used to making shows that they can sell to any network in the States without causing a hassle. And if Product Lazarus is putting in the dollars they don't see why *Vixens from the Void* should be any different.'

'What, and they can't show it because a man in a monkey suit isn't wearing trousers?'

'If Janet Jackson's nipple can cause a terror alert, then yes, they're not going to take any chances with naked monkeys. Bottom line is, we have to cover up their genitalia.'

'But they don't have genitalia.'

'Of course they have genitalia. Everything has genitalia.'

'Everything but the suits at PLM it seems,' muttered Mervyn.

'You're not being part of the solution, Mervyn,' snapped Randall.

Ken looked aghast. His eyes blazed behind his square glasses. 'We've shot days of footage with those bloody gonks. You're not seriously telling me we have to go back and do it all again?'

'Of course not. There's stuff we can do. The effects boys can add clothes digitally to the stuff we've shot.'

Louise and Nick became visibly tense.

'It'll be a bit expensive,' Randall continued, 'but they feel it's worth it to make sure the show gets an airing, so they're happy to find the extra budget to do it.'

Louise and Nick became visibly relaxed.

'But the question remains... What are they gonna wear?'

'A big sash?' suggested Mervyn.

'That's not gonna work. The suits will still say that the area where their genitalia is supposed to be is still unclad.'

'How do the suits know where a Gorg's genitalia are supposed to be?' said Mervyn.

'Merv, now is not the time to be cute. I don't give a shit where a Gorg's genitalia are, but I know where *my* genitalia are gonna be if I don't sort this out quickly; stuffed up my own ass.'

'Some kind of shorts, like boxer shorts?' ventured Nick.

'Marks & Spencers do wonderful pants. I swear by them,' said

Mervyn wistfully, picking his swimming trunks from where they were currently lodged. 'Very comfy if you're an active Gorg on the move, flying business class.'

Randall ignored him.

'How about hotpants?' Glyn giggled from the corner.

'Or a kilt?' said Mervyn.

'Lederhosen, my lovely,' said Glyn. 'They can wear the little hats too.'

Randall twisted his tie and stared despairingly at the ceiling. 'Am I the only one who is still acting like a professional here?'

Louise shrugged. 'Why not get Valerie in here? That's really her job. I'm not an ideas person.'

'Great,' said Randall. 'Glad to see someone is still trying to work towards the Solution Horizon here.'

The costume designer, Valerie Pemberton, was called in. After being told of the problem, she immediately realised that this was her moment to shine. She paced down the bus's gangway, rows of bracelets rattling on her wrist as she pressed her finger to her chin.

'Okay, let's throw some ideas at the Velcro, see if they stick... Perhaps some little toga type of thing, you know, an ancient Rome vibe?'

'PLM thought about that. All those little folds in the material... They think it might be too difficult for the computer boys to animate.'

'Animal skins?'

'Even worse. It's the little follicles.'

Valerie was not to be defeated. 'Okay, how about something a bit more ancient Egypt? Flat strips of shiny material? That shouldn't be too hard to animate.'

'Hmm...' Randall considered, absently curling his tie around his finger. 'That might fit the bill. I'll just e-mail my boss and see if that's acceptable. Can you get one of them in a costume like that for tomorrow?'

Valerie gulped. 'I think so. I'll get my boys and girls to pull an all-nighter.'

'Great.'

Ken scowled. 'And what are we supposed to do in the meantime? I've got scenes to shoot.'

Randall handed out a sheaf of script pages. 'Here are all the scenes we can do without the Gorgs. It's not much, but it should fill our afternoon.'

Ken went pale. 'But I haven't planned these scenes.'

You mean you actually plan the scenes you do shoot? thought Mervyn, and he knew everyone else was thinking it too.

The meeting over, everyone filed out of the bus. Randall stayed around, waving his Blackberry in the air, looking for life, and Mervyn saw his chance. 'Um... Could I get your keys off you again, Randall? I've left my notebook in your car.'

Mervyn rushed back to the car park, threw open the car door and found Maggie curled up asleep on the back seat. It was the most adorable thing he'd ever seen. She'd pulled Randall's leather coat over her, and her curls were draped across the seat like a pre-Raphaelite dog blanket. Her nose was squished up against the seat back. Mervyn wondered if he dared kiss her awake, but instead settled on giving her a gentle shake of the shoulder.

'W... whaddya want?' she slurred, in a strange American accent. She must have been having some odd, transatlantic dream.

'Maggie, it's me.'

'Oh, hello.' Her eyes fluttered. 'Have we got to Woodstock yet?'

'Time to go. Before Randall comes back.'

'What?' She sat up, startled, a fat red mark decorating her cheek. 'How long have I been in here?'

'Only 45 minutes.'

She looked at her watch. 'Oh my God... I thought I'd be stuck in here for days. I was frightened to try the door in case the alarm went off.'

'Don't worry. I'd never leave you in here. I'm aware of the danger. Dogs die in hot cars.'

As soon as he said it he knew it was the worst possible thing to say. He waited for the world to crash around him, but Maggie just snorted with giggles. 'Thanks,' she said, flinging her arms around him. 'Help me out of the car, Prince Charming.'

Mervyn pulled. Maggie slid out of the seat and allowed her drooping legs to hit gravel.

'I'll get my bag.'

'Mervyn!' she said suddenly, gripping his arm. 'While you were gone. There was a man by your bag. He was poking around inside it!'

Mervyn rushed to his bag and looked inside.

'Everything's here that should be. No bombs or spring-loaded daggers.'

'He was looking at your script, flicking through it. Then he put it back.' Maggie clapped her hand to her mouth. 'My God, I don't believe it.'

'Who was it? Was it a member of the production team?'

'How should I know? I've only met you and Roger. And it wasn't Roger.'

'Did you get a photo?'

'No I didn't. Your bloody battery's flat. Of all the luck.'

'What did he look like?'

'Ugly. Fat. He was a big fat guy. Really really fat and ugly. I mean really, really fat. The type of guy you'd never bring home to meet your mother – in case he ate her.'

Mervyn closed the car door and locked it. 'It doesn't sound like anyone on the shoot... unless Glyn's written in another alien monster.'

Maggie suddenly backed away from Mervyn. She seemed unnerved, and was looking over his shoulder. Mervyn glanced behind him, but could only see the production team; Roger, Randall, Glyn, Nick, Louise, Valerie and the Wagz, all walking from the location to their cars.

'I have to go. Now.'

'Wait, Maggie...'

'Sorry, I just do.'

'Look don't worry about Roger, I'll explain why you're here. I'll think of something plausible.'

'I'm sorry!'

She ran, stumbling, to the exit.

'I'm sorry about trapping you in the car...'

But she was already gone.

Louise and Nick came in Mervyn's direction, into the car park. Mervyn nodded at them cheerfully, swinging Randall's keys and trying not to act suspicious.

Louise unlocked her car door wearily. 'I'm going back to Truro to talk to Clockworks, tell them what we've discussed. Perhaps we can make a start on the CGI.'

'How can they do that?' said Nick. 'We don't know what the Gorgs are going to wear yet...'

'I have to do *something*!' she snapped, smacking her car roof with the flat of her hand. 'This is all we need. It's karma. We take on some stupid sci-fi shit and look what's happened. It's punishment. I've been cursed. I was the brains behind *That was Ben, This is Now,* for God's sake. I don't need this crummy remake.'

That was Ben and This Is Now was a comedy drama made by Attic Space Productions for ITV. It starred Martin Gable (a great character actor, considered a triple A list name by everyone in telly) and was about a man who'd lost his memory and accidently fell in love with his ex-wife. It was a huge ratings hit about three years ago.

Mervyn was stung by her dismissal of *Vixens,* and couldn't help himself. 'Oh really? I always though the writer was the 'brains' behind *That was Ben.*'

Louise threw Mervyn's knee a condescending look. 'I'm talking modern television here, Mervyn. Everybody in modern television knows what I mean when I say I was the brains behind *That Was Ben.*'

But Mervyn was friends with the writer, and he knew exactly what Louise had to do with *That Was Ben*. He was ready for her.

'Well, as you say, Louise, I'm not an expert in modern television, so I'm just guessing here. Does 'being the brains behind' mean 'chucking the script in a filing cabinet, forgetting about it and carpeting your assistant for fishing it out and showing it to Martin Gable's agent?'

Louis stuck her pointy nose in the air and glared at the clouds. She was obviously furious. 'I always suspected there was something wrong about you, Mervyn. I had grave misgivings. When Randall told me you coming down here to "advise" us, I smelt trouble. When Ken described you as a high-handed pompous shitty arsehole, I thought that was just bad blood from your history together on the show. But he was right. You know what you are, Mervyn? You are a troublemaker. A dinosaur. A relic. Guarding the old and jealous of the new. Yours is a life living off past glories.'

'At least I have past glories to live off,' Mervyn snapped. 'Not some illusion of achievement. The only work of fiction you've been the brains behind is your own CV.'

Louise's face turned brick-red. 'Thank God you'll be gone soon, Mervyn. The sooner this pet project of yours dies and you go back where you came from, the better.'

'*My* pet project? I didn't even want to...'

But she had already climbed into her car and was driving past, narrowly missing his foot. *That was interesting,* thought Mervyn. *Louise wants rid of me.*

He looked around. He was embarrassed by her outburst and by his own. Had anyone noticed he was blushing?

Nick was on his mobile, talking intently. 'Are you going back to the hotel? Do you want a lift? Glyn, are you sure you're alone? I can hear someone else...' He looked at his phone. Then pulled a face. 'Cut off again. Bloody reception.'

Mervyn suspected that a dodgy signal had little to do with the fact Nick had been cut off. But he still raised his eyebrows sympathetically.

CHAPTER THIRTY-THREE

That night, Mervyn dreamed.

He was back in the supermarket and he heard a scream coming from inside the freezer locker. He entered the locker and found boxes and boxes arranged against the wall, all with 'Frozen seagull portions' stencilled on them.

Maggie was dead, lying in the middle of a burst box oozing packets of icy breasts and frosty drumsticks. She had a 'Reduced' sticker on her forehead.

Mervyn started piling the frozen peas on her body. 'If I keep her fresh perhaps she'll come back to life,' he found himself muttering.

He heard a laugh, turned round and there in the doorway was Glyn Trelawney. 'Everything must go!' he laughed, and closed the door with a clang.

Then there was shouting outside the door. Someone was shouting. It was Nick, demanding that Glyn open the door. 'Open up!' yelled Nick. 'Open up!'

Mervyn awoke sluggishly, and realised he could hear Nick's voice. Nick was indeed shouting 'Open up!'

He looked at his bedside clock. It was 11pm.

He leaned over to the curtain and peered outside. There was Nick, standing in the car park, throwing handfuls of gravel at a first-floor window. 'Come on, I know you're in there!' he said in a drunken drawl. Lights were pinging on throughout the pub. 'Stop fucking her, you bastard!' He picked up a rock.

The window slid open and Glyn appeared, bare-chested.

Nick stretched his hands upwards. 'Romeo, Romeo, wherefore art thou, Romeo?'

'Just fuck off, Nick.' This time Glyn was a cockney. All trace of chuckly bonhomie had been stripped away. In its place was an aggressive thug who just happened to be a writer.

'It is the east, and Juliet is the sun!'

'Fuck off.'

'Come on Mr Writer. You can do better than that.'

'Piss off.'

'I'm not going anywhere.'

'Fuck... offff. This is nothing to do with you.'

'Yes it is. 'Sgot everything to do with me.'

'I am not doing this here. Go away, you sad sack.'

The window slammed down. Nick threw another handful of gravel. And another.

There was a door-slam from somewhere inside the pub, and angry running feet pounded past Mervyn's door. Mervyn peered out into the hallway to see what was happening but Glyn had gone. He looked back up the corridor, and there was Penny the script editor looking out from her door, swathed in a fluffy dressing down. She closed it quickly. No prizes for guessing where Glyn had come from.

Mervyn returned to his window and watched. Glyn burst out of the pub's front door. He hadn't dressed, just flung on a pair of jeans. His bare feet scrunched hard on the gravel as he rushed towards Nick, pushing him angrily square in the chest, punching him on the right shoulder.

'What are you doing? What are you doing to me? Can't you see I'm busy?'

Nick just took it, his head lolling forward on his shoulders, a defeated, punch-drunk boxer waiting for the bell to ring. Waiting for the abuse to stop.

'Come back to the hotel, please. Don't do this. Please stop.'

'Don't do what? Stop what? Stop screwing a woman? Is that what you want me to stop? Well sorry, I'm on a promise. She's up there and she's going off the boil, so if you'll excuse me...'

Mervyn looked across at the window from where Glyn's head had emerged. The curtain had been pulled back. Penny was watching, vaguely interested in the spectacle of her white knight charging out to fight for her lack of honour.

'You don't want to do this,' mumbled Nick. 'It's not you. It's not you.'

'Yes it is. I've told you a thousand times. I've moved on, my lovely. I don't do gay any more. It's boring. It's very last decade.'

This didn't register with Nick; obviously he was in so deep he was just ignoring things he didn't want to hear. He grabbed Glyn's arm. 'Come on. We can talk. We can sort it out.'

'Get off me!' Glyn shrugged off Nick's arm. He walked a few steps back to the B&B.

'Glyn!'

Glyn turned, but it wasn't a change of heart. Mervyn had seen enough of Glyn's technique; he knew that the man was a past master at closing down debates ruthlessly. This wasn't going to be any different.

'Why would I be with you, even if I was gay? Why would I waste my time being with you? Being your mummy?'

'Glyn, please...'

'Look at you, just look at you. You're pathetic.'

'No.'

'You're pathetic.'

'Don't say that.'

'Path-etic. So needy.'

'I'm not.'

'You're just my fucking glove puppet. Take my hand out of your arse and you cease to function.'

'You need *me*!'

'The fuck I do.' Glyn started to walk away again.

'I'll tell!'

Glyn stopped, turned. 'You have nothing to tell. You say anything – you hear me? – *anything*, and the party stops. For both of us. I go down. You go down. And you won't do that, my lovely. You know why? Because you haven't got the balls. So leave me alone and let me get on with my life. I've spent the last five years sleeping with an old woman, let me sleep with some young ones for a change.'

'GLYN!'

This time, Glyn kept walking.

Nick stood there, bathed by light from the windows. One by one the curtains closed and the lights went off again. Then he was in darkness. Like an actor leaving the stage, he trudged into the tavern.

Mervyn saw his chance. He pulled his trousers on over his pyjamas, pushed on a pair of shoes, threw on a shirt and jacket and ran downstairs.

Nick was at the bar. He was arguing with the landlord. 'I'm sorry sir, I can't serve you,' the landlord was saying.

Mervyn slid to Nick's side. 'Let me, Nick.'

Nick looked very grateful. 'Thanks, Mervyn. They won't serve me 'cause it's after hours. Residents only.'

Mervyn bought him a whisky, which he drank in one gulp. And then he wanted another. And another. By the time Mervyn came back from the bar for the third time, Nick was slumped low in his seat, rolling one of the glasses on its side along the table. It rumbled around in a wide arc and fell on the floor. Everyone was ignoring him, apart from the drunk's dog. It padded painfully over and lay near his feet, like an AA counsellor in mongrel form.

Nick was staring at the clock. It was 11.32.

'Are you expecting anyone?'

'I'm waiting for Glyn to come downstairs.'

'Are you sure he's coming down?'

'He'll come back. He'll get bored, and he'll come back. He always does.'

'I'm not sure he is.'

'What do *you* know?'

'Not a lot...'

Mervyn had a knack for needling people, for saying things that could make an embarrassing scene anywhere. If he volunteered a negative opinion on any actor/writer/producer, there was an almost 100% chance that he'd be talking to the wife/boyfriend/brother/sister of the actor/writer/producer and there would inevitably be tears/shouting/ fisticuffs, or probably all three. If he casually mentioned that due to heavy drinking the night before he was as sick as a pig, he would very likely find himself sitting in the foyer of a hotel playing host to the Biannual Conference for the Promotion of Positive Swine Health. It was only recently he had started channelling this great power as a force for good.

'I'm not sure. He seemed pretty cosy where he was.'

Nick's eyes widened with sudden fury, then he faltered, eyes falling back to the table. 'Yes...'

'But he'll be back.'

'Yes!'

'You seem pretty sure.'

Nick said nothing.

'It seems to me that Glyn does what he wants.'

'Yeah, he does that.'

'But he'll be back.'

'Yes.'

'How can you be certain?'

'I just can.'

'Can you make him come back?'

'No.'

'So how do you know he'll come back?'

'I didn't say I could make –'

'But if he does just what he wants...'

'Shut up.'

'And he's doing what he wants right now...'

'Just shut up. Shut up.'

'Then how can you know...'

Nick punched his knee. 'He's got no fucking choice!' They stopped talking for a moment, to allow time for Nick's words to sink in. Then Nick piped up again. 'I'm not saying any more. Go away.'

Okay, here we go...

'Nick... Did you save Glyn from some kind of trouble? Does he owe you?'

This completely threw Nick. His mouth opened and closed, but only a croak came out.

'Hello, hello, hello!'

Glyn was behind them.

Nick's expression cleared, confusion and despair banished from his face. It was the crazed optimism of the battered wife, ever hopeful for a new start. 'Glyn!'

'Hello you two dirty stop-outs! Having some all-night drinking session? Lovely!' Again, it was like that moment in the lift. A switch had been flicked, as if the row outside never happened. 'Shall I set them up? What are we all having? Trebles all round?'

Glyn bought drinks for all of them, and they all sat there, sipping hurriedly, wishing the time away.

'So isn't this exciting? I've seen the raw footage and it's fabulous. Really fabulous. Nick, we haven't talked about the series yet, have we, if it happens. Which it definitely will – we're really sitting on something special here. Tell me, Nick, are you up for it, my lovely? Get yourself a nice big office in LA, with your own swivel chair and all the biros you can eat?'

Nick flushed with excitement. 'You know me. If it's a Glyn Trelawney project then I'm certainly available.'

'And you, Mervyn – are you ready to chuck your hat into the ring and your balls into the fire?'

'Me? You won't need me.'

Glyn choked on his whisky and banged the glass down in an almost comical gesture of surprise.

'What nonsense! *Vixens from the Void* without Mervyn Stone, my lovely? It would be like *Star Trek* without Gene Roderick.' Glyn looked at his naked wrist. 'Goodness me, is that the time? Let's hightail it back to the hotel, Nick.' Glyn drained his glass, got up and left without another word. After a bare second, Nick drained his and got up. He gave Mervyn a strange, half-imploring, half-resigned look.

Mervyn had once seen that look on the face of an actress who'd married a famously aggressive actor. She was always turning up for work wearing more make-up than the TV lights needed; usually around the eyes.

Nick gave a shrug, and trotted after his master. Mervyn was left alone.

CHAPTER THIRTY-FOUR

Mervyn went back to his room, frustrated. He felt he'd been so close to finding out something important...

His mind flicked back through what he knew about Glyn; the conversations with Glyn; the row in the supermarket with Glyn; the threat in the lift from Glyn. What was Glyn prepared to do to get his own way? What was Nick prepared to do for Glyn?

He sat on his bed and pulled off his shoes, his trousers... Then he noticed the note.

It had been pushed under his door. For a glorious moment, he thought that Maggie had forgiven him. Perhaps she was feeling lonely and fancied a co-snuggler, volunteering to be a replacement for the badger in his lonely bed.

He read the note and his mind went numb.

It was a sheet of paper, with four sentences in a simple font that could have come from any printer. It read: YOU WANT TO KNOW WHO'S TRYING TO KILL YOU? LOOK OUT OF THE WINDOW. FOLLOW THE LIGHTS AT MIDNIGHT. THE PASSWORD IS 'PANDORUS'.

He looked at his watch. It was 11.56.

He crossed the room and moved the curtains to one side. It was like the window had been coated with oil, utterly and completely black. For a city-dweller like Mervyn, it was unnerving to see the night unpunctuated with points of light.

And then there were points of light. Two of them. They blinked into existence from nowhere; tiny, almost invisible.

Mervyn pulled his trousers back on over his pyjamas, shrugged on his coat and pressed his feet back into his shoes. He stood at the door, hand hovering over the handle, undecided and feeling rather foolish. *Think about this. I'm just about to charge into the night, pursuing a light in the sky. I'm behaving like some of the fans I meet at conventions; the ones who think the show's real, ask for Arkadia's astral address and demand to join the Vixos Space Force. I'm being stupid. Let's go back to bed and forget about it.*

He watched his hand.

His hand gripped the handle and pulled the door open.

Stupid hand.

He felt as though he was walking along the bottom of the ocean. His tiny torch created a fuzzy beam of light three feet in front of him. He twitched it one side; it showed him grass. He flicked it to the other; it showed him more grass. It was utterly useless.

He headed grimly towards the two points of light, knowing he'd feel a prize idiot if it turned out to be a pair of lighthouses.

The moon gave a cheeky peep from behind the clouds, and Mervyn fancied he heard a deep mournful howl. Now he felt like Dr Watson; blundering away without a clue as to what he was up to, a puppet doing the bidding of someone much cleverer than him.

Then he reached the lights. They were huge brass lamps, fixed on either side of black wrought iron gates. They were firmly shut, and there was no bell as far as he could see. Not very welcoming.

Well, there was no point wandering around like a tourist. He'd come a long way to look at these lights. He wasn't turning back now. He walked around the building, found the lowest part of the wall and clambered up, throwing himself over the top. He was fortunate; he landed on a compost heap and managed to scramble down to the ground, slipping and sliding on the decaying plant matter.

He was standing in the courtyard of a converted farmhouse, a building that had been beautiful once but had rashly succumbed to the surgeon's knife and had had expensive but not-very-classy plastic surgery. The mullioned windows had been punched out and replaced by large sheets of triple glazing. Rods of wrought iron poked out from the tops of the walls.

Then two huge Dobermans came round the corner. They stopped about 30 feet from Mervyn, looking intently at him, heads cocked to one side as if listening for invisible instructions.

Good, thought Mervyn hysterically. That's good. They're highly trained dogs, dogs trained to differentiate between undesirables and burglars and decent law-abiding writers like him.

The dogs started to growl.

'Good dogs. Nice dogs. Good boys.'

They kept growling.

'Umm... *Pandorus?*'

They didn't stop growling. There was an extra degree of growling, with a postgraduate certificate in snarling and snapping.

'*Pandorus?*'

Any second now, he thought, *they're going to realise that I'm just a friendly visitor who's happened to drop by at one o'clock in the morning, that I don't mean any harm and they'll... oh shit.*

The dogs were running towards him now, heads down, ears flattened.

Mervyn ran for his life.

CHAPTER THIRTY-FIVE

Where? Where could he go? He ran across the courtyard, aware of the skittering sound of claws on flagstones behind him. He hurled himself through a gap between two outhouses and ran alongside the rear, straining his eyes in the darkness, looking for something he could step on and use to launch himself over the back wall.

The dogs had oozed out of the gap he'd just emerged from, fighting with themselves in their eagerness to be the first to wrestle him to the ground and find out what his insides tasted like.

He flailed at the wall, but couldn't get a purchase on the smooth brickwork. He gave up and concentrated on running, pelting around the corner up to the house. He hoped the owner would be more reasonable about visitors than the dogs behind him, but he didn't hold out much hope.

He was an out-of-shape man running in the dark with no idea where he was or where he was going, so the inevitable happened. He skidded on something and collided with the ground. He lay there, staring at the moon, hoping he'd wake-up nice and warm in his hotel room in the Black Prince Tavern.

An outside light went on, spearing Mervyn with a blinding beam.

'Arkadia! Medula! Cease! *Daxatar*!'

The dogs stopped mid-charge, as if they'd been slapped in the face by an invisible force-field. They fell to their haunches and looked at Mervyn with doleful eyes, as cute as a poster on a kitten obsessive's wall.

A man clad in a dressing gown was in the doorway, grey hair sprouting in tufts above his ears.

'I've been instructed to bring you into the lounge, sir.'

Mervyn was invited into the house by the butler, who disappointingly introduced himself as Paul, not Jeeves or Crichton. Mervyn's muddy shoes were confiscated and he was given expensive slippers to wear. But before Mervyn could ask any questions about the owner of the house, Paul vanished.

Inside, the house didn't resemble a farmhouse at all. There was the occasional timber jutting out of the ceiling betraying the building's original purpose, but mainly the place had the antiseptic look and feel of a television studio; black furniture, glass coffee tables scattered with Broadcast and Variety, and large framed posters of old TV shows on the white walls.

Paul reappeared with a stiff drink and a steaming hot pasty, which

Mervyn consumed with gusto.

'Whose place is this?' Mervyn asked, spitting bits of potato on to a frighteningly expensive rug.

'It's not for me to say, sir. I'm sure my master would like to tell you himself.'

'Why?'

Paul arched an eyebrow. 'I'm sure he wouldn't thank me if I squandered his chance to be enigmatic.'

There was no answer to that. Paul disappeared again and Mervyn munched on his pasty thoughtfully.

Once he had finished, Mervyn got up and perused the room. There were several large glass cases transfixed by tiny spotlights. In the glass he saw his reflection; his nose was streaked with mud and his hair was even wilder than usual. Inside the glass cases were cheap and nasty lumps of polystyrene, fibre glass and scraps of costume.

It was all starting to feel horribly familiar.

'Hello Mervyn.'

The voice came from the adjoining room. Mervyn walked through.

Before him was a man sitting on a sofa. It was difficult to see where the sofa ended and the man began; both were lumpy, overstuffed and clad in a shit-brown hessian material that someone thought was a good idea in 1973.

It was Graham Goldingay. Of course.

Graham was holding a glass of something golden in one hand; it could have been whisky, but it could equally well have been apple juice or Lucozade. You never knew with Graham. In the other hand he had a TV remote, and there was an expensive set of headphones on his lap. A television dominated the whole of the far wall, and on it, actresses with 80s hairstyles and costumes mouthed silent, anguished words to one another.

The two dogs were panting amiably at his feet, looking benignly at nothing in particular, like they'd been taking lessons from Louise Felcham.

'Sorry I didn't hear you come in. I normally watch selected classic episodes of *Vixens* at this hour, and I use my Ultrasone headphones to completely immerse myself in the experience.'

Graham Goldingay was a *Vixens* superfan, but there was nothing particularly super about him. He had no X-ray vision, to the great relief of the female *Vixens* stars, and he couldn't leap tall buildings; in fact, if he'd entered a leaping competition he'd get out-leapt by pretty much anything; even tall buildings.

He was an unfortunate combination – an extremely anal fan with almost limitless piles of cash. He had set up a successful company that made millions, but he was never more than a spittle-flecked phone call away, always pestering the *Vixens* celebrities with demands to attend functions, dinners and charity events. Mervyn had been coerced into writing some Goldingay-funded bargain-basement drama that had died on its way to the made-for-video shelf.

'Mervyn Stone... I thought I recognised Paul's description, but I wasn't 100% certain; about 76 to 79% certain, I would say. This is a great honour, and quite a stroke of luck; you've already seen the props in my London residence, now you can see the ones I keep in my rural bolthole.'

Mervyn had last encountered Graham during the investigation of a perplexing mystery involving locker keys and old *Vixens* props. It had involved Graham showing Mervyn round his private collection of memorabilia.

Mervyn dusted himself off with shaky dignity. 'The only prop I need is my phone,' snapped Mervyn, pulling out his mobile. 'I'm going to ring the police now.'

'You can't.'

'Are you threatening me?'

'No, I'm just giving you a statement of fact. Mobile phones won't work here. You're welcome to use my landline. Why do you want to call the police?'

Mervyn looked astonished. 'Isn't it obvious? You've kidnapped me, attacked me with your dogs...'

Graham's mouth only usually opened for talking and tarka daal, but this time it dropped open in astonishment. 'What are you talking about?'

'They'll certainly be interested in what's just happened to me. I'm sure kidnapping and incarceration are crimes, even in these parts.'

Graham got out of his seat surprisingly quickly for one of such great size, and advanced toward Mervyn like an avalanche with a face. He might have been an adoring fan but he was still a film producer, and he'd been threatened many times before. 'You'll be surprised at what are seen as crimes in these parts; trespass definitely is, and they view it very seriously.'

'I was asked to come here and then I was ambushed by your bloody dogs!'

Graham's mouth, nose and eyes were pushed together in a frown. It made his head look even larger. 'Of course you've been asked to come here, on many occasions in the past, in fact. You've always said you were busy. But I didn't invite you here tonight.'

'I was slipped a note.' Mervyn fumbled in his pocket, produced the note and placed it in the middle of Graham's meaty palm.

Graham studied it, turning it over and holding it up to the light. 'I don't know anything about this. Did you really say the "P" word to Arkadia and Medula?'

'Yes.'

'That's their attack signal.'

'I sort of gathered that.'

Graham drummed his stubby fingers on the table. 'This is very worrying. Do you think someone tried to kill you using my dogs?'

'It looks like, doesn't it?'

'Who could have done such a thing?'

'Well... Does anyone know the attack signal apart from you?'

'Paul does, of course.'

'That narrows it down.'

'And I may have mentioned it on a few internet forums...'

Mervyn groaned. '... to several thousand *Vixens* fans...'

'The attack signal is common knowledge; whereas the signal to cease attacking is less so, for obvious security reasons. Only Paul and I know that. You are indeed fortunate that we were present at the house when you called.'

'I feel very lucky indeed,' Mervyn responded drily.

'This is indeed a heinous act, to think that I, Graham Goldingay, would be wielded as a weapon in the destruction of the most valuable piece of *Vixens* memorabilia of all time...' He pointed between Mervyn's eyes. '... Mervyn Stone's brain.'

'I think they were more after my guts, Graham, but I appreciate the sentiment.'

CHAPTER THIRTY-SIX

'This is indeed a fortunate meeting, Mervyn. We have much to discuss. Allow me the honour of bringing you into my humble abode and cleaning you up. You must be quite shaken up by your ordeal. Let me show you to my executive bathroom.'

Mervyn carefully stepped over Medula and Arkadia – uncomfortably aware his testicles were dangling within their chomping distance – but the dogs just stared at him happily, pink tongues dangling from their panting mouths.

Graham guided Mervyn's bedraggled form through his house but was obviously in no hurry to get to the executive bathroom. He was eager to continue where he left off a year ago and show off the rest of his collection to his special guest. Mervyn couldn't help but notice that the dogs had trotted after them and were following at a distance.

He was led through corridors festooned with recording equipment; cameras on tripods stood to attention on either side of them. They went past recording suites and a TV studio decorated with green screen. It was much better resourced than the *Vixens* shoot.

They came out into what had once been an open courtyard but was now a covered walkway encased in glass and steel. Suspended above them was more of Graham's collection, much bigger than the battered chunks of fibreglass in his London home. They were hanging like hunting trophies. Mervyn hoped they were fixed more securely than his kamikaze badger's head.

'That was the machine that stopped the Styrax attack in "Acceleration Switch". The one buried in the heart of Ventricula, left there by the Ventriculans.'

'The Magnotron?'

'The Magnotron. They found that inside Ventricula, and lo and behold it just happened to be the right kind of machine to stop the Styrax. It was such a convenient plot device. Such a deus ex machina. Such lazy writing.'

Mervyn had written that episode. Not for the first time, he marvelled at the disconnection fans had when they talked about the show, not realising that the work they dismissed with such casual brutality was the work of human beings with feelings, usually human beings standing right next to them.

'Such a cop-out. I got so annoyed about the ending to that one. I hated that ending. I hated that machine.'

'You hated it?'

'Oh yes. Hated it. Hate it, hate it, hate it.'

'But you bought it.'

Graham ran his hand along the bottom edge of it, caressing the cheap fibreglass. 'Of course I bought it. It cost me £8000 at auction at a Nostalgia convention. I was in a fight to the death with Simon Josh, but it was worth it.'

It's a strange world, the world of a fan, thought Mervyn. *Passionately loving and hating something all at the same time. I used to be so amused by their funny mindsets when I was making the show. But now? Just look at me. I both love and hate Vixens too. So I sympathise, I really do.*

'Now *that* was a good Nostalgia convention,' Graham ploughed on tediously. 'One of the great Nostalgia conventions. The best Nostalgia convention I ever went to. Nowadays there's not much to buy any more. I really miss the old days, when Nostalgia conventions were really good.'

'You have a very nice house.'

'Thank you. I come here for the peace and quiet and to work on my edits.'

'So it's just a big coincidence your place is just a stone's throw from where I'm staying?'

'You still think that I had something to do with attacking you? Oh no, not at all. It's not a coincidence I'm here, but not in the way you might think. I actually bought this place during the last *Vixens* shoot in Cornwall, back in 1990, to be near the filming, and goodness me I've had it ever since. But it *is* a funny coincidence that you've returned to the same place to film again, isn't it? It's very poetic, I think. I approve – of that aspect of the new production, anyway.' Graham ushered him into a sumptuous bathroom with gleaming taps and fat towels.

When Mervyn emerged, pink-faced, Graham was still waiting there, like a toilet attendant waiting for a tip; alert, ready to pick his moment.

'It's very fortunate you coming here.'

'You said.'

'We both need to work together, to stop the remake of *Vixens from the Void,*' he said. 'We need to stop it before it's too late. And only you can do it, Mervyn Stone.'

CHAPTER THIRTY-SEVEN

Mervyn was almost amused. Just moments ago they were talking about an attempt on his life, and now Graham had switched back to his usual preoccupation, *Vixens from the Void*. The man's bizarre priorities never ceased to amaze him.

Graham continued. 'I am begging you, I am imploring you, you can stop this madness, you can do this.' His least pudgy finger hovered in Mervyn's direction. 'You own the rights to the Styrax. You can take the Styrax away from the show.'

'No I can't.'

'Yes you can. You can stop the whole thing in its tracks, and then they can listen to you and you can tell them how the show should be brought back. You owe it to your loyal fans.'

Mervyn sighed. 'In the first place, Graham, the Styrax are not essential to the relaunch. I suspect a lot of people on the production team would be dancing the Macarena if they were prevented from using them. And in the second place, even if I *did* do anything like that and it *did* bring the production to a halt, wouldn't there be a completely different set of fans threatening to lynch me? The ones that might be keen for this project to go ahead?'

Graham snorted and tilted his huge head down like a charging rhinoceros. 'Darren Cardew's mob, you mean? Those people aren't relevant. They're idiots. They have no idea how this new show could shred the legacy of *Vixens*. I believe that this is a disaster in the making and alien to the spirit of the original show, and so does everyone who has lunch with me.'

'Just what is your problem, Graham? What's your huge problem with this relaunch?'

'What is my problem? I have many problems. I can make a long list.' *Of course you can.*

Graham's fat fingers on his left hand were prodded in turn with the index finger on his right as he ticked off his points. 'The lesbian bits, the profanity, the silly dialogue about sex tapes, the boyfriend stuff, the silly fat-looking Styrax, the clumsy references to terrorism... I could go on. This has nothing to do with the spirit of *Vixens*.'

'Graham, there's no "spirit" of *Vixens*. It was just a piece of 80s telly that was influenced by the fashions, politics and other television programmes of the time. If you revive the programme now, it's bound to be influenced by the politics, fashions and television of now. It can't be just the same. There's no point just trying to recreate the past exactly. If you do you're bound to fail.'

Graham ignored him. He was in full flow now and he wasn't about to stop any time soon. 'Eighteen years I've begged the BBC to let me have the rights. Eighteen long years. I poured half my fortune into setting up a film production company just on the off chance that they would ask an independent company to remake the show. I've asked 14 times, but each time the BBC said no they've given a different reason. Reason one: we have no plans to bring *Vixens from the Void* back; reason two: we are planning to bring *Vixens from the Void* back and talking to an independent film-maker would jeopardise negotiations with the other independent film-makers we are talking to; reason three: the negotiations with the independent film-maker have fallen through, and for that reason we are no longer considering approaches from any independent film-makers; reason four...'

'Oh God,' groaned Mervyn. 'Please stop with the lists. It always happens. Have any conversation with any fan and it'll inevitably degenerate into bloody lists...'

Graham blinked. He had lost the place in his speech. 'Lists are very important,' he said. 'They organise the thoughts; they present information in an easy-to-digest form. If it wasn't for lists I wouldn't have known when the edits were and I wouldn't have saved all the original unbroadcast studio footage by stuffing them down my –'

'And now you're making a list about how lists are important!' Mervyn wasn't a man who liked confrontation, but once he was angry enough he could quite happily scream like a hangover-encrusted Vanity Mycroft who'd been handed a glass of Shloer instead of a vintage Roederer.

'Graham, I really can't help you. And if I could, I don't think I'd want to. My job revolves around making money from my work. And if a bunch of nice television people happen to want to pay me good money for my creations then I'm there in the queue banking the cheque.'

Graham looked sulky; he looked like he wished he hadn't saved Mervyn from the dogs.

A thought struck Mervyn. He slapped his head in realisation. 'Wait a minute... Did you ring up my son and ask him about the rights to the Styrax? Did you ask him if he was prepared to sell you the rights in the event of my death?'

'The rights of the Styrax are incredibly valuable to me. I want them. I made enquiries, just like I do with any piece of merchandise. It's what any sane person would do.'

'Oh my God. You bloody nutter. You give no consideration between the thought and the act, do you? You think of something, you do it, and hang the consequences.'

Graham was about to retort, but he was interrupted by the *Vixens from the Void* theme emerging from nowhere. Graham rushed to a model of the *Hyperion*, picked up its top engine and held it to his mouth.

'Hi. Yes of course, glad you could ring. Don't worry about how late it is. I was up anyway. No, really. Glad to. I'm sure you're very busy.' Graham listened. 'No, it wasn't inconvenient in the slightest. I needed to stay in tonight anyway to listen to a dub.' It was as if Mervyn had suddenly ceased to exist. He was almost hurt. 'Really? Oh fantastic. You won't regret it. I'll be ready. Goodbye. And thanks a million. Bye. Thanks again. Bye.'

Graham Goldingay put the phone down and turned back to Mervyn, his face triumphant.

'I've been waiting for that call all night, trembling with anticipation. Do you know who that was?'

'Meals on wheels?'

'That was your executive producer, Mr Randall Angelford. You'll be seeing a lot more of me in the future. A lot more. My new job, as of now, is continuity advisor on the revamped *Vixens from the Void*.'

Mervyn didn't know what to say to that.

Eventually, he said 'Bollocks.' Sometimes the simple retorts worked best.

'It's true Mervyn.' He pulled his day pass off his collar, and showed it to him. It was definitely a real one, not one of the home-made photocopied ones Graham made in the 80s. 'I was meeting your producer yesterday and I start tomorrow.'

Another thought struck Mervyn. 'You were there yesterday? *That* was you too, wasn't it? You were going through my bag, looking at my script!'

'You'll find that difficult to prove.'

'That's how you knew about what was in the show! I should have known! Have you been leaking stuff to the press? Have you been taking footage of behind-the-scenes arguments and putting them on the web?'

Graham sniffed. 'More accusations. Of course I haven't, I've only managed to visit your set yesterday. I have not had access to filming yet, a point I made forcefully to your executive producer.' Graham moved his considerable weight from foot to foot. 'And I repeat what I said just a moment ago for the record. I'm not happy with aspects of the reboot, but I'm very excited and delighted to get this opportunity to shape the production and to work from within to bring it up to an acceptable standard.' Bizarrely, Graham saluted. 'I look forward to working with you on this new project.'

Mervyn said his goodbyes and left Graham's house, his head swimming with shock. Graham had been made continuity advisor to the new show? By the executive producer? Mervyn assumed that it might be Louise who wanted to sabotage the shoot, or some mad fan, but now he realised that the evidence had been staring him in the face all along. Who was really trying to sabotage the production? Who had decided to employ Ken Roche? Who was antagonising Glyn by insisting on using the Styrax? Who had just appointed Graham Goldingay as 'Continuity Advisor'?

It was Randall Angelford.

CHAPTER THIRTY-EIGHT

>CLICK<

[SIGH]

Jesus Christ. He's back.

Graham Goldingay is on set, that walking lump of cholesterol is here, I saw him, poking around.

[SIGH]

The fat fuck. I should kill him. But no. If I stabbed him he'd probably fall on me and kill me too.

Anyway, relax. Mervyn died tonight, and that's what I set out to do. One death on set is enough. Can't raise suspicions. Mervyn died out on the moors last night. Everything's fine.

He's gone.

CHAPTER THIRTY-NINE

Mervyn woke up, saw the badger snarling on his stomach, screamed, threw it off, and lay there, heart pounding.

He was still wearing his clothes; he'd just collapsed on the bed the moment he'd got in last night.

Last night.

He thought about the events of last night. Randall Angelford. It was obvious now. Everything he'd done seemed to plunge the production into more chaos.

Of course the same might be said of me, thought Mervyn guiltily.

He looked at it from a slightly different point of view, that of an outsider, and easily fitted the evidence together to make it look like *he* was the saboteur, bent on bringing the production to a halt. It was *him* who caused rows on set, ruined Glyn's plans to revamp the Styrax his way and caused Holly to cry in her trailer for a morning. Perhaps Randall wasn't a saboteur; perhaps he was just guilty of being naïve? He would have to tackle him about Graham's appointment at the earliest opportunity.

But – Graham Goldingay?

Was Graham genuine when he said he didn't know about the note, or was he just playing mind games? It was certainly part of Graham's character to put pressure on celebrities in subtle ways so they'd do his bidding. Was all that business with the dogs part of the softening up process, so Mervyn would gladly remove the Styrax from the new series? Or was there a darker reason? This was the third time in two days he'd had an 'accidental' brush with death. Was Graham behind it all?

But Graham had been at home. Who could have pushed the note under his door? Who had been here, in the pub that night? Had the butler done it? Nick had been here. Glyn Trelawney had been here. Should he go to the police with what he had thus far? He'd had an encounter with the boys in blue during that bloodbath of a sci-fi convention, and regarding that DVD commentary murder, the year after. He knew how they responded when he – a writer well known for his far-fetched stories – arrived with a far-fetched story of murder.

They either ignored him or arrested him.

He didn't feel that the cornish constabulary would be any more helpful. He was on his own. He had to sort this out and sort it soon.

He wondered who was doing the leaking. He stared at the badger. He'd seen a lot of spy films; perhaps he himself was spilling the beans? He examined the badger for bugging devices, tried to dig one of its eyes out, but no; it was just a rather mangy stuffed badger.

He got up and looked at his underpants, which were soaking in the bathroom sink. The heating had kicked in now because the timer had worked out it was October, so he'd decided to wash his pants and dry them on the radiator. Of course, he'd forgotten all about them and left them there. Even if he put them on the radiator this minute, there was no way any of them would be remotely wearable in time. He'd catch his death of cold. His swimming trunks were in no fit state to be worn again, so he made an executive decision; he would go without today. It was not a decision a man of his age took lightly. He felt his unfettered penis drag against the inside of his trousers as he went downstairs and flinched at the unusual feeling.

Mervyn had woken up late and missed breakfast. He'd missed Maggie, too. He wished he could have talked to her. He realised he was too blasé about this potential murderer stuff. He had scared her, and he was deeply sorry about it.

His lift to work failed to turn up, too. After half an hour, he came to the conclusion that Randall had forgotten him. He'd tried to call him, but alas, no signal. There was no sign of Penny. Perhaps she was feeling hurt that Glyn ran off into the night with a man? Perhaps not; she didn't seem energised about anything much. It was likely she'd realised Randall wasn't turning up and made her own arrangements without telling Mervyn. And perhaps it was just as well he had no lift. If Randall was some psycho saboteur, perhaps it would be better to tackle him on it when he wasn't behind the wheel of a fast car.

So Mervyn took a taxi. For once he was thankful that his driver kept up a jolly stream of gossip about new parking restrictions in Newquay and how the rugby clubhouse in Falmouth had been painted. It all felt blissfully normal.

The filming had moved to Truro. Large green screens had been erected in the Royal Cornwall Museum on the high street. They were close to the Product Lazarus building, which meant no need for catering vans and other location vehicles. The crew were running out of the Oo-ar Bar, clutching clotted creamoccinos.

Randall and Nick were outside the library when Mervyn found them. He walked up to them and gatecrashed their conversation.

'Randall, I want a word with you.'

Seeing Mervyn, Nick gave an embarrassed smile but said nothing.

Randall slapped his forehead in an exaggerated fashion. 'Oh Merv! I'm sorry I didn't pick you up this morning. I had such a lot on my mind, Valerie wanted to talk to me first thing about the Gorg costumes.

and I just rushed out the door, I didn't think...'

'I don't want to talk about that. What the hell is this about?' Mervyn flapped the call sheet under his nose, making Randall's fancy green tie shudder in the breeze it made. On the call list were the words 'Graham Goldingay – Continuity Advisor', and a contact phone number. 'Graham Goldingay? Are you serious?'

'Oh yeah. Yes. That's right. Graham Goldingay. I hired him last night. Don't worry Merv, you officially outrank him. I made that very clear.'

'Do you know who he is?'

'Of course I do. He was Continuity Advisor on the old series. You used him in the past. I've read your production notes.'

'We didn't use him at all. We gave him the title "Continuity Advisor" so he would stop ringing up the production office and annoying the secretary. A move that completely failed to work, I might add. He's a gossip, he's an attention-seeker and he's completely hostile to the whole concept of the relaunch.'

'I know that Merv. I've had about 300 letters from him since we got announced. I thought if I brought him inside the tent then he'd stop pissing on us. It worked for Harry Knowles.'

'Harry Knowles?'

'He runs a powerful website in the US, puts out reviews that a lot of suits think can make or break a movie. He's a big fat fan who spits his dummy out a lot – sound familiar? But the bottom line is, the suits think Harry can be bought by freebies and flattery. They work on the assumption that he can be swayed by a pat on the head and a plate of free cookies. They think the same will be true for Graham.'

'Graham can't be bought. He's a pathological headcase who cannot be swayed. No matter what you do, he will eventually take offence at you; he will find something you've done that he thinks is unacceptable, scream the internet down, throw his expensive collectable toys out of his pram, blame you for making him break them and buy some more expensive collectable toys to throw at you. There's no telling what mischief he's been up to since he's been on set.'

Nick looked alarmed. Randall just shook his head and smiled. 'Mervyn, you're exaggerating.'

'I only wish I were.'

'He's harmless, I'm sure.'

'That's what you said about Ken.'

At the mention of Ken, Nick's left eye twitched.

'Yeah, you were right about Ken, Merv, and I salute you for your wise counsel, but Graham's okay. He's promised to be good.'

'Graham can't promise anything. He has no control over what he does.'

As if saying his name conjured him from thin air, Graham appeared, like a killer whale launching on to a glacier ready to consume an unsuspecting sealion. He was caressing his crew pass with his thumb.

'Hey Randall, Mervyn, Nick.'

Mervyn flinched. Nick stared. Randall just gave his winning grin. 'Hey Graham. How's it going?'

'Wonderfully. This is so wonderful, Randall, a dream come true. Hey, I love your tie,' he said. 'Is it for sale?'

'Perhaps,' grinned Randall. 'I normally auction them for charity at the wrap party. You could be in with a chance.'

'Fantastic. It'll be mine.' It was a statement of fact, not intention. 'Thank you so much for giving me the opportunity to take part in this enterprise and be a part of television history.'

'Great. So what's on your mind, Graham?'

'Oh, nothing much. I've had a quick read of the script, and it's great, really great. I've just noticed a few things...'

Here we go, thought Mervyn.

'Elysia says in scene 19 that "The Styrax are going to be through that door in minutes." Glyn might not know this, but they don't have "minutes" as a measurement of time on Vixos. They say "klakks".'

'Okay. That's good to know.'

'Of course, I thought you might have decided to use "minutes" anyway. I know this is for a mainstream audience, and they might get turned off by weird-sounding names for everything, so I thought I'd flag it up with you, in case you want to raise it with Glyn. No worries either way. Just thought I'd mention it.' Graham ambled off.

Randall looked at Mervyn, a faint twinkle in his eye. 'He just thought he'd mention it?'

'Well...'

'He thought he'd "flag it up" with me, in case I want to raise it with Glyn...?'

'It's a ruse. He's pretending.'

'As long as he keeps pretending like that, he'll be just fine. Perhaps you can take a leaf out of his book, Merv? After all, "flagging things up" with me before tinkering around with a script... well it's more than you did, isn't it?'

Mervyn's face flushed with anger and embarrassment.

Randall looked at his watch. 'We've got another hour 'til lunch, and then I want the senior staff back to the office. We've got a Gorg to accessorise.'

CHAPTER FORTY

>CLICK<

WHAT THE FUCK?

FUCK!

FUCK!

FUCK IT!

FUCK!

I failed. I was so sure it was going to work this time. I was just *waiting* for the morning papers to arrive, so *sure* there'd be something in it about his death. I was so *sure* they'd find his mangled body.

When he didn't turn up to the production meeting that morning, I was so sure. So sure he was a bloody stain on the moors.

[SIGH]

Fate, you have a cruel way of taunting me. You made him come in late this morning? Of all mornings? You made me think he was dead for a whole blissful couple of hours, and then make him shuffle in like nothing has happened?

So he's still alive. Three times! Three times I've tried to kill him! And there he is again. Jesus wept.

[SIGH]

God, Mervyn, just fucking die, why don't you? Show some good manners and realise when you're not wanted. God, he's fucking indestructible. It's like trying to wash a spider down the plughole.

[SIGH]

Perhaps God is protecting him.

Oh no.

Perhaps he *is* God.

He is creator of this world. He created the Styrax. He created this show. He's the reason we're all here.

Perhaps there *is* no world outside his world. Perhaps we're all figments of his imagination. Yeah, that's it. He has to die, so we can all be released from this hellish shithole.

There's only one way to find out. For the sake of all of us, I have to kill him, I have to succeed and I have to do it soon.

For all our sakes.

I've got to do something!

CHAPTER FORTY-ONE

Lunch was called and everyone dashed back to the Oo-ar Bar to stock up on pastinis. Mervyn headed over to the Cornish Business Village. The big metal shoebox was still half-encased in scaffolding and he hadn't seen a single workman on either of the days he'd been there.

Mervyn was sent to the top floor of the building, which was open-plan and much lighter than the dingy room where they'd held the read-throughs. It had a corporate feel, of course – a huge black table dominated the room with phones fixed to it. Black swivel chairs skulked around the outside, some of them still covered in protective plastic. Small glass-panelled offices were hidden away in the corners. Wide sash windows looked out onto the river.

Nick, Ken, Louise and Randall were already there when he arrived and joined them at the table. The male runner was handing out coffees. Mervyn had just missed out again.

Randall was on the phone. 'Okay. Great. Look forward to it.' He put down the receiver. 'That was Valerie. The Gorg's costume's all ready. They're sending one up now.'

There was a frisson of anticipation. After about two minutes the Gorg strode in, brandishing a huge black pistol. It was dressed in a faux-Egyptian style, bare-chested with a huge brass belt and simple skirt fashioned from strips of golden cloth.

'I like it,' said Randall.

'It's a bit camp,' mused Louise.

'Hey, this is science fiction. Everything's a bit camp. What do you think, Merv?'

'I think it works. It's possible. I wonder... are we straying into "unintentionally funny" territory, here?'

'How do you mean, Merv?'

'I mean, would people be reminded of Carry On films, you think? Or Morecambe and Wise sketches?'

They all stared at it again.

'No, I don't think so,' said Louise, staring at the Gorg's foot. 'Those things are quite old...'

'But repeated an awful lot,' said Nick.

They all had another stare.

'Maybe we should add some science-fictiony things. Shiny coloured panels or some squiggly runes or something like that,' Ken mumbled.

'That might work,' Nick nodded. 'It would be better than a complete redesign, if only for reasons of time.'

Louise clicked her pen. 'Right. What do we all think about that?'

There were vague nods of assent around the room.

'Shiny's good,' said Randall. 'Not too shiny, though, don't want to pick up the cameras in any reflection.' He paused, thinking. Then he slapped his hand down flat on the table. 'Okay, that's the one. I'll tell Valerie to make up some more.'

The relief in the room was tangible once they realised they'd actually managed to get something done without disaster falling from the sky.

'The gun's wrong,' said Mervyn.

Everyone sighed.

'Mervyn. Do I take it that you...?' Nick began.

'If you're going to ask if I own the rights to the Gorgs as well then yes, I do.'

Nick looked weary.

'But I'm not just being obstructive for the sake of it. I'm just making an observation to help the programme. Is that supposed to be a space rifle? It just looks like an ordinary gun.'

'Mervy's right,' said Randall. 'It does.'

They all stared at the Gorg again.

'Okay,' said Randall to the Gorg. 'We've made a decision. Costume – good; gun – bad. I'll ring the props guys. You can go back to costume now.'

The Gorg didn't move.

Steel entered Randall's voice. 'Excuse me, buddy? Off you go. Time's a-wasting.'

The Gorg didn't move.

'Is this a joke?' said Nick nervously. 'Glyn? Is that you?'

Then Glyn entered the room. 'Hello my lovely boys and girls!' He spied the Gorg in his new costume. 'Hey that's just... Just so Spartacastic! I love the Carry On look! He's hairy, huge and camper than a row of gays!'

'*Vixens from the Void* died for me today!' the Gorg cried and aimed the gun straight at Glyn's head.

Everybody froze.

'What?'

The Gorg didn't say anything else. He just pointed his gun at Glyn.

'What did he say?'

'He said "*Vixens from the Void* died for me today",' repeated Mervyn, helpfully.

'Oh, okay, I thought he said "*Vixens from the Void* – formidable!" Like in the French. It's difficult to understand you, my lovely. Your mask. We can't hear you very well.'

'Shut up or I'll kill you.'

'Oh, lovely, I heard that loud and clear. Lovely enunciation.'

The runner in the corner did something stupid. He actually started running – towards the Gorg. Perhaps being a runner he'd had it drummed into him that his life was about as important as an insect, so he decided it was worth throwing it away with a futile gesture.

The Gorg saw him coming and slapped the gun across his head. The runner dropped to the floor, arms and legs splayed like a starfish.

'Oh fuck,' said Glyn.

'Oh Jesus,' said Randall.

'Oh hell,' said Louise.

'Oh,' said Mervyn.

'Oh my God, oh my God,' whimpered Ken. 'This is just about pissing *it* for me. A piss awful shoot with Mervyn fucking Stone, and now I'm being held hostage by a pissing gonk!'

'It's a GORG!' screamed the Gorg, aiming the gun now directly at Ken. 'For crying out loud just get it right once! I'm a fucking GORG!'

At that precise second, everyone knew that the Gorg was going to shoot Ken.

He fired.

Randall ran, stumbling for the door, but only succeeded in ending up in the line of fire. He span around to protect himself, but was too slow. The bullet tore into the shoulder of Randall's jacket and sent a fine spray of blood along Ken's face. Randall slumped, dragging Ken down by the dead weight of his body.

Ken lay on the floor, stunned, then realised he was coated in blood. He screamed, twitching and convulsing, rubbing at his bloody face with his hands and then rubbing his bloody hands on his jeans.

The man who *had* been shot, Randall, lay on the floor, panting, his face wiped clean of colour. His pretty tie was miraculously unscathed and it looked deeper and greener than usual against his grey suit and his white face.

'Randall, are you all right?'

'I'm okay.' Randall's voice was strained. 'It just grazed my shoulder. I think it looks worse than it is.'

Nick was uncharacteristically pugnacious. He got to his feet, the barrel of the Gorg's gun pointing directly at his chest. 'Did you see what you just did there? Do you realise what that could do to our schedule? What the hell do you want?'

The Gorg pulled up his mask a little so his mouth was unimpeded by the latex.

'Mervyn Stone... stand up.'

Mervyn looked up, surprised at hearing his name, and then slowly and clumsily he got to his feet.

The gun moved to Mervyn's head.

'This thing is all bollocks,' said the Gorg. 'I got a job as an extra because I loved *Vixens from the Void* and everything I've seen since I've been here tells me this is going to be a load of old bollocks. A complete insult to the subjects of Vixos.'

It's a mad fan, thought Mervyn. *Of course it is.*

'I have told the world of the disaster that is befalling *Vixens from the Void*. I have posted videos and facts designed to make the BBC – or anyone – do something about it. And it has come to naught. I have only one option left to me...' He swung the gun to cover Mervyn. 'Mervyn Stone. You are the guardian of classic *Vixens from the Void*. You can save us before this farce goes on any longer.' He raised the gun so it was aimed squarely at Mervyn's forehead. 'You are going to write a proper *Vixens from the Void* script for them to film. And if you don't, I will shoot you and everyone here.'

CHAPTER FORTY-TWO

'No,' said Mervyn.

'What did you just say?' hissed the Gorg.

Yes, what did I just say just then? thought Mervyn. *I could have sworn I just said 'No'.* 'I mean "no",' he repeated. 'That is to say, I can't.'

'Yes you can. You're Mervyn Stone.'

'I really can't. I've got writer's block. I can't write a word. Haven't done any writing for years.'

'But... You can try... Can't you?'

'I've tried, believe me I've tried. Writer's block is a serious condition. Why do you think I'm not writing this new episode?'

'Well, I did wonder...'

'There's no other possible explanation, is there?'

'I suppose not... I'm sorry to hear that, Mr Stone.'

The Gorg believed it. As improbable as it sounded, he believed it. The idea that Mervyn might be seen as too old or unfashionable to write for modern television didn't occur to him. In the fan's-eye view of television, there were actors, writers and directors who'd worked on *Vixens from the Void*... and then there were the rest. Mervyn was the obvious choice to write the new pilot because there was NO ONE ELSE in television who could do it. And OF COURSE there was only one possible explanation for Mervyn not writing the new pilot. He'd refused because he'd got writer's block. That was the ONLY explanation.

'Right...' The Gorg seemed to deflate slightly, then he shrugged. 'So if you can't write the episode, there's only one way to stop this.' He raised his gun until its line of fire nestled between Glyn's eyes. 'I'll have to kill you, Mr Trelawney...'

Oh dear. That was unexpected.

'... So they'll be forced to find a better writer. Someone who worked on the show. Someone like Andrew Jamieson or Stephen Dickson-Bailey.'

Mervyn made a huge effort to make his voice sound casual. 'Someone who worked on the show? Do you know who Glyn is?'

'He's some kind of writer, who writes about girls doing sex with each other.'

'Oh that's just what he's *famous* for. That's how the media pigeonhole him. Why do you think he's here writing the pilot for the new series?'

The Gorg shook its head vigorously, as if trying to dislodge something. 'I don't know.'

'It's because he wrote for the original series, of course!'

Glyn gave Mervyn an outraged look. Mervyn knew, in that split second, had Glyn been able to make a choice between being called a writer on the old *Vixens from the Void* and getting a bullet between the eyes, he'd go for the extra eye-socket every time.

The Gorg looked doubtful. 'I don't know his name. He's not been on any credits.'

No you don't. Think, Mervyn, think. Find a story in that sluggish old head of yours.

'Well of course you haven't. Of course you haven't seen his name. And do you know? There's a very good reason for that.'

'Yes? What reason?'

'Well, I'll let you into a little secret. Do you remember the episode 'Wings of the Warlock'? By Gareth Lyons?'

'Serial 7G? Yes I know it.'

'Glyn wrote that episode.'

'Seriously?'

'Absolutely.'

'I... thought that was you, under a pseudonym.'

The Gorg was right. It was an emergency episode written in an hysterical blur by Mervyn because a writer had suddenly found himself unavailable to finish a script (he'd been used as a drugs mule and ended up in a jail in Honduras). 'Gareth Lyons' was a fake name, put together using Mervyn's uncle's first name and his mother's maiden name. 'Oh that's not me,' he said. 'What nonsense. I didn't write it. If you just look a little closer, "Gareth Lyons" is an anagram of "Glyn Trelawney".'

'Oh. Oh yeah! So it is.'

Phew. Thank God he didn't ask him to spell it or write it down.

The Gorg peered at Glyn. 'I liked that episode. Did you write that?'

Glyn's survival instincts bobbed to the surface. His face twisted into a grisly parody of a smile. 'Yeah, that's right. That was me, my lovely. Just a little bit of nonsense I knocked off in an afternoon.'

'Don't do that!' the Gorg snarled. 'I hate that. I hate the way some of you who worked on the series dismiss what you did, like it was rubbish. Like it was the worst job you ever had. It was the best thing you did, and you know it.'

'He's a writer,' soothed Mervyn. 'Writers are modest people. They can't help but be self-deprecating about their work. That's why Glyn used a pseudonym. He hates the adoration. It doesn't mean to say he's not very, very proud of it.'

'Okay. I know that.' He waggled the gun at Glyn. 'Just try, okay? Just stop being so bloody modest.'

'I promise,' said Glyn solemnly, the irony of the moment whizzing over his enormous head.

'Right, I've come to a decision,' said the Gorg, still waving the gun at Glyn. 'You're going to write the *Vixens* pilot again, and this time you're going to do it properly. And I'm going to watch you to make sure you do it properly.'

It was Glyn's turn to say something mad. 'I need coffee. I can't work without coffee.'

'What?'

'Everyone knows that, my lovely. It's on my Wikipedia entry.'

Everyone looked tense. They didn't know what the Gorg was going to do next. The Gorg didn't know what the Gorg was going to do next. It seemed to be thinking hard.

'Fine. Get coffee,' it said.

'There's no coffee in the building,' said Nick. 'We send out for it.'

'Okay, go and send out for it.'

Glyn sighed. 'You've just knocked the runner unconscious, lovely. How on Earth can we get coffee now?'

The Gorg thought hard. 'We could get it delivered.'

Glyn barked a mirthless laugh. 'No one delivers coffee in this part of the country, my lovely. This place is a cultural wasteland.'

Nick piped up. 'The Oo-ar Bar does. If you order food.'

'But does anyone want food?'

'I could go for a pastini,' said Louise

'Actually, I'd like a clotted creamoccino,' said Glyn.

'Well I'd like a cider smoothie,' said Nick.

'That's not food,' Glyn replied.

'I'd still like one, and if you're getting a clotted creamoccino, then I want a cider smoothie.'

The Gorg snapped. 'Shut up! One pastini and one plain coffee. That's it, all right?' He picked up the phone on the table.

'That's just an internal phone,' said Mervyn. 'If you need an outside line you have to go into an office.'

The Gorg glared at him but couldn't prove Mervyn was lying. 'Okaay...' he said, subconsciously mimicking Ken Roche. 'I'm going into that office. I can see everyone from the door, so don't get any ideas.'

'I'm not an ideas person,' said Louise, instinctively.

The Gorg jabbed his gun in Glyn's direction, and then twitched the barrel to the glass-panelled office adjoining the meeting room. 'You come with me to that office. You've got work to do.'

'Okay my lovely, but will I need coffee very soon.'

Glyn was frog-marched into the office and sat at a desk. The Gorg perched on the corner of the desk and stared intently at him.

'Okay, start writing – and don't try anything funny. No farting spaceships. No musical numbers. No silly references to Ant and Dec.'

Glyn started to write, reluctantly at first, typing one grudging keystroke at a time, but then faster, his fingers pitter-pattering across the keyboard. Mervyn looked at the Gorg. It was on the phone, running through the order with the Oo-ar bar.

'I hope the Gorg has the exact money,' babbled Nick. 'Those delivery people get very irate if you give them a £20 note.'

'I think we have a chance,' hissed Mervyn. 'Look, the door to the office isn't completely open. My guess is he can only see that corner of the room. If one of us stays in plain sight the rest of us might be able to creep out.'

'But he's right next to the door. He's bound to see us.'

'We're not going out of the door. We're going out of the window.'

'What?'

'There's builders' scaffolding all the way to the corner. If we get outside we may have a chance to go along the outside of the building and get down on one of the ladders,' whispered Mervyn.

'Do you know what floor we're on? We're on the fifth floor!' snapped Nick, answering his own question for reasons of time.

'I *know* we're on the fifth floor. But it's our only hope. It's only a matter of time before Glyn writes something that the Gorg finds unacceptably cheesy and does something we'll all regret.'

'What about Glyn? We can't leave him?' Louise posed it as a question rather than a statement, hoping that someone else would say 'Yes we can leave him' and absolving her of any responsibility.

Mervyn obliged her. 'The only way we can save Glyn is by raising the alarm.' He snaked over to where the runner lay, tapping the young man's cheeks lightly but firmly. The runner's left eye slowly opened.

'Are you all right?'

'Hrrr.'

'Do you know where you are?'

'Hrrrrr.'

'Do you know your name?'

'Toby. 's Toby.'

Mervyn looked up. 'He says his name's Toby.'

'Right.'

'So? Is that his name?'

Louise shrugged. 'I don't know.'

'It might be...' said Nick

'I'm not sure,' said Randall

'Does anyone know this man's name so we can verify he knows who he is and doesn't have concussion?'

There was a symphony of shrugs and confused faces.

Mervyn gave up. 'Okay Toby, well done. Can you get up? Can you walk?'

The runner staggered to his feet.

Mervyn went to the window and gently pulled it open. 'Okay. Nick, stay sitting near the doorway so he doesn't see an empty room and get suspicious.'

'But you can't leave me!' Nick whimpered.

'Not so loud!'

'But you can't leave me!' he hissed.

'We're not leaving you. You're just going to wait until the last possible minute and then you can make a move and join us. Just act like you're having a conversation with us, like we're in the room.'

'But why can't the runner stay?'

'Because that's who he would expect to stay behind.'

'That makes no sense.'

'Oh God... Nick...' sighed Louise.

'I still don't see why it has to be me!'

'Because you're good at talking and pretending that people are listening to you,' she snapped.

'Oh thank you for that, you cow.'

'Glyn needs you, Nick,' said Mervyn simply.

That did the trick. Nick nodded his head and slouched in the chair, in plain view of the Gorg.

'Okay, be quiet, all of you,' Randall pulled himself up, clutching his shoulder. 'Let's do it.'

Mervyn looped his leg over the window sill and looked down. The planks on the scaffolding were about a foot wide. Oh dear. Oh bugger. He wasn't good with heights. He hoped he wasn't going to lose control of his bowels, especially with no underwear to contain the fall-out. The wind charged up his trouser leg and caused his balls to shrivel.

'Come on!' He gestured to Louise, who climbed on to the window sill. He edged along to give her the room to get on to the scaffolding. She didn't move.

'Take my hand,' said Mervyn.

'Oh, God!' she wailed. 'I get vertigo!'

'Don't look down. Just look straight into my eyes.'

Louise looked straight into Mervyn's eyes for the first time ever, and

Mervyn saw her fear. Not just fear of being five storeys up on a tiny length of plank; fear of not knowing what she was doing. Fear of being found out.

'You're going to be fine,' said Mervyn.

'No I'm not!' she hissed.

'You're going to be fine Louise. Listen to me. You're going to be just fine. And do you know why? Because you're a TV executive. You're telly management. You will always survive, you hear me? If you get shot, you will survive. If you fall, you will survive. You can walk away from any appalling accident, any disaster, any epic tragedy because you're a bloody TV executive and that's what you bloody well do!'

She seemed to take strength from the idea, and grabbed his hand. She started to inch forward again. Mervyn saw Ken stumble on to the scaffolding and then Randall emerged, his face creased with pain. Then Toby – if that was his name – climbed on to the ledge and followed Louise. Then, finally, Nick's head popped out of the window and brought up the rear.

We're nearly there, thought Mervyn. *We're going to get through this.*

He was nearly at the corner of the building. He was groping along the wall, feeling for a large vertical pole to anchor his body. He couldn't find anything but rough brickwork. Then he touched something large and soft.

'Go away Mervyn,' said a familiar voice.

He prised his eyes from Louise and slowly turned his head.

There was Graham Goldingay, standing on the ledge, chained to the scaffolding. He was wearing a tent-sized T-shirt with 'GLYN MUST GO' printed on it. A megaphone was embedded in his warty fist. 'This is my protest. You can't stop me.'

'Graham, get off the bloody ledge! We need to get past!'

'You're not getting rid of me like that.' He aimed his mouth into his megaphone and blared his words to the world below. 'I want concrete assurances that Glyn Trelawney be removed from the relaunch of *Vixens from the Void*, or I, Graham Goldingay, will jump!'

Mervyn looked down. A few people were gathering on the pavement below, casting their eyes upwards and watching the show. They heard Graham talk about jumping and backed away from the pavement. Well away. That was a lot of man to fall out of the sky.

'Graham, there is a mad Gorg with a gun in there. He has already shot one person and has threatened to kill more.'

'That doesn't happen in my copy. What page of the script is that? Is that a rewrite?' Graham sounded hopeful.

'This is *real life*, Graham. Remember that? Now get out of the fucking way!'

The Gorg's head poked out of the window. 'Where the bloody hell are you lot going? Come back here! Come back here now or I shoot Glyn Trelawney!'

'Don't shoot Glyn Trelawney you idiot!' yelled Graham. 'You'll make him a martyr! They'll be even more certain to film his rotten script if he dies!'

The Gorg did a double-take.

'What are you doing out there, Graham?'

'What are you doing in there?' said Graham.

'I'm holding hostages. I'm making a protest about the new *Vixens from the Void.*'

'With a gun?'

'Of course with a gun!'

'Are you mad? It's just a television show!' said Graham – probably for the first time in his life. 'Why don't you protest like me? I've got more T-shirts.'

'Thank you, but no. I won't intrude. I'm forcing Glyn Trelawney to write a proper episode of *Vixens from the Void.*'

'That's a terrible idea. You should have got Mervyn Stone to write it.'

'That *was* my original idea, actually,' the Gorg grew petulant. 'But he's got writer's block.'

Graham frowned. 'Your voice sounds familiar.'

The Gorg froze. 'No it doesn't.'

'I know that voice! I was watching the video of ConVix 12 just the other week. That voice interviewed Suzy Lu on the main stage. It was one of the worst interviews in fandom's history.'

'It wasn't my fault no one could understand what she was saying!'

'It is you! Darren Cardew!'

'No I'm not.'

'Yes it is you. What are you doing protesting? I distinctly recall that you're in favour of the reboot.'

'I'm not.'

'You are. I remember your posting on Voices from the Void last year. You were dismissing anybody with reservations, calling them "moaners" and said they were "living in the past".'

'You're distorting my postings. The main point I made was: If other forum-frequenters are negative whenever any new programme is announced then nothing will ever get made.'

'That's a straw man argument and you know it.'

'No it's not! "Wait and see" is a perfectly reasonable position to take.'

'That's what they said about Hitler.'

'Godwins! Godwins! You mentioned the Nazis! You lose!'

'Ha! You always invoke Godwin's Law when you've got no argument! The fact remains: you pissed in those collectable Medula knickers you wear when Glyn Trelawney was announced as show-runner.'

'I did not! I was open-minded and relatively positive about the possibility of a relaunch with Trelawney at the helm, and now, in the light of the evidence, I have taken the stance you see now.'

'You squeed!'

'I did not squee!'

Graham huffed. 'I can provide documentary evidence.'

'Oh yes, we know all about your "documentary evidence"; your programme guides are a tissue of lies and inaccuracies.'

'How dare you, you... you... insect! Come here and say that.'

'Right! You lot on the scaffolding. Come back in here!' Admitting defeat, the production team reluctantly edged back along the planks and clambered in through the window, bottom first, expecting dire reprisals for their rebellion. They needn't have worried; the Gorg, or Darren as he was apparently called, leapt out of the window and climbed along the ledge.

'Watch it!' protested Mervyn. He was the last to come back inside and was nearly edged off the building as Darren shoved past.

'Out of my way!'

Glyn greeted them as they came back inside. 'What's going on? Where's the Gorg gone? I've finished the first three scenes already.'

'I don't think the Gorg has any time to read your first draft,' drawled Mervyn. 'He's in conference outside the window.'

'Oh.' Glyn almost sounded disappointed.

They watched as the Gorg crawled along to Graham, straightened up and wagged a hairy finger in his face. 'Your accounts of the production meetings are spurious and your documentary about the episode *The Burning Time* was a bigger work of fiction than your infamous "interview" with Tara Miles in *Into the Void 15*.'

'At least I get to speak to the stars, when did you last have anyone of note in those events you hold in Coventry? You'll be holding them in the hotel lift next year if your attendances get any smaller.'

'What!' the Gorg shouted back at his long-disappeared hostages: 'Hold me back someone! Hold me back!'

'There's no one to hold you back, Darren. Your hostages have escaped and are no doubt ringing the police as we speak. Your so-called "siege" was as badly organised as your so-called "conventions".'

'Right! That's it, Goldingay. You're retconned, mister! You're in for a serious reboot!' They grappled with each other on the side of building; a cheap remake of *King Kong vs. Godzilla.* The Gorg's hairy fist embedded itself in Graham's vast stomach, disappearing up to the wrist. Graham gasped and grabbed at a length of loose pipe. He swung the pipe at the Gorg, but missed, hitting the window and cracking it. The Gorg grabbed Graham around the waist and tried to give him a bear hug.

Graham tried to turn, they overbalanced, and then they both fell off the ledge with a scream. They hung there, dangling by Graham's handcuffs for a few endless seconds, and then the chain snapped and they pitched off the building with a scream...

And into the firemen's net that had just been pulled out below them. The net bulged with the force of catching Graham, but the firemen held fast.

Still swapping insults, statistics and tiny historical footnotes from the world of *Vixens*, the two superfans were retrieved by the Cornish police and bundled into a car.

Mervyn went with Randall to the hospital. He was swaddled in a blanket, pale and suffering from shock, but he seemed okay.

'Well, you were right about Ken, and you were right about Graham. I should listen to my personal morale-booster more often, right?' Randall gave a weak smile. 'How cursed am I, Merv? Crappy director, crazy writer, mad fans holding the show to ransom, dickish bosses who worry about non-existent dicks, and now I get myself shot into the bargain. This is a major setback, Merv, I don't mind admitting it.'

'Well, yes. I suppose...'

'No suppose about it. I'm one Gorg short.' Randall spluttered with hysterical laughter, interspersed with huge hacking coughs. The ambulance siren drowned out his insane giggles, but only just.

Mervyn wondered if the stress of it all had finally gotten to Randall.

CHAPTER FORTY-THREE

Mervyn took a bus back to Truro city centre from the hospital in a mad dash to find some underpants. His quest was in vain – by the time he got there the shops were closed again. Mervyn dug his hands in his pockets and moved his penis to a more comfortable position for the 93rd time.

He wandered over to the Cornish Business Village with the hope of cadging a lift home. There was a *Points West* van parked outside; it had deigned to travel down from Bristol and a reporter was talking to a camera, gesticulating at the scaffolding as he did so. The story would hit the region tonight, and it had enough entertainment value to reach the national media by the morning, or at the very latest the day after.

Internet or no internet, thought Mervyn, t*he world will now know how much of a fiasco this production has become.*

There was nobody left except the costume department, frantically sewing Gorg kilts together. Valerie pointed him in the direction of a nearby pub, where the senior members of the production team were coping with delayed shock via the medium of alcohol. Mervyn felt like a stiff drink too, and followed Valerie's directions.

Nick was there with Louise. Ken too. They were huddled together, sipping their drinks and looking ashen like they were guests at their first science-fiction convention.

Mervyn cleared his throat. 'Hello everybody. How are we all?'

'I'm fine. Nothing wrong with me,' said Louise bullishly. 'They build us hardy down here.'

'You're not Cornish, Louise,' snapped Nick. He still looked hurt from being forced to act as decoy.

'I know I'm not, but I've been down here three months. I'm practically accepted as native now,' she downed her cider and allowed a belch to erupt from her mouth, as if to emphasise the point. 'Anyway, I'll bet money my ancestors came from here. I bet I have true Cornish blood pulsing inside me.'

'How's Randall?' asked Nick.

'He's fine,' said Mervyn. 'Don't worry about him. He's American. They get shot all the time. It's like having a bit of a sniffle with them.'

'That's not funny,' Louise scowled.

'Sorry.'

He sat down, bracing himself, ready to be glared at by Ken, but Ken didn't even acknowledge him. *He looked like one of the episodes he'd directed for Vixens,* thought Mervyn. *Sort of half-finished. Queasy.*

Badly lit. A sickly mixture of shame and resignation that this was as good as it was going to get.

'Are you okay, Ken?'

Ken didn't respond.

'Ken?'

He still said nothing.

'Don't worry about him,' sighed Louise. 'He's been like this all afternoon.'

'I looked death in the face today,' droned Ken. 'I stared into the face of death... and it was the face of a bloody gonk.' No one corrected him this time. 'It was the biggest moment of my shitty life, and it was death. I looked at the end of that gun pointing straight at my face...' he moaned. 'It was like what they said, everything flooded back, like sewage. My shitty, shitty life sloshed before my eyes, like effluent in a waste pipe. I wouldn't wish that on anyone.' He staggered to his feet and lurched away.

Louise harrumphed unsympathetically. 'It's a bit late for him to not wish it on anyone. I *have* seen parts of his life flash before me – when he sent the video of his holiday in Luxor to BBC Bristol instead of his showreel. I was the producer who had to watch the whole bloody thing, to make sure it wasn't some kind of clever naturalistic play. Two bloody hours of him wandering around the temple of Karnak, buying wooden camels and complaining about the heat. Never again.'

Nick smiled weakly. 'Oh, you got his holiday tape? My mate at Sky got sent his wedding video. He'd taped over the vows with twenty minutes of him screaming "No!" on a hill painted blue. That is, he was painted blue, not the hill.'

'Is Ken okay?' Mervyn asked, looking at the exit.

'Not really. Post-traumatic stress, I reckon.'

Mervyn sniffed Ken's drink. 'Oh. It's water.'

'He's teetotal. Didn't you know?'

'He mentioned he was clean, but I didn't know what he meant by it. I thought he was just off the drugs.' Mervyn got to his feet. 'Perhaps we should go and see if he's all right.' Louise and Nick both looked at him.

'Okaay...' they both said, unconsciously echoing the absent director. But they didn't move. Mervyn left the pub without them.

Outside, it was cold and dark, and Ken was nowhere to be seen. 'Ken?' Mervyn hissed. 'Are you out there? Are you all right?'

He was feeling utterly ridiculous. Why was he out here? He'd warned them all about Ken! He'd warned them about Graham, too. And now he was the one outside in a freezing car park, cleaning up the mess.

How could that be? He supposed that there were two types of people in the world; the type of person who goes out into a freezing pub car park to find a shell-shocked maniac, and the other type of person; the type who lets them.

'Ken? Are you all right?'

No one about.

'There's blood on my hands, Mervyn.'

Ken's voice was terrifyingly near. Mervyn screamed.

Ken was less than three feet from him. He was crouching in the beer garden like a tasteless ornament. He had a pub umbrella over his shoulder, holding it as if he were a soldier on a parade ground.

'I saw the blood on my hands. I stared at my hands and saw the blood on my hands.'

'That was Randall's blood, Ken.'

'I did it. That's why the blood was on my hands.'

'You didn't do anything to Randall. It was the Gorg.'

Ken laughed, a tiny girlish giggle, and shook his head. 'No, not him. I saw her fly through the air. Like Mary Poppins. She had an umbrella like this, and she danced in front of me, and her little dog laughed to see such fun.' He walked around in a wide circle, and pointed the umbrella at Mervyn 'You don't know how lucky you were, Mervyn,' he said sadly. 'I stared death in the face today, and I walked away. I know how lucky I am. But you've done it three times, and you didn't even know.'

'What?'

'One day you will find out how lucky you were.'

'Ken!'

Ken ran off into the night, hopping over walls and skipping along the pavement, stabbing his umbrella into the pools of light cast by the streetlamps. 'Blood on my hands!' he screamed into the night.

Three times? I faced death three times? Mervyn felt sick to his stomach. At last he knew the truth.

It was Ken.

Ken was the one who'd been trying to kill him.

CHAPTER FORTY-FOUR

Faced with the brutal truth of his no-longer mystery assailant, all of Mervyn's bravado dribbled out of him. His legs forgot how to keep him upright, although somehow he just managed to stagger back into the pub and over to his barstool by grabbing the backs of chairs and tables. He dimly heard an 'Oi!' as he fumbled past and nudged someone's pint.

'Where's Ken?' asked Louise.

'I don't think Ken's coming back.'

'Are you all right?' asked Nick.

'I'm fine,' he said in a dull monotone.

'No you're not. You're shaking. You've got delayed shock.'

'Okay, not so fine,' he moaned.

'You need to get to bed.'

'No, I'm all right.'

'No, you need to get to bed, seriously. I've seen this happen before...'

Louise sighed. 'Yeah yeah, cos you had this big a shock once...' she intoned, '...and it took you weeks to calm down, your hair fell out in lumps, and you were on all these anti-depressants...'

'Shut up, Louise...'

'... And after the trial, you flew straight back to England with Glyn, who looked after you, and that's why you'll never be apart. I've heard it all before. Sooo many times.'

'Just shut up for a minute and help me with him.'

'I've had a long day,' snapped Louise, 'and it ends now. You help him. I'm going home.' She picked up her bag and vanished into the ladies.

Nick pulled Mervyn up and tried to carry him out. A man saw him struggling and helpfully grabbed Mervyn's other arm.

'Had a bit too much, has he?' said the man.

'He's from London,' explained Nick.

Nick leaned him up against the wall.

'Now just breathe deeply.' He nipped back inside to get their bags.

Mervyn breathed deeply and tilted his head back, staring up at the stars. How weird to see them so clearly; artificial light didn't fill the sky and overwhelm their twinkle. He wondered if there would be a point in the future when the only stars kids saw would be computer-generated lights on silly science-fiction shows.

He clutched his head. His brain was screaming at him to do something;

to tell someone about Ken. Then something else was screaming at him. Outside his head. A real scream, long and loud.

It was Louise. She was in trouble. He staggered upright, lurched around the corner of the pub. There were the toilets, quaintly situated outside the pub, in the corner of the car park. Then Mervyn stopped dead, as if he'd been punched in the mouth. What he saw filled his vision, and he recoiled.

Louise was jammed up against the wall of the women's toilet, a young unshaven man wearing a leather jacket and jeans around his knees had skewered her on the brickwork. Her hands were gripping him hard, scarlet fingernails decorating his shoulders like epaulettes. 'Oh! Oooh! Oh! Fuck me hard Jim, you rough hairy bastard! Fuck me till I fart!'

Mervyn hurriedly crept away. No good would come of the situation if either of them saw him. Nick came out with the bags and heard the noise. 'What's that?'

'Nothing.'

'That's Louise!' He moved to the corner, but Mervyn grabbed his arm.

'She's not in any trouble. Well, not in any physical danger. She's fine.'

Nick stopped, realising what he was listening to. 'Oh.'

'It seems Louise has found a way to have true Cornish blood pulsing inside her.'

Nick handed Mervyn his satchel and together they hurried out of the pub car park, Louise's lustful moans echoing into the night.

CHAPTER FORTY-FIVE

It was only after they'd been walking for five minutes that Mervyn asked the question he'd been burning to ask since they hit the cold Cornish air.

'Where's your car?'

Nick looked at him, surprised. 'I'm in a hotel a mile away, on the outskirts of Truro. I didn't drive in today, I walked.'

Now he tells me, Mervyn thought, relocating his penis for 218th time. They'd walked out of town and Mervyn didn't know where he was.

'I'd better go back to the town centre. Get myself a cab.'

'Come back to my hotel. You can ring for a cab from there.'

'Ah... Okay.'

They walked in silence across the pedestrianised roads and past the ghostly orange shape of the cathedral. They huffed up the hill, until the lines of big brightly-lit shops with comforting names like Carphone Warehouse and Dorothy Perkins gave way to small shops with strange names that were either dark or had closed down. The edge of town was quiet and dead, and soon they could see nothing but cones of light spilling onto the pavements from the streetlamps.

Mervyn had calmed down now. He could deal with Ken. He would confront Ken tomorrow morning, and felt sure that Ken would break down and confess all and the Cornish police would turn up on their bicycles, licking their pencils and stroking their huge moustaches, and take him away. He felt much more serene about things.

'So what about Louise, eh? She seems to have got over the events of today pretty quickly.'

Nick laughed. 'She likes a bit of rough. I was told that.'

'Did Glyn tell you that?'

'No,' he gave a flaky laugh. 'And before you say anything, she's not his type.'

'I thought everything was his type. If it's got a pulse...'

'No!' Nick was stung. 'No it isn't. Leave him alone.'

'Okay, okay, fair enough. No need to be defensive. I get the message. Glyn's a good guy.'

'Well...'

'Glyn's been a good friend to you, hasn't he?'

'Yes. Yes, he has.'

'Louise said he had been a good friend to you. When you had that bad shock.'

'Yeah. I was pretty bad, really shook up. My hair started falling out from the stress. I lost three stone. He looked after me, because the

205

doctors wouldn't.'

'No medical insurance?'

'I didn't even get an aspirin. I was skint.'

'But Glyn pulled you through it.'

Nick laughed. 'He pulled me out of it, too.'

'He sounds like a good friend.'

'He has been. He looked after me when I got the shakes.'

'Oh, the shakes! Don't remind me. That happened to me when I crashed my car too.'

'You too? I swear my hands were like rubber. I couldn't even open the...'

He tailed off.

'You couldn't open the car door?'

'No.'

'Glyn pulled you out. Out of what? The car?'

'What?'

'Were you grateful to him? Did you do something for him in return? Something that kept Glyn out of prison?'

'You conniving sod. You're just talking to me to get to Glyn. That's all you care about. You bloody conniving sod.'

Nick turned and ran, full pelt up the road, and disappeared around a corner.

'Nick. Wait!'

Mervyn was alone, in the dark, with no idea where he was.

Good move, Mervyn.

CHAPTER FORTY-SIX

He started walking, looking for a cab; of course there were none. He was idiotically still thinking like a Londoner, expecting to see dozens of orange taxi lights clustering like fireflies along the streets.

He kept walking, up a vertiginous hill crowded with terraced houses. He missed a few turnings and found himself slightly more lost; he was no longer surrounded by picturesque seafront buildings but plain council boxes stretching to the edge of town. There was nothing for it, he was going to have to admit defeat and turn back. That was all he needed; his penis was flopping around uncomfortably in his trousers and his bottom felt numb with cold.

Then he saw them.

They were hanging outside the back of a particularly unkempt property with a scrappy garden that grew nothing but rusty buckets and children's trikes. Hidden between a pair of nasty cheap knickers and a baby's T-shirt which said '007 months old: Licensed to spill'.

Underpants.

A pair of the biggest, greyest nastiest underpants he'd ever seen.

There was a hole in them. 'ALRITE MOI LUVVER!' was stencilled on the front. 'CORNWALL 4 EVER' was stencilled on the back. But they were clean. And probably warm.

Could he? Should he? Dare he?

He was sure that, if the owner of the underpants knew of Mervyn's dire need, he'd happily donate them to a worthy cause.

Or perhaps he wouldn't. Perhaps he'd be very cross that someone had stolen his underpants.

Sod it. Just look at the state of them! They were ancient! The owner probably bought them with shillings and sixpences. It was about bloody time whoever it was got a new pair. Mervyn was doing him a favour.

It was very late. There were no lights on in the house. The washing line was tied to its back wall and the other end to a post in the middle of the garden. Stepping over the low garden wall, Mervyn reached as far as he could, stretched out his hand, plucked the pants from the line, pushed them frantically into his trouser pocket and sauntered away, whistling, into the night.

CHAPTER FORTY-SEVEN

Mervyn finally got back to his room. He wearily sank on to his bed, his eyes resting on pictures of lobster pots and fishing nets, cheery bewhiskered fisherman chuckling on their clay pipes. He needed to prepare for tomorrow. He needed to screw up enough courage to do something about Ken. It was already very late. He had to get to bed.

There was a knock on his door.

'It's me.'

The voice was muffled, but it was definitely Maggie. He opened the door and she came in.

'Hello there,' he gabbled. 'Sorry about the other day. I'm didn't mean to spook you...'

He allowed his voice to drain away. Something was up.

Maggie smiled at him, a bright smile; but there was something not quite right about it, like a pretty picture that had been hung on the wall slightly crooked.

'Mum's dead,' she said, simply.

'Oh God. Oh I'm sorry.'

Her smile grew brighter, too bright. 'No it's fine. It's really fine. She'd been in pain a long time. It's a good thing. I'm happy about it, really...' She walked into the centre of the room, arms wrapped round her body as if to hold herself together. Mervyn felt like a lumberjack at the foot of a tree, waiting for the moment to shout 'Timber'.

'She was a good woman, a jolly giving person who gave everything of herself to everyone she loved... And she had a great life. Now the pain's gone. She's happy now, wherever she is...' The last three words came out as a high-pitched wail, because her composure finally collapsed. Her face folded in despair, and so did her body, doubling over, expelling the pent-up grief as great mucus-filled gasps wrenched her throat.

Mervyn instinctively went to comfort her, but she was juddering and quivering, a moving target, difficult to embrace. He moved this way and that, circling her like a clown in a rodeo trying to distract the bull.

She solved his problem by launching herself at him, grabbing at his jacket and holding on grimly. The sobs grew muffled.

'I'm sorry. I'm sorry. I'm not normally like this,' he thought he heard her say. 'I'm normally the one that keeps it together. I'd be the one in the death camp organising the bring-and-buy sale and looking after the coffee kitty.'

He could feel his shirt getting damp. He wondered how long she wanted to stay there; the small of his back was starting to ache. Her head was almost trying to burrow into his neck. Her lips were resting on his Adam's apple.

Her face was warm on his neck. She smelt nice.

'You smell nice,' he said, feeling he ought to say something.

'I'm not wearing anything. It's my shampoo.'

'Fair enough. It's still nice.'

'It's herbal. Honey and orange blossom. For normal hair.'

'I wouldn't call your hair normal.'

'I wouldn't call your hair normal, either.'

'Thanks. I think.'

There was a half-sob under his chin which Mervyn took to be a damp giggle.

Her lips started to move. They walked their way up his neck, under his chin, on to his cheek. He felt her tears there, her lips on his lips. He responded slowly, but she plunged her tongue into his mouth, her nostrils stretching and contracting as her breathing quickened. Suddenly, his belt was undone, and she was tugging at his flies. He was steered toward the bed.

Mervyn didn't want to let the lady take all the initiative; he was too much of a gentleman. He tugged the tail of her blouse from her skirt and pushed his hand inside, snaking up her back, exploring the catch on her bra strap. Thank God – it fell open at his first touch, without the embarrassing tugging and fiddling women had usually had to endure at his hands.

She tore her blouse off without undoing the cuffs, hurling it and her bra behind her. She pulled his face into her breasts and forced his mouth on to her nipples. They had blossomed like roses, wide and large and angry. She screamed, almost with rage, as his mouth enveloped her. He worked her with his tongue, moving from one to the other. She pushed him harder against her, unzipping and pulling down her skirt, knickers too, revealing a beautifully manicured bush of pubic hair.

Mervyn was surprised at this; he didn't expect Brazilians from British women, not any over the age of 25 at any rate. They normally looked like swarthy unkempt Mexicans down there. He appreciated the effort, and showed his appreciation by inserting his fingers into her; she moaned and started biting his neck with terrifying ferocity.

They collapsed on Mervyn's bed. Now it was his turn to tear his clothes off; pulling off his jacket, shirt and jumper and hurling them into a corner. Then she was kissing and nibbling the area around his belly button, licking and tracing the tiny trickle of hair that meandered from the navel and joined the estuary of his groin.

Now for the difficult part. He had to get his trousers off without revealing the appalling underpants he'd stolen less than an hour ago. The pair he was wearing were definitely not of broadcast quality, as they said in television, and if she carried on the way she was going Maggie would get the full 3D experience of them, with high definition thrown in for good measure.

What to do? He could make his excuses and go into the bathroom, but no, that would ruin the moment. Many was the time he'd comforted some young production assistant in the tearful aftermath of a freshly-shredded love affair and disappeared off to the bathroom only to return in his shirtsleeves and find the PA lying in bed with the covers firmly welded into her armpits, an apologetic what-were-we-thinking? smile on her face.

There was only one thing for it. He tried to take them off inside his trousers while kneeling on the bed, which was a physical impossibility. He knew it was a physical impossibility. Every man knew that.

But Mervyn was reckless in the bedroom. When he was in the throes of passion, he often tried doing things that were a physical impossibility, and at his age he almost always regretted it.

Like now.

He couldn't maintain his balance. No man could. He fell backwards, off the bed, hitting the wall. The badger was dislodged from its lofty perch and descended, hitting Maggie square on the forehead and knocking her to the floor.

'Maggie?'

Maggie didn't move.

'Maggie?'

He refastened his flies and rushed over to her.

Oh my God, Mervyn thought. *I've killed her. Her mother has just died and now I've killed her.*

He felt her neck. There was a slow throb of a pulse. She was unconscious. Just unconscious. Thank God. There was no alternative. He'd have to call an ambulance. There was an unconscious woman in his bed with a head wound and he'd have to get her to hospital. His mind rushed to the darkest corners of his imagination and he envisaged angry mobs outside his house, screaming in estuary accents, throwing stones and waving badly-spelled placards saying 'Prevert Go Home', 'Our kids will be next' or 'No sex pests in our nayborhood'.

For a few silly seconds he contemplated bundling her up in his carpet, carrying her back to her room, leaving her tucked up in bed and hoping she'd wake-up with a nasty headache and complete amnesia. But no. That would be an appalling thing to do. And if she didn't get better? If she had a skull fracture and died there?

He worked out his story, and called the front desk. 'Hello, Mr Stone here, room 34. I'm afraid there's been a bit of an accident here. I was sharing a glass of wine with a friend of mine in my room, when this badger fell off the wall and struck her on the head. She's been knocked cold.'

There was a noise of resignation from the other end of the phone, a clattering sound like cutlery falling on a plate, and eventually a woman's weary voice in Mervyn's ear. 'Oh bugger. Not again. How many times is this going to happen before Clive throws the bloody thing out? We've got casualty on speed-dial here. They'll be here in ten minutes, going by their usual run time.'

'Thank you.'

'You'd better get her decent, in case the other residents look out their windows.'

'I beg your pardon?'

'Oh. I'm sorry sir. I didn't mean. Well... It's over the bed isn't it? The badger. The others were all... Um. Well, it's where the badger lands. About halfway down the bed. You wouldn't have your head there unless... Well, I'd think she'd appreciate it if you dressed her.'

'Actually, we were just sitting on the bed sharing a bottle of wine when it hit her. And for your information, she is dressed.'

'Of course she is.' The woman sounded like she didn't believe it for a second.

Mervyn put the phone down and looked at Maggie, stark naked save for stay-up stockings, earrings and a necklace.

Nine minutes. Bugger.

He frantically went to work, trying to dress her to the best of his ability. Naturally, what seemed so easy when driven by hormones was a damn sight more difficult driven by sheer blind panic. Her knickers were a nightmare; trying to lift Maggie's dead (don't even think it, Mervyn) weight and slide them up her legs was so back-breakingly frustrating he was almost crying by the time he slipped them over her hips.

Five minutes. Shit.

He knew that bloody bra came off too easily – it was saving itself for the rematch, when it was time to go back on. He almost had it attached when the demonically-possessed piece of elastic pinged off and bit him, snapping on his fingers. The sudden surprise of pain made him let go of her, and she fell backwards, her head thudding on the carpeted floor.

Three minutes. Oh fuck a duck.

The bra finally went on, and the skirt slid up without incident.

Two minutes. Sod.

The blouse was an insane world of intricacy; cuffs to undo, sleeves to pull out... He was shaking too much from delayed shock to cope. He might as well have been asked to solve a Rubik's Cube in less than 30 seconds. But somehow he managed it.

One minute. He could hear distant howling from across the darkened landscape; not a fearful feral beast but an even more dreaded ambulance.

Thirty seconds. He'd done it. He hoped so. He threw a shirt on and scoured the room for any tell-tale bits of evidence missed; he felt like he was covering up a murder, and the irony didn't escape him.

The ambulance chugged into the hotel's driveway, wailing and flashing and setting all the lights in the hotel ablaze, and soon the woman at the reception desk was knocking on Mervyn's door, two paramedics looming behind her. They placed a large metal contraption on Maggie's head that made her look part robot, part American football player, lifted her efficiently on to a stretcher and carried her down the hall, scrutinised by at least a dozen pairs of eyes.

The woman was at the door, looking around the room like a policeman with a search warrant. 'Don't worry. She'll be fine. They always are.'

'I hope so.'

'You must have enjoyed your wine.'

'We did, thank you.'

'You've drunk the bottle as well.'

And with that crisp little comment ringing in his ears, Mervyn followed the paramedics out of the tavern.

Mervyn went with Maggie to the hospital. He rode in the back of an ambulance with the two paramedics, who grinned at him in a conspiratorial way.

'Badger, eh?' said one.

Mervyn didn't know what to say, so he just nodded.

'It's always the bloody badger,' said the other.

'Bigger passion-killer than socks with suspenders.'

Mervyn wanted to defend his and Maggie's honour. He stuck to his official story. 'We were just sharing a glass of wine on the bed when it fell down and hit her on the head.'

The paramedics didn't believe him for a second.

'Don't worry she'll be right as rain. They usually are.'

'Thanks,' muttered Mervyn uncomfortably.

'They're all right. It's the collateral damage that causes the most grief.'

'Oh yes. Collateral damage.'

'One woman got knocked on the head at a vital moment.'

'Very vital.'

'She almost bit it off.'

'Very nasty.'

Mervyn crossed his legs.

CHAPTER FORTY-EIGHT

The rest of the journey was conducted in relative silence. Maggie seemed to wake-up at one point and ordered a dry Martini in an American accent, but the paramedics assured Mervyn that she was still under and just talking in her sleep. Mervyn hoped she wasn't going to say anything about the events that brought them both screaming towards casualty.

Maggie was whisked into the bowels of the hospital while Mervyn was left in a corridor with just a Polish woman prone to tearful histrionics and two angry tramps for company.

This is the second time in six hours I've ended up inside this hospital, he thought.

An hour later and he was desperate to talk to anyone who spoke English. It occurred to him to see if he could find Randall.

He wandered up and down, his footsteps sounding incredibly loud in the empty corridors. Randall wasn't where Mervyn had left him, but after a process of elimination (twitching open the curtains on several grey-faced old men snoring in their beds) he discovered that Product Lazarus had found him a private room; a large impersonal space with cream curtains and a photo of a sunrise on the wall. At least, he assumed it was a sunrise; a sunset would seem tasteless.

Randall's face was as white as his blankets, his eyes were pink and watery. He was awake, staring at a television. His pretty green tie was curled up neatly and placed on his bedside table, alongside his watch and cufflinks.

'Hi Randall.'

'Hey Merv,' he croaked. He switched the television to mute. 'What brings you here at this hour? Does Ken want you to wheel me out for a night shoot?'

'Nothing so dramatic. A friend of mine has been injured and I'm just waiting for the verdict from the doctor.'

'Sorry to hear that, Merv.'

'So... How are you doing?'

Randall shrugged. 'Not bad. The doctors seem nice, and I'm reasonably certain the nurse who changes my bandage doesn't wear any panties. Thank the Lord for socialised medicine.' He gestured to his bedside table. 'I'd offer you some fruit, but some little bastard came around and confiscated it because they were worried about germs. Shit. They've got a Burger King by reception and they're worried about dangerous fruit! The world's gone completely nuts. Or I've gone completely nuts and the docs haven't bothered to tell me.'

'How's the shoulder?

'Good. Just a flesh wound, thank God. So glad I didn't get shot in the gut. I consult my gut about all my major decisions. I wouldn't know what to do with a damaged one.'

'Very lucky.'

'Even luckier – the doctors in this hospital are about the most expert in treating gunshot wounds outside the US. Of course, they mainly treat hikers.'

He sighed, and clicked off the television. 'I feel like such an asshole, letting Graham on set like that. What was I thinking? What the hell was I thinking?'

'Well... Look at it this way. If it wasn't for Graham distracting the Gorg we probably would have all got shot.'

'Thank you for that observation, my little morale-booster,' snapped Randall. 'That cosy thought will keep my mind off the ruins of my career and the oozing hole in my shoulder.'

'Sorry.'

They sat without talking, the silence punctuated only by the sound of nurses passing in the corridor outside the door and the rattle of medicine trolleys.

Finally, Mervyn said 'There've been two more attempts on my life since the incident at the supermarket.'

'What?'

'Someone poisoned my sandwiches at Trebah Gardens, and then I was lured to Graham's place so I could be torn apart by angry dogs.'

'Don't do this to me, Merv. Please don't say this stuff. I can't cope with your shit on top of everything else.'

'I wish it wasn't so, but I'm telling the truth. He told me himself.'

'Who told you himself?'

'Ken Roche. He mentioned me "staring death in the face three times." He knew how many attempts there'd been on my life.'

Randall sighed and sank back into his pillow. 'Mervyn, he's an asshole. He's just winding you up. He hates you, so he's playing mind games with you.'

'I don't think so. I'm convinced he's trying to kill me. I'm going to the police with what I know tomorrow morning.'

'The fuck you are. You're not going to the cops – they'll be all over us, and we'll never finish this damn show. I've come this far with this shitty project. I'm not gonna let you close us down.'

'He tried to kill me!'

'So you say.'

There was an awkward silence.

'Look Merv, I'll do a deal with you. I'm gonna send Ken home anyway. He's fucking useless. He won't be able to do anything to you once he's back in London.'

'I suppose... But...'

'We get him out the way, finish the shoot – just a couple more days – then you can talk to the cops, and they can lock him up and throw away the fucking key for all I care.'

'Okay. It's a deal.'

'Great. Wonderful. Hallelujah. Praise the Lord. Now get lost and let me get some shut-eye.'

Randall thrust his head in his pillow and closed his eyes. He instantly fell asleep, the breath escaping from his mouth in a slow peaceful hiss.

Much reassured, Mervyn went back to wait for news about Maggie.

CHAPTER FORTY-NINE

He stayed in the waiting room for another 45 minutes, reading the signs about heart conditions and breast screenings. So he was doubly relieved when a nurse came up and told him that yes, Maggie was okay, that there was no physical damage, she was just suffering from concussion, she'd probably be ready to see him soon.

Mervyn kept waiting but he needed to feel useful, so he asked reception for a Yellow Pages and looked through it to find the number of Maggie's mother's nursing home. He thought he'd try to make amends in a small way, and tell the home about Maggie's accident. They might be waiting for Maggie to call to confirm funeral arrangements.

Millpond Retirement Cottages, that's where she said her mother was. He found the address and number – it was only a couple of miles from the hospital. That made sense. He went outside, waving his mobile phone around like a Geiger counter. He squeezed a signal out of the night sky and dialled the number.

'Hello, is that Millpond Retirement Cottages?'

'Yes it is. Hello.'

'Hello, yes, I'm calling on behalf of a friend. Maggie Rollins. She's had an accident. Her mother was a resident of yours. Apparently she died today.'

'Oh dear. A daughter of one our residents died today? That will be upsetting.'

'No, sorry, I'm not making myself clear. Maggie's had the accident, but she's not dead, just concussed. It was her mother who died today. She was one of the residents in your home.'

'No. Sorry. You're mistaken, I'm glad to say no one has passed away here in months.'

'Really? Are you quite sure?'

'Well, I can never be absolutely sure; it's an inexact science. But unless the duty nurse sounds the alarm in the next few seconds, then I'm pretty certain we've not lost anyone recently. What did you say her name was?'

'Maggie Rollins.'

'Rollins... I don't recognise the name. Are you sure her mother was here?'

'I saw Maggie go into your place just a few days ago. This is the Millpond Retirement Cottages on Tregower Street?'

'Yes.'

'Wait. I remember her mother's name. Mavis. She's Mavis Rollins.'

'I'm sorry. We don't have anyone of that name.'

Mervyn went back into the hospital, his mind groping for a plausible explanation for what he'd learned. He couldn't find one. He didn't know what to do. The nurse came up to him and told him that Maggie was still unconscious, but comfortable, and could he come back tomorrow?

He left. He got a cab and was heading back to the Black Prince, but he knew he couldn't leave it like that this. On an impulse, he asked the driver to head to the outskirts of Falmouth. Soon he was standing in the foyer of Millpond Retirement Cottages, looking around him. Looking baffled.

An old woman in a dressing gown made her way slowly over to him, big furry slippers gliding across the lino.

'Are you all right, sweetheart? Are you lost?'

Mervyn stared at her blankly. 'What?'

'I can get Jenny. She can take you back to your room, sweetheart.'

'No it's all right...' He shook his head, recovering his wits. 'Don't worry about me...' He sighed. 'I'm sorry, I don't quite know why I'm here.'

'That goes for most of us, sweetheart.'

Mervyn was on the point of leaving, but then hovered agonisingly in the doorway. He came to a decision. 'Can I take-up a bit of your time, please? I only need a minute.'

'I think I can just about spare a minute, sweetheart, I can fit you into my busy schedule...'

Mervyn produced his digital camera and bleeped through the recent photos. But he couldn't find any of Maggie. Where had they gone? She'd deleted them, of course. Double chins and all. Thank heavens he'd taken a sly extra one of her when she wasn't looking, and saved it in his favourites. He bleeped the camera until he found it.

'Do you recognise this woman?'

The old woman's face exploded into a thousand wrinkles as she grinned. 'Of course I do. That's my daughter.'

'Seriously? She's your daughter?'

'Oh yes. She was here just yesterday with a big bunch of flowers. She never misses a day.'

'Kath, what are you doing up?'

A stout woman in an ugly uniform was standing by the front desk, hands on hips, looking concerned.

'I was helping this man, Jenny. He's lost my daughter.'

'Has he indeed.' Jenny took the old woman firmly by the arm. 'Well, he can find her without your help. You should have been in bed hours ago.'

Mervyn followed them. 'I'm sorry. Can I talk to you?'

'Visiting time was six hours ago. Unless it's a matter of life and death, then no.'

'It is actually. This woman's daughter has been involved in an accident.'

'What?'

'I said...'

'Shh!' she angrily thrust her finger against her lips. 'Come on Kath, here we are, home sweet home...' They reached Kath's room – which was more a hospital bed with a few faded wedding pictures on a side table than 'home sweet home' – and went inside. Jenny closed the door on Mervyn, mouthing 'five minutes' at him before it clicked shut.

Mervyn waited outside, in an agony of anticipation, listening to Kath being put to bed. Finally the door opened. The room inside was dark.

'Okay,' said Jenny. 'What's your problem? Why are you trying to upset Kath?'

'It's true,' said Mervyn. 'I don't know why but she pretended she was dead.'

'Who pretended who was dead?'

'Maggie pretended her mother was dead. And that she was called Mavis. Anyway, Maggie's had an accident, but she's fine. Tell Kath she's just had a knock on the head and she'll be okay.'

'I'll do no such thing.'

'She would want to know her daughter was all right.'

'Kath doesn't have a daughter.'

'Yes she does. I showed her this photo. She recognised her daughter.'

'If you showed her a picture of the Mona Lisa Kath would say it was her daughter. That's what she does. It's called old age. But Kath has never had children of any kind.'

'But... Maggie had her mother here. She came in here and visited her mother. I watched her.'

Jenny sighed. 'Let me see that picture.'

She looked at the screen of Mervyn's camera. Her eyes narrowed. 'Oh yes. I recognise her. She walked in a couple of days ago, hung around the entrance. I asked her if I could help, but she just shook her head. She stayed there for a few minutes looking out the window and then she left.'

CHAPTER FIFTY

The following morning, the senior production staff were all phoned at their hotels, digs and rented cottages and asked by Randall to come in for an emergency meeting.

When Mervyn found the message waiting for him at the front desk of the tavern he assumed that Randall had decided to cancel the whole shoot, or at the very least suspend filming because of what had come to light about Ken.

To his surprise, new scripts (coloured orange) were waiting on the table. Louise was there, as was Nick. Ken was there too. None of them seemed the worse for wear after their ordeal yesterday. Ken was looking through the script, his face drained of colour. 'It's all changed. It's all different. It's all changed.'

Randall walked in, holding himself surprisingly well considering he'd taken a bullet only the previous day. He wasn't even using a sling. He was wearing a different jacket as his earlier one had been ruined; this one was a slightly darker grey. It looked like it didn't fit him quite as well, but then Mervyn realised he'd got padding on his shoulder where the bullet had struck.

Mervyn mouthed 'When?' to Randall. Randall mouthed 'After lunch' to Mervyn, and gave him a reassuring wink.

Louise was angry. 'What's going on Randall?'

Randall straightened his tie. 'Glyn rang me last night. He wants to incorporate the rewrites he did yesterday into the final script, and I've agreed.'

'The rewrites he made yesterday? The ones he did while being held at gunpoint by a lunatic?' spluttered Louise. She was being bypassed again and the fury was apparent in her voice.

'I'm serious. Glyn discussed the changes with me, and they all sound good.'

'This is ridiculous. I should have been consulted.'

'That's why you're here, Louise. To go through them with all of us here. There's the script in front of you.' He flapped his own script like a flick-book. 'Orange – my favourite colour.'

'This is really irregular, Randall; what about this morning's filming? It's just not the way to do things.'

'Bryony is more than capable of handling it this morning, and it's good for her to do it on her own.' Mervyn guessed there was an unspoken clause after that which went: *because she's going to be doing a hell of a lot more filming on her own after I sack Ken.*

'And,' Randall continued, 'it may have escaped your attention,

Louise, but I've just been shot. In the circumstances, I feel like being a bit irregular.'

Louise fixed the water jug with an angry stare.

'I'm sure Glyn has his reasons,' Nick blurted. 'After all, if it improves the final product...'

Product. Project. When did TV people get scared of the word 'programme'? thought Mervyn.

'Oh shut up Nick. Is there anything he'd dream up that wouldn't get your cringing support? If he asked you to throw yourself under a bus, would you do it? If he said it was in the interests of the show for you to jump off the building, would you go for it?' said Louise.

Nick stuck his bottom lip out and played with his water glass.

Louise sighed. 'Fuck it.' She took out a small tub, popped open the lid and threw a couple of white capsules down her throat. Mervyn thought they were chewing gum, but she didn't chew. She just took a swig of water.

'Hello, hello, hello!' Glyn bounced in, clutching his own script. 'Sorry to be a pain in the arse, my lovelies, but this script is turning into something really special. Dull warty chrysalis to sexy butterfly in one bound.'

Mervyn wondered how long Glyn had been behind the door, listening to Louise's protests, waiting to make his entrance.

They buried their noses in the script, flicking through it and finding the revisions, which were in a bold font. The changes seemed very sensible, beefing up Holly's part because it turned out she could act, and paring down Gemma's because it turned out she couldn't. Mervyn noted wryly that the scene inside the airless spaceship was now much clearer, and made it apparent that Medula's spacesuit was also out of oxygen. Part of his emergency rewrite was still in there, but in an edited form. Everything after the word 'cellulite' was removed. He felt slightly better about his unwarranted interference.

Ken obviously didn't think the changes were very sensible. He was looking at his old script, then the new one, then the old one again. 'This bit's different. This bit's different. What the fuck? What's *this* scene?'

After about an hour Randall, Nick and Louise were twitching the pages on their scripts, which meant it was time for a ten-minute fag break. They pulled cigarette packets out of their bags and headed for the lift. Mervyn wasn't sure where Glyn or Ken had gone. The runners stopped off in the Oo-ar Bar, but Mervyn didn't feel like being sociable. He stayed in the room, pacing round the table.

Louise had left her pills behind. He picked them up. He knew what they were; he'd taken them once. Anti-depressants, and very powerful ones at that. He wasn't surprised. Louise's hands had been shaking ever since day three. He carried on round the table, flicking through the scripts. Glyn had left his behind, and he couldn't resist having a peek.

He didn't expect to find what he found. On a dead page, about halfway through, Glyn had written his name. He had written 'Mervyn'. And then he had written it again. And again. And again. He counted about 200 versions of his name on the page, some in capital letters, some in italics, some in huge fat cartoon lettering.

In the middle of the page, across the script was the word: 'NO!' written in huge letters about eight inches high, scribbled so intensely it had made huge grooves in the paper. Then... 'HE CAN'T DO THIS TO ME!' was written on the bottom. Mervyn wondered if Ken was the only person who wished him harm. He flicked through Glyn's script, looking for more evidence.

On page 103, the page they were reading when they broke for smokes, there were the words 'Sorry Nick'.

Something flashed by the window, then a second later there was a crash, and a tinkle –

WHUP-WHUP-WHUP-WHUP-WHUP-WHUP-WHUP – and a car alarm blared in pain.

Mervyn rushed to the window and looked down. There, splayed on the wreckage of a car, was Nick.

Mervyn stared, stunned. People were already standing round the car, like maggots collecting around a piece of rotting meat. Nick stared back up at him, mouth open, as if to say 'Watch that last step, Merv, it's a killer.'

Some of the people clustering around the car looked up at Mervyn and he instinctively stepped back, as though he'd done something wrong by being in the building.

More people rushed to the car from inside the building. There was an animated conversation – 'Has anyone called 999?' – 'I thought someone would have'– 'I haven't...' – three of them fished out their mobile phones like cowboys going for their guns. They were all very keen to make the call; probably because it was the only phone number that didn't need a signal.

WHUP-WHUP-WHUP-WHUP-WHUP-WHUP-WHUP – and the bloody car alarm kept going.

Louise rushed in, then Randall. They ran to join Mervyn at the window.

'Oh my God, what's happened?'

'It's Nick.'

'No way.'

'No, it can't be.'

'Oh hell, it is. It's Nick.'

'He was on the roof. He must have...'

'Jesus Christ.'

'Oh my God. No!' shrieked Louise. 'This show is cursed! It's bloody cursed! We have to stop it right now!'

Glyn sauntered in. 'What's going on, my lovelies?'

'It's Nick,' said Mervyn. 'He's fallen off the roof. I'm sorry Glyn. He's dead.'

Glyn moved to the window. He didn't run; he practically strolled. He leaned on the window, resting his chin on the sill like a boy contemplating spitting on the pavement.

'My God...' he breathed.

Glyn's brow furrowed. Angry more than horrified. Mervyn took the expression to mean 'How dare he die without my permission?'

'He was with us on the roof having a fag,' Randall said. 'He was right behind us.'

'He had his extra fag,' said Louise. 'He needed his extra fag.'

Ken came in. 'What's going on?'

'He should have used the stairs,' said Glyn softly, 'but you know Nick, always looking for ways to save time.'

Everyone looked at Glyn with their mouths open. Mervyn thought people only did that in cartoons and sitcoms, but here they all were, gaping at Glyn. Glyn didn't seem to notice.

'What's happened?' said Ken. He ran to the window. Mervyn watched his shoulders sag as he saw the chaos beneath.

WHUP-WHUP-WHUP-WHUP-WHUP- WHU-

The car alarm was put out of everyone's misery. In the blessed silence that followed, Mervyn could easily hear Ken's muttered words.

'Oh pissing, shitting hell,' said Ken. 'More blood. More blood.'

The rest of the day went by in a blur. The Cornish police came. They didn't lick their pencils. They didn't come on bicycles. They drove cars and they took statements. Very detailed statements.

They questioned everyone, the smokers in particular, who had been the last to see Nick alive. Nick always needed his extra fag, Randall told them. He always hung back for an extra five minutes, Louise informed them. It must have been a tragic accident, they both opined.

The police left, but not before cordoning off the roof with bright yellow tape. They obviously wouldn't finish their inquiries any time soon.

Nick's body was levered out of the roof of the dented Toyota very quickly and whisked away to where dead bodies go. The problem was that it took considerably longer to find a breakdown truck to take away the car. It was a good hour before a rusty pick-up truck growled along the street to drag it away, by which time Mervyn had looked out of the window at least half a dozen times to check it was still there, to see if it was real. Nick's imprint was still in its roof, like the remnant of a cartoon character who had done one crazy stunt too many.

Mervyn didn't even ask Randall about confronting Ken. It just wasn't the right time.

Everybody went home. So did Mervyn.

He sat on his bed, tried to think, tried to move. He couldn't do anything. He didn't know what to do with himself. His mind gradually searched for something practical to do.

Maggie. He could ring Maggie and see how she was. He could ask her about her mother. There must be some misunderstanding about that. It was the wrong nursing home; must have been.

He pulled out his phone. No signal. Of course. He risked an extortionate room service bill and used the phone by his bed. He waited on the line for ages, edging past receptionists and crawling through switchboards before his call finally arrived at its destination.

'Mervyn?'

'Maggie, are you all right?'

'I'm fine. What happened to me? The last thing I remember was, we were, you know...'

'You got hit on the head by a badger. Are you sure you're okay?'

'I'm fine, really. The nurses seem to be smiling at me in very odd ways, but apart from that, I'm comfortable. A what? A badger?'

'Yes. I'll explain later. Look. I went to your mother's nursing home, to let them know you were hurt but there seems to have been a misunderstanding. They'd never heard of her. Was it the Millpond Retirement Cottages? It was, wasn't it?'

'You... what?'

'I'm sorry for everything that's happened to you. I wanted to call you earlier, but it's been a hellish day. Nick, our producer, has been killed. He fell off the roof of the building. They don't know if it was an accident or suicide or, you know... And guess what else? I found out who was trying to kill me...'

Mervyn realised there was silence on the other line. No 'What?' or 'I don't believe it' or 'My God.'

Just silence.

'Maggie?'

The line had gone dead.

He called back, couldn't get through. He tried again, pleaded with the receptionists, frantic she'd had a relapse or a brain haemorrhage, begged them to check on her. Finally, a nurse came to the phone with an answer.

Maggie had got dressed and checked out a bare few minutes ago.

She was gone.

CHAPTER FIFTY-ONE

>CLICK<

Oh my God. I've killed him. I've killed Nick.

[SIGH]

Shit. What was I thinking? What have I shitting well done?

I didn't mean to do this. I know he swanned about, telling me what to do, trying to direct my shots for me, but I didn't mean him any harm.

[SIGH]

I hate Mervyn and I hate Vixens and I hate Styrax but I didn't hate him. I saw him sitting there, and I just pushed him. It was just an impulse. I was so frustrated about not killing Mervyn. It was an impulse. Over he went...

[SIGH]

... and I finally came to my senses. I realised. I've been trying to kill someone! And I was so annoyed about NOT killing them I went and killed somebody else!

I have a problem.

Okaay...

I know it's the coke. It's the coke that did this. I'm sick. I've got to sort this problem out, I've got to end this right now.

>CLICK<

CHAPTER FIFTY-TWO

There was another emergency meeting scheduled, to discuss the events of the *last* emergency meeting. This time, the day's filming had been cancelled.

'Okay everyone,' Randall said to the subdued collection of people before him; this time, they were joined by Bryony, Valerie and the runners, and even two of the Wagz had made an appearance. The only ones not there, and conspicuous by their absence, were Ken and Glyn.

'I'm sure we're all shocked and distressed by Nick's death,' said Randall. 'But I'm afraid we can't stop to mourn him. We have a show to finish, and I'm sure that's what he would have wanted.' Mervyn was sure that Nick wouldn't have given a toss either way but he probably *would* have liked to have had a few days mourning on his behalf – although he didn't think it wise to raise that now. Randall continued. 'Louise is now series producer as well as being actual producer from this moment on, and Bryony is to take over full-time as our director.'

A murmur passed round the group – part surprise, part excitement but mostly relief as they slowly realised what he was saying; they were finally going to be free of Ken Roche.

'Sorry?' said Louise, exasperated, out of the loop again.

'What's happened to Ken?' said Gemma. 'I liked him. He was sweet.' Everyone looked disbelievingly at her.

'Don't worry about her,' said Holly. 'She loves hopeless cases. She goes out with second division footballers.'

Gemma looked shocked, then she punched Holly playfully on the shoulder, and everyone gave a relieved laugh. The tension in the room seeped away.

'Ken is taking a short sabbatical,' said Randall evenly, giving Mervyn a quick conspiratorial glance. 'I'm sure we all hope Ken gets some much-needed rest, and wish him a speedy return to our happy band. I was hoping to talk to him this morning. Has anyone seen him today?' Everyone shook their heads. 'Okay. I should speak with him real soon. I'll drive over to his B&B right now. Mervyn, would you like to accompany me?'

All heads turned to Mervyn, intrigued. What had Mervyn to do with Ken's removal from the programme? Mervyn felt a tiny glow of power as the Wagz stared at him with slight awe.

'Thank you, Randall, I'd like that very much.'

They took a runner, the female one with the purple hair, as a witness, in case there was any unpleasantness.

'I want to make it clear that I'm just giving Ken some much-needed leave – on full pay. That's the official line. He's not being sacked, and we're not mentioning anything about incompetence or attempted murders or any shit like that,' barked Randall as he drove along the tiny roads. 'It's expensive, but not as messy as a lawsuit for wrongful dismissal or slander.' Mervyn nodded reluctantly. He desperately wanted to confront Ken, but he owed it to the show (and his ample fee) to play it the way Randall wanted.

The 4x4 glided into the B&B's drive. The tiny saucer above Randall's head bleeped and they listened to an angry voicemail.

'Randall this is Louise, ring me now and explain to me what's happening to Ken,' she grated. 'Ring me RIGHT NOW or I quit. And you won't find any exec down here stupid enough to take my place.'

Randall harrumphed. 'I'm gonna have to call her back. You two guys head on in and check if he's still in bed.'

Ken's B&B was much nicer than Mervyn's. There was waitress service for one thing, and the waitresses wore frilly aprons and stockings. Mervyn liked frilly aprons and stockings. The nice old lady who ran the B&B hadn't seen Ken. 'But it is only nine o'clock – still very early for most of my residents.'

'He should have been at a meeting an hour ago. So you can understand we're quite worried,' said the runner.

'Hmm. He's probably dead, then.'

'I'm sure he's okay,' said Mervyn, shocked.

'Do you think so? That would be a first.' The nice old lady sighed. 'Every time someone calls for a resident who hasn't turned up for a meeting, I usually find they've popped off in the night. The undertakers make the beds here more often than the chambermaids.'

'How very interesting,' said Mervyn, squeezing out the minimum of politeness.

'Well anyway. Not to worry. I can soon check. I have my special key right here. I call it my "skeleton" key, on account of every time I use it...'

'I get the idea.'

They reached Ken's room. But they didn't need the key. It was open.

'What are you doing in there?' said Mervyn.

Glyn was inside the room. He spun round, guiltily. 'Ah, hello, Mervyn my lovely... And you, my purple-headed beauty... Now I know this looks a bit odd, but don't be shocked and don't jump to any conclusions...'

'Oh God, oh fuck, oh God!' shrieked the runner.

About two feet from Glyn was Ken. He was splayed across the duvet cover, feet on the headboard, head dangling off the bottom of the bed. The blood had settled inside his face, giving it a ruddy complexion. He would have just looked like a drunk sleeping it off were it not for the yellow eyes bulging sightlessly out of their sockets and the large syringe sticking grotesquely out of his arm.

'I knew he'd be dead,' sighed the nice old lady.

CHAPTER FIFTY-THREE

The runner couldn't cope. She was incredibly young and to her death was still a fantasy concept that only happened to people who were evil. She stared at Ken, clutching her purple hair and going 'Oh God. Oh fuck. Oh God,' over and over again like a sample in a dance track.

Mervyn took charge. He grabbed the runner by the shoulders. 'Go back to Randall. Tell him what's happened.'

She staggered off. Mervyn could still hear 'Oh God. Oh fuck. Oh God,' as she disappeared down the corridor.

'Oh dear,' said the nice old lady, clicking her dentures in irritation. 'I'd better ring for the police.'

'You still haven't said what you're doing here, Glyn,' said Mervyn.

'Ah, well, I was, I was, in Nick's room...'

'This isn't Nick's room, Glyn.'

'He's two doors along. I have a spare key to his room...'

Of course you have.

'... And I was collecting Nick's things, my lovely. I think I owe it to him to sort out his stuff. You think? Of course you do. I came downstairs and I packed his stuff...'

Mervyn glanced in the corridor and saw that there was indeed a suitcase standing guard outside a room two doors down.

'Well I saw Ken's door was ajar, I came in and, well, here he was... Like this. Who'd have thought it?'

'So you were just "finding the body"?' said Mervyn, quizzically.

'I don't have to answer questions from someone like you, my lovely,' Glyn retorted. 'I've been nominated for BAFTAs. Now I'd better get on, I've got Nick's things to attend to.'

And off he went, past Mervyn and down the corridor with barely a backward glance, wheeling the suitcase down the hall as though he was checking out. Mervyn was astonished.

'This is really going to upset the day,' the nice old lady sighed. 'We serve breakfast until 9.30 so the girls are going to have to cope without me. And take it from me, they're thick as shit.'

'There's no point leaving the girls to serve breakfast on their own,' Mervyn found himself saying. 'You go back and sort them out. I'll sort this out for you.'

The nice old lady was obviously delighted at the offer of help, but looked wary. 'But I don't think... Is it your place to...?'

'I'm the television company's risk assessment officer so it's my job to look after all dead bodies found during location filming. I'll ring the police and hold the fort here.'

That clinched it for the nice old lady. 'Wonderful! Would you like a cup of tea? Or coffee? I won't be specific because whatever the girls bring up will be anybody's guess.'

Mervyn always craved coffee, but he controlled himself. 'No thank you.' So off she went. He went further into the room, looking around, staring unwillingly at the body. Then he noticed the CD player on the bookcase tucked behind the door.

It was a shiny compact thing designed for portability; it was sitting on Ken's suitcase and attached to two tiny speakers. There was a Post-it note with 'PLAY ME' written on it stuck on the lid. Mervyn did as he was told and pressed play. First there was silence. Then there was a

>CLICK<

and Ken's weary voice floated into the room. A message from beyond the grave.

Oh God. I'm still here. I'm still in Cornwall. Oh God. I thought it was a terrible dream. Oh... God.

It continued. He listened in stunned disbelief as Ken described his deep hatred for Mervyn. The director recounted the 'rehearsal' murder, the hit and run on that poor woman and her dog, the attempts on Mervyn's life and the growing frustration at him not being polite enough to die.

All this was shocking, but nothing compared to the spontaneous murder of poor Nick.

I saw him sitting there, and I just pushed him. I was so frustrated about not killing Mervyn. It was an impulse. Then I realised. I've been trying to kill someone! And I was so annoyed about NOT killing them I went and killed somebody else! I have a problem.

Okaay... I know it's the coke. It's the coke that did this. I'm sick. I've got to sort this problem out, I've got to end this right now.

There was another

>CLICK<

and the CD finished.

Mervyn stood there, scarcely able to believe it. He always knew Ken to be a hopeless case, a lazy, incompetent, petulant man with a temper. He was alarmed when he suspected Ken of being his mysterious assailant, but all the way through this business he'd never seriously thought of Ken as capable of doing anyone real harm.

But he *had* murdered someone.

Two people.

That poor woman walking her dog. Dead.

Nick. Dead.

It was the coke that did it, he said. But he said he'd been clean for two years hadn't he? Was he lying? That's what addicts do...

He noticed that there were no other puncture marks on Ken's arm. Odd. Well, that didn't mean anything. There were other ways to take coke, weren't there? But it was odd he'd do it a different way just the one time...

Nobody seemed to be in a hurry to return, so Mervyn was left alone with Ken. What was the runner doing? It didn't take that long to get to the car park. And what had happened to Glyn?

He sat there and waited, staring at Ken's body. Ken seemed to be staring at the CD player. His outstretched arm, the one with the needle sticking in it, was also pointing to the spot behind the door, where the CD player was. Mervyn wasn't given to superstition, but the body looked like it was asking him to play the CD again.

Mervyn counted to ten. No one turned up. He counted to ten again. When he still found himself alone, he went back to the CD, stood in front of it, and, very gingerly, like he was arming a bomb, pressed play again. Ken's life-shattered voice coursed through the speakers, frail and tinny and hopeless, raging at Mervyn from beyond the grave.

There was something wrong about the CD. Something that was just... wrong. He couldn't get any more specific than that.

Of course it's wrong, you idiot. It's a recording of the last desperate words of a crazed and desperate multiple murderer. You would hardly expect it to sound right, would you?

Then he did something insane and spontaneous. He pressed eject, pulled the CD out of the player and slipped it into his pocket.

As soon as he'd done so, Randall walked in.

'What's going on?' Randall saw the body and jumped out of his skin, his tie flapped in alarm. 'Jesus! Ken! My God! Why didn't someone get me?'

'Didn't the runner tell you what had happened?'

'The runner? She just... ran away. Jesus, I don't believe it. This is insane. Has anyone called the police?'

Mervyn remembered he'd promised to do so and fished out his phone.

CHAPTER FIFTY-FOUR

Mervyn felt guilty. His conscience grumbled at him.

Fancy nicking a man's final agonised message to the world, it nagged. *How ghoulish. I'm only surprised you didn't stuff some of his clean underpants in your pocket on your way out.*

Mervyn convinced himself he'd done nothing wrong. *It's just evidence that hasn't come to light yet,* he replied. *I can just 'discover' it again in a couple of days. If I need to.*

He listened to it on his laptop that night but still couldn't hear anything wrong with it. It was definitely Ken's voice. Old curmudgeonly Ken, still banging on about how crappy location shoots were after 20 years, still raging about actors and producers... Still hating Mervyn.

Mervyn wondered how someone could stay like that for so long.

The production team of *Vixens from the Void* was stunned, but nothing could actually surprise them any more.

Randall and Louise were obviously relieved. Ken had ruled himself out of launching a messy and expensive lawsuit for wrongful dismissal.

Bryony took over the filming; and aside from Chrissie disappearing without notice for a day to hold a tearful publicity conference with her footballer husband in London, everything settled down. It almost felt like a normal production again. They had a post-Ken summit meeting, where everyone looked very grave and agreed that the credits for the pilot should feature a dedication to Nick and Ken. The credits at the end of the show, of course. Not at the beginning. That might cause channel-hoppers to switch over. Then everyone forgot about Ken.

Until the package arrived.

It was bunged in an in-tray that morning, in among a huge pile of letters from fans. The post to Product Lazarus had reached epic proportions; news of the hostage situation and Graham and Darren's subsequent arrest had been nationwide news. One 24-hour news station gleefully re-enacted the incident using a cuddly gorilla and a Homer Simpson doll. Some letters demanded the release of Graham and Darren because they were political prisoners; Darren was rumoured to be heading for a 20-year stretch for aggravated assault and sources alleged that Graham was to be given a relatively lenient 18-month sentence for trespass and threatening behaviour.

The letters demanding Graham and Darren's release were in the minority; most demanded the return of this or that monster, demanded that they write for any new series that would certainly be commissioned, demanded that there should definitely be no kissing between ladies, demanded that there definitely *should* be kissing between ladies, and so on and so on and so on. After all that had happened, the production team were under a lot of pressure. It wasn't surprising that the package sat there unnoticed until the afternoon.

The production office was almost empty. Everyone was on location, trying to film material to stitch together the shreds of footage they'd got in the can when Ken was at the helm. The only people in the room were Mervyn, Randall and the female runner. The runner had been delegated to open the post. She unwrapped the little Jiffy bag and found a CD inside.

She played it – and within a few seconds her knuckles were crammed into her mouth as she tried to stifle a sob. She tried to speak, but since her mouth was full of fingers Mervyn couldn't decipher what she was saying. He guessed it was 'Oh God. Oh fuck. Oh God.'

Ken's recorded voice floated out into the office. By now, Mervyn knew what it was saying word for word.

>CLICK<

Oh God. I'm still here. I'm still in Cornwall. Oh God. I thought it was a terrible dream. Oh... God.

Randall was sitting in his partitioned office, looking through his emails. He heard the voice and he leapt to his feet. 'What the hell is going on?' he shouted over Ken's voice.

Mervyn shushed him, and they listened to the CD in silence. He pretended that he was hearing it for the first time, and looked suitably shocked when he 'discovered' that Ken had killed Nick.

'Oh Jesus. Call the police,' said Randall. He ran his fingers wearily through his thinning hair. 'I'm so sorry, Mervyn. I feel so bad. I employed this guy. I had no idea. I just had no idea. This guy was one sick puppy. You could have been killed.'

'Well, I wasn't. It wasn't your fault. No one could have known about Ken.'

'That's nice of you to say Merv, but the very first meeting, the moment you clapped eyes on him, you told me he was unsuitable. I should have listened to you, Merv. I should have taken your advice.'

'Randall, it's not like that...'

'I should have got rid of him. It's down to me. It's my fault that Nick's dead...' Then Randall started to cry.

CHAPTER FIFTY-FIVE

Mervyn went home before the police arrived. He'd met some of the constables far too many times already. It was never a good thing to end up on first-name terms with the police.

When he got home, he listened to Ken's CD again. And again. He was in danger of becoming obsessed, he knew it. But he felt he was getting close to something important; some part of the story buried in the narrative. If he could just find it and dig it out... He felt he'd been keeping hold of the CD because he was waiting for something to happen. The arrival of the other copy of the CD in the post had been just that. But *why* did it happen? Did Ken *know* that Mervyn would take the CD out of his room? Was that why he sent a copy to the office as well?

Then there was Nick. It just didn't make sense. The CD claimed the murder was a spontaneous act on Ken's part, but did going up on the roof, pushing Nick off, coming back down and pretending nothing had happened *really* count as *spontaneous*? Was Ken just making excuses in his head for what was a planned, premeditated act?

It crossed his mind that the CD was a forgery, but it definitely sounded like Ken, even down to his trademark 'Okaay' at the end.

It's either him, or a brilliant impression of him, Mervyn thought.

Ken was obviously distressed about the whole situation; he still hated Mervyn with a passion, just like the last time they both went on a location shoot together. He still hated working with the Styrax, and he still hated Mervyn. He hadn't changed a bit in 20 years.

That afternoon he went for a final drink with Steve O'Brien; Steve was leaving for London the following morning.

'Product Lazarus have had enough of the whole thing,' Steve explained, cheerfully. 'They don't want any more publicity about this show, good or bad. They're closing me down, and they're closing down the DVD documentary. They're going to bury this show so deep the cable channels will have to invent an extra hour between one and two o'clock in the morning to show it in.'

'You don't seem very unhappy about it.'

'Well no, not really. I've got my notes, and as soon as they officially kill it I'm released from my contract and I can write a book about one of the biggest disasters in sci-fi history since *Matrix Revolutions.* Anyway, it was good to meet you, Mervyn. We should do it again sometime. Only without so many deaths.' Steve paused to sip his lager. 'The fans are going mental out there. Half of them want the production halted and the other half are so crazy to see it they're walking round with raging hard-ons. If this doesn't get shown, the bootleg tapes alone will be worth hundreds of thousands.'

Mervyn wondered how much the recording of Ken's final words would fetch. Then he wished he hadn't. 'It sounds crazy,' he said.

'It always is. I tell you, the fans never know what they really want.'

'But you do.'

Steve chuckled. 'Ha! Nice one Mervyn! Nice come-back!'

Mervyn was mystified. He wasn't trying to be funny.

'Yeah, you're right. I'm a sad fan too. Hands up, I'm guilty. Shoot me now...'

Not the best choice of words in the circumstances, thought Mervyn.

'I had the posters on my wall, *Vixens* figures and annuals on my shelf... I'm such a saddo fanboy at heart, and you'll hate me for this, but when I saw the words "Nick dies during *Vixens* production" on Twitter my first thought was "Who's going to do the Styrax voices now?"' Steve laughed into his empty glass, making a big echoey chortle. Mervyn chortled too, humouring him. Feeling stupid, as usual.

'I don't get it.'

'Oh come on! Nick? Which Nick did I think of? Nick Dodd, the producer, or Nick Briggs, the Styrax voice man?'

'Oh, I'd forgotten about the other Nick. I'd forgotten there were two Nicks on the show...' And then something in Mervyn's mind clicked. 'I have to go,' he said suddenly. 'Sorry.'

This time Steve was bemused. 'Okay...'

Mervyn collected his coat and bag and shook Steve's hand. 'Thanks. Thank you very much. I should talk to fans more often.'

'Right... where are you going now?'

Mervyn stopped. His mind was suddenly in so many places at once, he didn't know where he was going to start. 'Umm... the library, I think.'

He knew what was going on. Everything made sense. But now he knew he had a murderer to deal with. He had to prepare.

He'd blundered into situations too many times without the facts. The murderer didn't know that Mervyn suspected; now was the chance to gather evidence. To build a case.

In the library, he called up back copies of the local newspapers. He needed to go back a week, to the morning of the hit and run headline, the headline on the paper on the table of the location bus, back when they were filming at the supermarket.

There was the story; 'HIT AND RUN DRIVER KILLS MOTHER

OF TWO'. It was tragic and upsetting. No wonder Randall got so mad.

Everyone assumed that Ken had done it. It made sense. He'd said he knocked a woman over – the Mary Poppins figure dancing over his bonnet, the little dog. He said it to Mervyn. He said so on the CD...

Mervyn read the story thoroughly. There was no mention of any little dog. The paper claimed the woman was jogging, not walking her dog.

Okay, he thought. *That doesn't prove anything. The newspaper must have left out some details. They sometimes do that to help the police.*

That was Monday's newspaper. Reading Thursday's newspaper proved his theory beyond a shadow of a doubt.

'HIT AND RUN DRIVER WAS EX-HUSBAND, SAY POLICE.'

The woman's former spouse had confessed. He had lain in wait and run her over. Just as tragic and upsetting, but Ken hadn't done it.

Okay, Mervyn thought again. *That still doesn't prove anything. We just assumed that Ken ran over the woman in the paper. There must have been another hit and run killing, in another part of Cornwall.*

But there was no other accident that even resembled the hit and run Ken described. Mervyn looked very hard. He read through all the local papers for four or five days after the incident, just in case the body hadn't been found, but there was nothing. Then Mervyn asked for some more newspapers. What he found suggested that his theory was right. He just needed to make one more call.

'Hello, Nicholas Everett speaking.'

'Hi Nicholas, it's me, Mervyn.'

'Mervyn? Mervypoos! Darling! How lovely to hear from you again! I was afraid we weren't talking any more, after that unpleasantness at the convention.'

'Life's too short, Nicholas.'

'Bless you for that. What brings you to the electric telephone?'

'Just a question about the old days, Nicholas.'

'The only questions we get asked any more, old fruit. Fire away.'

'Now, do you remember the location shoot, down in Cornwall, back in 1990?'

'How could I forget? The *Titanic* had fewer casualties.'

'Now think hard. When you fell off the boat that day, and landed in the water; was it an accident?'

'Well I think it was... I assumed so... I had such a terrible bout of the dreaded lurgy afterwards I didn't know which way was up... Which is crucial when it comes to my manly preferences, as you well know, Merv.'

'But you're not sure.'

'About my manly preferences?'

'Not that! About whether it was an accident!'

'Not really. I assumed I slipped. Why are you asking?'

'Oh no reason...'

'Oh, I know the reason! The fearless sleuth Inspector Stone is on the trail of a miscreant again!' Nicholas affected a gruff cockney accent. '"That's him officer! That's the man, the one with the limp, I saw him through the curtains of Lady Agatha's boudoir, standing over her slumbering form! He was painting her fingernails with strychnine because of that nervous habit of hers!"'

'Something like that, Nicholas. Bye-bye now...'

'Don't forget to keep me apprised of the case, Inspector. Toodle-pip...'

CHAPTER FIFTY-SIX

The runner who was probably called Toby folded his arms and stood in the doorway of Randall's office (the runner with the purple hair had finally run away for good).

'He's not up to seeing anyone. He's in a shocking state. He's punishing himself over letting Ken on to the production.'

'I'm sure he is,' said Mervyn, 'but I have to see him about this.'

The runner frowned, but he had no choice. He stood to one side.

Randall looked shocking. He was unshaven; grey stubble covered his chin and stretched up into his moustache. His tie hung loosely around his neck and the knot was thin and ugly. His rich tan had long since faded and he looked just as pale and unhealthy as everyone around him.

'Yeah,' he croaked.

'Randall, I'd like to ask you a question about America.'

Randall's eyebrows crawled up his forehead. 'Okay...'

'The drink driving laws – how strict are they? I mean, if you were involved in an accident in America, and you were drinking?'

'We take our DUIs seriously in most of the country. It depends where you are.'

'Los Angeles.'

Randall gave a little whistle. 'Well, they have the most severe penalties.'

'And let's say the other driver was badly hurt.'

'In LA? Then they'd almost certainly be looking at some serious jail time. Why?'

Mervyn paused for dramatic effect. 'Randall,' he said at last, 'I don't think you should beat yourself up about Ken.'

'How can I not? I should have sacked him. I didn't, and he killed Nick.'

'I don't think he did kill Nick.'

'What?'

'And I don't think Ken committed suicide either. I think Ken was murdered.'

Randall froze, a cup of coffee an inch from his lips. 'Murdered? You can't be serious.'

'I'm very serious.'

'But you heard the CD.'

'I did.'

'Ken killed himself. He was completely nuts, Merv. He tried to kill you, he killed Nick...' Randall started to crumble again. Mervyn continued. 'I think someone else killed Nick. I didn't tell you this, but on the first day, after the first meeting, I heard Nick and Glyn in the toilets.'

Randall managed a weak smile. 'Hey, what they got up to in their private lives is no concern of ours...'

'No – I overheard a conversation between them. Glyn talked about Nick saving him from "jail". About being a "con". I thought it was odd, saying "jail" and not "prison", "con" and not "inmate"...' He pulled a sheaf of papers from his briefcase. 'I've done a bit of research on Nick. He had a car accident in LA ten years ago. He was working with Glyn on some kids TV show and it was after a wrap party. They were up in the mountains going home when Nick's car collided with another on a quiet country road in the hills. A woman got badly injured.'

Randall scanned the papers. 'I didn't know about this.'

Mervyn continued. 'The woman claimed Nick was driving erratically, but it was just her word against his. They eventually recorded it as a simple accident, one of those things. I just wondered... What if Glyn had been driving instead of Nick? If he'd been drinking. What would have happened then?'

Randall frowned. 'Glyn would have certainly gone to jail. His career would have been over.'

'Exactly. Nick was nothing without Glyn, he was using Glyn's coattails to go places, and so his career would have been over too.' Mervyn went to the door. 'That would explain what I heard in the toilet. I think Glyn needed Nick's silence. That's why he took Nick around with him. Wherever he went, Nick appeared one pace behind him. Every job Glyn's done he's there as producer, no matter how dreadfully out of his depth Nick was. Perhaps Glyn just decided that Nick couldn't be trusted any more, or perhaps he just got sick of Nick dragging him down. You have to admit, Glyn is the ruthless type.'

'Yes, you could call him that. Sonovabitch...'

'I think he killed Nick, and framed Ken. I think he impersonated Ken's voice on the CD. Glyn is an excellent mimic, isn't he? We've all heard his impressions. He probably impersonated you, so he could get that runner to lure me into the supermarket freezer.'

'Can you prove any of this?'

'No.'

'So it's just a theory. It sounds a bit far-fetched. But all your other instincts have been right so far. What the hell. I'll look into it.'

'Thanks.'

'No Merv, thank you.' Randall gave out a huge sigh. 'If it's not one damn thing, it's another.'

CHAPTER FIFTY-SEVEN

It was the last day of the shoot, and Louise had organised a wrap party in Falmouth in a cosy little pub called the Chainlocker that overlooked the quay.

Mervyn expected it to be more like a wake after everything that had happened, but when he arrived he was surprised to see the crew laughing, joking and giving each other presents, just like any other wrap party. He guessed everyone was just relieved to be going home. Happy to escape the madness. Louise put money behind the bar and the younger members of the production team were eagerly knocking back bottled lagers. Roger was hovering around them, trying to interest the make-up girls with stories of the times he'd worked with Benny Hill. The catering was done by the 'Oo-ar Bar', with little breaded bits of fish, and (of course) tiny spicy pasties. How Mervyn was sick of those pasties. Louise was chatting up one of the bar staff, a hairy young man who looked like he had plenty of true Cornish blood pulsing inside him.

Amazingly, the Wagz had also all turned up. Mervyn was glad. Mervyn liked them the more he got to know them; they turned out to be really nice, hard-working girls, grappling semi-successfully with the pressures of fame. He watched them as they shrieked with laughter and knocked back beers. He smiled indulgently, like a proud father at his daughter's 16th birthday. He must be getting old. He only slightly wanted to go to bed with any of them. They looked like too much hard work.

They'd come dressed down in jeans and T-shirts; the only evidence of their superstar status was the large silent guy sitting at the corner of the pub, not drinking, just watching. He watched silently as Roger staggered across the pub and engaged the blonde one in conversation. He watched as Roger laughed heartily, patted her shoulder and kissed her on the cheek. Then the large silent guy silently got up, silently took Roger by the collar of his jacket, and silently steered him back to the Ordinary People. To his credit, Roger didn't miss a beat, and carried on chatting to the make-up girls waiting for an opportunity to try again. Randall and Mervyn watched the dance of Roger and the bodyguard with quiet amusement.

Glyn was acting very oddly. He was being even more jovial than usual, throwing out 'lovelies' with much greater frequency. He practically fell on Mervyn and clinked their bottles together.

'You and me, my lovely, you and me!' he guffawed wildly.

The danger signs were really apparent when he took to the dancefloor, gyrating insanely and swinging his arms like a gibbon – and there was no music to dance to.

Soon the party ended, faltering and waddling to a halt like an old dog staggering to its basket. Hugs were exchanged, as were insincere promises to keep in touch. There was no farewell speech from Louise and Randall even forgot to auction his tie. Cars revved out of the car park. But Mervyn was following Glyn.

Glyn wandered up the high street. He was being deeply obnoxious, laughing and pointing at the teenage girls out on the town, singing Wurzels songs and making 'Oo-ar' noises. He blundered down a back street and along the quay, sitting on a bollard and throwing his empty bottle into the water. It landed with a distant ker-plop sound. He was now mumbling to himself, singing an old Coldplay song about being a superhero.

Time passed. The night was dark and cold.

Mervyn wondered how long he would have to wait. He was just about to walk into the light and talk to Glyn when someone beat him to it.

'Glyn Trelawney.' Someone had stepped out of the darkness.

'What?'

'Glyn Trelawney. I'd like to talk to you.' The voice was unmistakable. It was American. Randall had decided to play the hero.

'Leave me alone, Yankee boy.' Glyn was now American too. Mocking Randall's voice.

'I'm afraid I can't Glyn. Certain facts have come to light that compel me, as executive producer, to act. Mervyn's told me a little theory of his. About how you hurt someone in an automobile accident...'

'What the hell are you talking about? Have you been following me?'

'Back in LA, ten years ago. He thinks Nick covered up for you.'

'Fuck you. I quit. If we get a series, you can get someone else to write your space bollocks.'

'You see, it seems like I made a mistake, and it's your fault. It's a bit embarrassing really. Here's the thing; I killed Nick, because I thought he crippled my girlfriend, but I guess it's you I should have killed.'

Glyn tried to stumble to his feet, failed, and fell to his knees.

'It's your fault, Glyn. To think – I've been keeping an eye on Nick all this time, watching him. After all this time, I finally manage to kill him, and it looks like I got the wrong guy. Ironic, right? And you guys think we Americans don't do irony...' He pointed a shaking finger at Glyn. 'I always thought it was Nick who smashed my girl's spine into little bits on that road. After all, he went to court over it. Why would he go to court if he hadn't done it?'

Glyn wasn't really listening. He was sagging, sinking on to the floor, grabbing a bollard for support. *No one gets that drunk so quickly*, thought Mervyn. *He's been drugged. He didn't listen to me. He didn't listen to my warning about Randall.*

'Here's the maddest thing,' hissed Randall. 'All this. Vixens from the goddamn Void. This whole TV project, all it ever was, was a way to kill Nick and make it look like someone else did it. And I was after the wrong person all the time. I should have been after you.'

Randall pulled something out of his pocket. Mervyn thought it might be a gun, but it was smaller, something that he held in between the thumb and first finger of his hand. Lights flashed in the corner of the car park. Mervyn realised that Randall's 4x4 was there and he'd just unlocked it.

'Come on Glyn, time to go for a little car ride.'

He grabbed Glyn's flaccid form and dragged him towards the car, his tie swinging from side to side with the effort. He stuffed him into the driver's side, then he walked back to the quay, scouring the ground with a torch to clear up any evidence that Glyn had ever been there.

CHAPTER FIFTY-EIGHT

The 4x4 sped into the night.

Mervyn peered through the gap between the seats. He'd slipped into the back of the 4X4 while Randall was struggling with Glyn's body. He was just starting to realise that it was the stupidest thing he'd ever done in his life. The trees ran towards them like crazed crones in the headlights, talons wagging, warning them to slow down. Glyn was slumped in the passenger seat, face flattened against the window, dribble oozing out of his mouth towards his left shoulder.

'Hey Glyn,' said Randall. 'Wanna see a movie?'

Glyn went 'Hrrr.'

'I'll take that as a "yes".' Randall pressed a button and a television screen whirred out of the dashboard. 'This is the best show I've ever seen, and I didn't even produce it.' He pressed another button and Ken Roche appeared on the screen.

'Oh God,' said Ken, with sepulchral weariness. 'I'm still here. I'm still in Cornwall. Oh God. I thought it was a terrible dream. Oh God.'

And Mervyn's suspicions were confirmed. The Ken on the screen was younger, with a square moustache. His square hair was dark and his square glasses were large and chunky rather than small and wiry. He was slumped in a chair, in what looked like a hotel room. He stared hopelessly out of the screen. After the last 'Oh God', he leaned forward and turned the camera off. There was a jump cut, and there was Ken again, same features, same glasses, same room, different shirt.

'I'm almost glad I got the wrong man, Glyn,' said Randall conversationally, glancing at the screen. 'At least now I get the chance to explain how I did it all.'

Glyn didn't appear in any condition to listen, so Randall gave him a rabbit punch in the cheek. 'Wake-up Glyn, I'm talking to you! I'm explaining stuff to you, don't fall asleep!' Glyn opened his eyes, groggy, blinking. 'Let me spin on a bit,' said Randall.

The DVD lurched to another track. There was the younger Ken again, but wearier, more strung out, unshaven. The words were familiar to Mervyn but they were slightly changed. There were more of them, and the conspicuous sighing had vanished.

'Oh my God. I've killed him. I've killed Nicholas. Shit. What was I thinking? What have I shitting well done? I didn't mean to do this. I know he swanned about, telling me what to do, trying to direct my shots for me, but I didn't mean him any harm. Why should I? He gave me my first break in television, back in '86. I hate Mervyn and I hate *Vixens* and I hate the Styrax and bloody Vanity Mycroft, but I didn't hate him...' Younger Ken thumped his hand on the arm of the chair in frustration. 'I saw him sitting there, and I just pushed him. He was just sitting on the side of the boat all alone, fag in his mouth. I was so frustrated about *not* killing Mervyn. It was an impulse. Over he went. Splash. And when he hit the cold water, it was like I'd had cold water thrown into my face. Vanity Mycroft screamed, Samantha threw out a life-belt, Roger and Mervyn pulled him out – and I just stood there, and I finally came to my senses. I realised. I've been trying to kill someone! And I was so annoyed about not killing them I went and killed somebody else!'

Younger Ken took his huge 80s-style glasses off, rubbed them on his chunky 80s-style jersey and put them back on his 80s-style head. 'He's lying there in the hospital now and the doctors say he's really weak. He's going to die. I know it.' He slumped down further in his chair. 'I have a problem. Okaay... I know it's the coke. It's the coke that did this. I'm sick. I've got to sort this problem out, I've got to end this right now. I've got to get help, break the habit, wean myself off this shit, and get my life back. Lay off the booze, too. Start afresh. God, Mervyn. How did he get away with it? Mervyn will never know how lucky he was. Maybe one day I'll tell him.'

The screen went back to the menu. Randall flashed a grin at the unconscious Glyn. 'Poor Ken, sending out those tapes, desperate for someone to give him work. More irony, Glyn "my lovely". Ironic that he sent the wrong one out to me and guess what? It still got him work. Even though I planned it to be his last job on this Earth, it still got him a job!'

The car glided to a halt. All Mervyn could hear was the roar of the sea all around them.

'Sorry to hear about Nick, Glyn,' Randall quipped. 'You look really cut up about it.' Glyn stayed stubbornly unconscious. 'He must have meant a lot to you,' Randall continued. 'I know you're upset, but don't do anything stupid, like stealing your boss's car and driving yourself off a cliff or anything...'

Mervyn felt terror grip his brain with icy fingers.

'I can tell you're not listening to me Glyn. Well hey, I did warn you... You know what this stretch of coastline is called? "The Lizard." Kind of apt, you being a cold-blooded sonovabitch and all.' Randall opened his door and got out. Mervyn tried to embed himself in the upholstery as Randall walked round to the passenger side. Glyn's door opened and Randall grabbed the snoozing writer, struggling to drag him out. The passenger door closed and Mervyn watched Randall drag Glyn's lifeless body around the front of the car.

Mervyn saw his chance. He struggled into the front seat and frantically pressed the 'lock' button on the dashboard.

Randall dragged Glyn to the driver's side where Mervyn was sitting. He did a double-take when he saw Mervyn sitting inside the car. 'Mervyn? Is that you?' He peered into the driver's window.

'Hi Randall,' said Mervyn. 'Thanks for the lift.'

'Were you in my car all this time?'

'Oh yes.'

'Cool. What did you think of my explanation?'

'Very impressive. Certainly held my attention. I liked the visual aids. You should have done some PowerPoint.'

'Thanks.'

'You're welcome.'

'Now, please... Come out of there Merv.'

'Now why would I do that?'

'Don't be tiresome, Merv.'

'I'm not tired. I can sit here all night.'

'I do have a spare set,' he grinned. He pointed another key at the car and the doors unlocked.

Mervyn gasped, dived for the button and pressed 'lock' again. Randall pressed his keys and unlocked the car. Mervyn pressed the button. Randall pressed his keys. Mervyn pressed the button. There was a frantic game of keys–button–keys, until they both gave up.

'This is getting us nowhere, Merv.' Randall was starting to get exasperated. 'Come on, help me out here. Surely you can see this little shit has to die? He crippled my Sarah, put her in a wheelchair.'

'We don't know that.'

'Yes we do. I know it in my gut. You know it in your head.'

'I'm not having this conversation.'

'I need a break.' Randall leaned against the car. He lit a cigarette. The end glowed furiously in the wind, which whipped away the smoke.

Mervyn looked around. The car was only a few feet away from a sheer cliff edge. The waves crashed far below them.

'So,' Randall said calmly, his tie fluttering against his shoulder. 'It was you who took the CD out of Ken's room.' It was a statement, not a question.

'What made you suspect?'

'Nothing, at first...'

'Come on Merv, you heard my little explanation. Least you can do is give me yours.'

'Okay. It just crept up on me. I knew there was something wrong with Ken's message on the CD, but I couldn't work it out. It was just

Ken, as usual, moaning about the Styrax, like he did before, moaning about Cornwall, like he did before, moaning about me and Graham Goldingay and Roger Barker, like he did before... Then I realised, he was doing *everything* like he did before.' Randall smiled and smoked and said nothing. 'And once I noticed that,' Mervyn said, 'I realised everyone he talked about on the CD were people from the original location shoot, such as me and Roger and Graham... He didn't refer to you or Louise or Glyn, or anyone from the current shoot... All except one person.'

Randall supplied the name. 'Nick.'

'Yes. But he wasn't talking about "Nick" Dodd, was he? He was talking about "Nicholas" Everett. You edited it down to say "Nick".'

'Sure did. Didn't take me long. Took me an hour to edit the whole thing down, another hour to transfer it from video to CD, so no one could see how young Ken looked and how 80s his hair was...'

'And hey presto! You had a recorded confession about a man who'd murdered someone called "Nick".'

'*And* someone who sounded like they were ending it all as a result. A ready-made murderer, who'd recorded his own suicide note. Very neat, I thought.'

'You weren't running for the door. You deliberately threw yourself between Ken and the gun. You saved him from getting shot. Ken wasn't supposed to die then. Not yet.'

'Yep.' Randall felt his wounded shoulder tenderly. 'Yep. The things I let myself in for...'

'You killed Ken in cold blood. Just as an instrument of revenge.'

'He was just like the others!' Randall was suddenly angry. 'You heard the CD. He took his car and he ran over someone, and he didn't even think about what he left behind, just like Nick and Glyn. Even worse, Ken did it as a bloody rehearsal! These guys don't think about the pain they leave receding in their rear-view mirrors. I was with Sarah through the physio, the operations, the drugs, the tears, locking the hockey trophies away because she couldn't bear to look at them... Well let me tell you this, Mervyn, I've given them justice – one by one, Ken, Nick and now Glyn, they've all found out; objects in that mirror are much closer than they appear...' Randall went quiet.

Mervyn felt he had to keep him talking. The longer Randall leaned against the car in silence, the longer he had time to think. How long before it would occur to Randall that it would be easy just to toss Glyn's lifeless body on the bonnet of the car and push the car over the cliff?

'So the video. Ken sent it to you?'

'Sure did. Ended up right on my desk at my old TV company. I thought it was a gag at first, then I did some research and realised it was complete dynamite; a real account of a man planning and failing to commit a murder.'

Mervyn shrugged. 'I'm impressed.'

Randall turned to him, flicked his cigarette away and leered through the windscreen. 'You're impressed? You're impressed with *that*? Now came the *hard* part – manipulating events to fit the CD so it looked like Ken wanted to kill you *right now*; so it looked like he killed Nick. Manipulating *everything* to make it look like the events on the tape were being played out in the here and now, not 20 years ago. So what did I have to do, Merv...?'

'You had to revive *Vixens from the Void*.'

'Exactly. That's exactly what I did. I joined Product Lazarus and persuaded my bosses to revive your shitty little show. Didn't have to push too hard, my friend; in the States, it's all the rage to asset-strip and renovate creaky old sci-fi.' He took a cigarette packet from his shirt pocket and tapped it on the roof of the car. 'It was all a means to an end. Filming in Cornwall, giving Ken a job, getting Graham on set, using the Styrax, hiring Roger Barker – in a very weird role, granted, but it was the best I could think of – but it fitted it with the "old woman" line on the CD, didn't it? That was cute. And, most importantly, I got Nick to come and work for me. And all I had to do to get him here was hire his master, this lying asshole lying at my feet.' He gave Glyn a kick and Glyn gurgled helplessly. 'And you, of course, Mervyn. You had to join us too.'

'Because Ken said on the tape he tried to kill me in 1990?'

'Yep. Three times, and you didn't even notice. Poor old Ken. What a useless excuse for a guy.'

'And you faked three attempts on my life, to fit his words on the CD.'

'Now that was fun. I lured you into that meat locker, closed the door on you, waited five minutes and opened it again. Easy. I was just standing there, listening to you shout your guts out.'

'And the poisoned sandwich?'

'There was nothing in the sandwich. I was carrying that dead seagull around for days in my refrigerator box, waiting to find an opportunity to use it. When you skipped off into the garden to pick flowers with "Maggie" I just ripped up your sandwich and planted the seagull.'

'Yes, now...' Mervyn braced himself. 'What about Maggie?'

'Poor, lovesick Merv. I had to keep you down in Cornwall. Had to keep you on site, even when you were being stalked by a so-called murderer. I couldn't have you running out on me. So I did my research. I found the best way to keep you in one place was a nice plump piece of tail to flirt with.'

'You bastard.'

'Ha! Come out here and say that.'

Mervyn felt like he'd been punched in the stomach. He sagged in his seat, staring bleakly at the rocks and the black sea. He could cope with being stalked by a potential murderer, but this was something that really hurt. But Randall didn't even notice that Mervyn wasn't saying anything; he'd lit another cigarette and rattled on, more to himself than to Mervyn.

'The dog attack at Graham's was a stroke of genius, though I do say so myself. When Graham boasted about his "little pets" I thought it was Christmas. I got "Maggie" to put a note under your door, got you right in the middle of Graham's place, using the attack signal for the dogs. I knew Graham was there, so I was sure you wouldn't get eaten by hounds. Well, reasonably sure, that is.' He moved his face up against the window and grinned. 'Don't worry Mervyn, you were completely safe with me. Up till now...'

Randall grabbed the door handle and Mervyn realised with horror that the door had been unlocked the whole time. All Randall's talk had simply been a way to distract him and take his finger away from the 'lock' button. The door was wrenched open, and Mervyn was hauled out.

'Such a pity, Mervyn. All those fake murder attempts and you were never in danger. But now you've just gone and got yourself killed.' Randall punched Mervyn to the ground and Mervyn kicked upwards for his life, but Randall was an incredibly strong man. He beat Mervyn savagely until the fight went out of him, picked him up and slammed him against the car. 'I don't know how I'm gonna explain *two* people in the car. Writers' suicide pact? I dunno. I'll think of something. I always do.'

And then Glyn Trelawney was behind Randall.

'At last,' gasped Mervyn.

Glyn swung Randall round and punched him – not in the face, but on the shoulder where the Gorg's bullet had entered. Randall howled and collapsed against the side of the car – which was where Mervyn wanted him. Mervyn slammed the driver's door shut, trapping Randall's pretty green tie. He dived at the ground where the car keys had landed and locked the car again. Randall strained against the tie, stretching the little Styrax patterns out of shape, but he couldn't free himself. He started pulling the knot from around his neck.

And then Mervyn realised what Glyn was doing. He was behind the car, heaving with all his might.

'Glyn, no!'

Glyn wasn't listening. The car moved very, very slowly. Randall had left it in neutral, in preparation for Glyn's 'accident'. The car was huge and heavy, but it was on a slope and it didn't have far to go.

'Mervyn! Help me!' cried Glyn.

'I can't!'

'Help me, Merv!' croaked Randall.

'This is murder! Stop!' Mervyn shouted.

'It's survival. He did it to Nick...' He gave a huge heave. 'So he fucks with me, I fuck him back,' grunted Glyn.

'He plays games with me, I play games with him. That's television,' said Randall in a tiny voice, whispering like a man already dead. The car moved and Randall staggered alongside it, clutching his neck, trying to wrench free. He sobbed in frustration. It glided smoothly to the very edge and stopped, as if wondering whether to take a late-night swim or not, and then it tipped over.

'Farewell, my lovely!' yelled Glyn.

There was a gurgling scream, which didn't last long. It was submerged beneath the crash and tinkle of the car as it cracked apart on the rocks below.

CHAPTER SIXTY

Mervyn and Glyn agreed a story to tell the police. Somehow Glyn convinced him it was the simplest thing. No need to make things 'messy'.

Randall planned the whole thing; he killed two people and he tried to kill Mervyn and Glyn. He attempted to escape when they got the better of him, but left his car in the wrong gear and ended up lurching over the cliff.

End of story.

Mervyn hoped he'd done the right thing.

Mervyn finally realised why Maggie looked familiar when he checked out of the Black Prince Tavern.

'Maggie' had left her bag behind, and when she realised 'Maggie' wasn't coming back the woman at the front desk gave it to Mervyn for safe keeping. After all, given the badger incident, 'Maggie' and Mervyn were obviously close.

The bag contained clothes, a few towels, nothing much of interest – except a DVD. It was lots of clips of US shows with their names scribbled directly onto the disc in felt marker. To his surprise, one of the names was the US cop show he'd vainly tried to watch on Channel Five a week ago (it felt like a lifetime).

He slid it in to his computer and was treated to a pin-sharp image. How interesting – so the male detective had a moustache? And the female one had glasses – and was black? Well, well. It was a completely new viewing experience, watching them investigate that woman's murder without stretching into nightmarish shapes or turning electric purple.

After about ten seconds, he paused the DVD. Yes, there was no mistake about it. No wonder she looked familiar. The dead body in the episode, the one lying by the trash can? The one whose death the amazingly attractive cops were investigating? It was 'Maggie'.

He played it through; there were sitcoms, cop shows, true-life dramas. In all of the clips, there was 'Maggie'. Sometimes she was lounging at the back in a crowd of bystanders, sometimes standing in a room full of cops. In one sitcom she was a silent woman who threw a jug of water out of an upstairs window on to the head of the star.

It was a showreel. Of course.

CHAPTER SIXTY-ONE

Nick's funeral was a quiet affair. Mervyn was struck by the similarities with Ken's service: both had a scattering of family members, but neither was well attended by the production team of *Vixens from the Void* – classic or remake. It seemed that Ken and Nick had not made a habit of forming friendships at work. Mervyn was the only one who made it to both services. He felt he was obliged to.

He was expecting Glyn to make a speech, some sparkling eulogy that sounded sincere and was beautifully written but always somehow led back to Glyn's feelings about Nick, Glyn's experiences with Nick, how important Nick was to the Glyn Trelawney project. But he couldn't see Glyn anywhere; he was still craning his neck and looking around for him when a man shuffled to the lectern. He was a sweet, baffled man, dressed in a shapeless black jacket, like Mervyn, crumpled black cords, like Mervyn, and his hair sprouted shamelessly in all directions. Just like Mervyn's.

'I knew Nick for a long time, but I didn't really know him at all. I was too self-obsessed to bother hearing about his life, his hopes and fears...'

The man lost his place, inspected his notes, frowning. *Who was this guy?* wondered Mervyn. A feeling of horror grew inside him. He didn't know why he had the feeling, or who the guy was, but he got the sense he was going to find out both very soon.

'Anyway, I didn't know Nick, but I talked to a lot of people about Nick who really knew him, and this is what they all said. His sister Mary said he was the kindest, sweetest brother who ever walked the earth. He protected her on her first day at school, and got her Barbie back from the gym's guttering where some bullies had stuck it. He didn't care that all the teachers were watching...'

It was then that Mervyn realised that the shambling figure at the lectern was Glyn.

After the service, Glyn shuffled up to him and whispered in his ear. 'Are you going to go to the wake, Mervyn?'

'No, I don't think so.'

'Good. My thoughts exactly. Let's go and slip into a pub and drink to the memory of Nick Dodd.'

'And Ken Roche.'

'Of course! Can't forget Ken.'

Mervyn reached unconsciously for the beer mat on the table, only to find it sliding out of his grasp. Glyn had retrieved it and was starting to tear it into little strips. Mervyn wished he'd been quicker; he wanted something to tear up right now. Glyn sighed. 'You've got to help me, Mervyn. Can't you see? I'm turning into you!' He touched Mervyn's sleeve. Mervyn recoiled as if Glyn were a leper.

'What?'

'I've copied them all, Mervyn, all the writers. I've aped the best. I've morphed into writers that were cool. Writers that are "now"... Pinter, Potter, Davies, Bleasdale... God that was tough. Try being an angry Scouser when you come from Cheam. Family Christmases were a nightmare.' He ran his fingers through his newly-unmade hair. 'I first started to get a sneaking respect for you when I was forced to rewrite that bloody script at gunpoint. I thought, Christ, this is hard, making this work as crappy space opera with cardboard cut-out characters shouting gibberish. Mervyn must be better than I thought. I tried to resist it...' Mervyn remembered the angry scribbles on Glyn's script. '...Then, when you worked out who the killer was and when you saved my life... I sort of started respecting you properly, Mervyn. For the first time in my career I actually started admiring someone like you, a has-been loser writer...' He shrugged. 'As you do.'

As you do. Mervyn said that kind of thing. It was just the kind of empty silence-filler Mervyn specialised in. Glyn frowned in a very Mervyn-like way.

'I find myself trying to have sex with people who are completely useless to the furtherance of my career. I'm being modest for God's sake! I was so self-effacing back there at the funeral!'

'I'm sure you'll snap out of it,' said Mervyn reassuringly. 'Why not go to America and become Charlie Kaufman or JJ Abrams?'

'That's a good idea. Perhaps I will.'

They sat there, drinking. Not speaking. Finally, Glyn said: 'We did good work that night, Mervyn. If you hadn't told me your suspicions about Randall, I wouldn't have avoided drinking that beer he gave me... And if I hadn't faked being drugged we would have both gone over that cliff. Hey, we caught a killer! How about that?'

No, you killed a killer.

'A great result,' agreed Mervyn warily.

'What a team!' Glyn made a great show of savouring his whisky, pressing it to his nose, making smacking noises with his lips. He seemed to be waiting for the moment to say something, but – and this was very unlike Glyn – he seemed embarrassed about coming to the point.

He did, finally. 'Mervyn, I'm still confused about the CD... Ken's

CD. I don't suppose you could tell me... um...' Of course. Glyn was now Mervyn. He was curious now. He wanted to know everything.

'So you want an explanation of the plot?'

'Um... Please.'

'Really?

'Oh yes.'

'Even though it might be boring, might slow down the climax of our little adventure?'

Glyn gave him a look. 'Very funny.'

'Because I'm told that a lot of talking at the end about plot points can just lose the audience's attention very quickly.'

'You've made your point. Look, I know that Randall was a man driven by revenge. He'd been watching Nick for years, thinking about ways to get him, and I know that Ken sent him a recording by accident. But what *was* this recording? Was it really made in 1990? What was all that stuff about Ken trying to murder you?'

Mervyn grabbed a bit of remaining beer mat and shredded it. 'What dropped on Randall's desk was a private video diary Ken made during a *Vixens from the Void* location shoot in Cornwall. Yes, it was made in 1990. It was a video of Ken, pretty strung out on coke, staring into a camcorder, recounting the hell of each day's filming, how he hated me and was planning to kill me, how he hated the Styrax robots, Cornwall and everything else.'

'But what about his "rehearsal" murder – when he talked about running over someone walking a dog?'

'Yes, that actually happened. I looked it up in the newspapers of 1990 and there was indeed a hit and run during our original location shoot; but the woman was just injured. Ken didn't stop to find out whether he killed her or not. He just assumed he had.'

'So trying to kill you three times? He did that?'

'And I didn't even notice, yes.' Mervyn sipped his drink, thinking about the horrific location shoot from 20 years past; all the innocent incidents that now carried so much more significance for him. How odd. He was so blasé about the inept attempts on his life he thought were taking place just a few weeks ago. The realisation that his life might have been in danger back then and he had been blissfully unaware... His hand started to shake. He quickly put down his port and drew in a calming breath. 'Did you notice, on the CD, how much sighing Ken was doing?'

'Yes I did, now you come to mention it.'

'Ken sighed a lot anyway, but even for him I thought he was overdoing it. The sighing on the tape was sampled, covering up edits Randall made on Ken's original recording. The police found the unedited version on Randall's laptop, and thanks to my – ahem – sources on the force, I know *exactly* what Ken did 20 years ago.'

'So what exactly did he do?'

'Luckily for me, he was so out of it on drugs that he made a very lousy murderer. First, he tried to drop an arc light on me. It missed. When that didn't work he had a go at cutting the brake cables on my old Fiesta Popular. Unfortunately for Ken, in that type of car the brakes are right next to the tube that supplies the windscreen cleaning fluid; Ken cut the wrong one. The worst I got was a muddy windscreen.

'Then he had another go. This time he *did* cut my brake cables, but luckily for me the minute I got in the car it slid down a mud bank very slowly and went into a tree. I never found out about the sabotage because I just gave up on the car and left it where it was. I phoned some garage and got it towed away for scrap.'

'So three attempts, three failures. It's almost funny.'

'Finally, in sheer frustration, he pushed Nicholas Everett off a boat on the way to an island location shoot. Nicholas caught pneumonia, ended up in a coma and was very bad for weeks; Ken thought he'd killed him, came to his senses and panicked, hence those last lines on the CD about 'doing something about it'. Basically, he was going to clean up his act and get off the coke, which he did...

'Nicholas Everett recovered, but thanks to his fever, he couldn't remember anything about the circumstances of his unscheduled swim...'

'I don't know how you put this all together, it just sounds mad to me.'

Mervyn shrugged modestly. 'There were discrepancies... Randall couldn't research everything. Ken's comment about Roger Barker taking amyl nitrate was wrong. Roger doesn't use that stuff any more. All the world and his ex-wives know he takes Viagra nowadays...

'Once Randall got us all together on the shoot, he subtly manipulated events to match up with the account on the CD. On the first day of filming, he threw a newspaper down on the table and made a big issue about a hit and run story on the front page. The hit and run wasn't anything to do with Ken; it was just a story Randall had picked out, but he let us make the connection that Ken had hit the woman with his car *the night before*.

'Then Randall failed to pick me up one morning; which meant I was late. As you can hear on the CD, I was also late one morning in 1990 too, after Ken's third attempt to kill me. Randall started talking up the friction between Ken and Nick, pretending that Nick was calling him all the time about Ken on your behalf. Enough to make me think Nick was riding Ken's back quite hard. Nonsense, of course.'

Glyn grinned. 'The friction was fiction. A fictional friction.'

'And it was quite easy to stage a death for Nick Dodd which involved pushing; mainly because Nick went on the roof to smoke. Then after that it was off to Ken's room to stage his "suicide" the following day.

'It was then I put a minor spanner in the works by taking the CD from the scene of the crime. I can imagine it would have been quite frustrating for Randall to have his master plan almost complete and then the final "confession" wasn't discovered.'

'So Randall sent another one to the production office.'

'Yep.'

'And then we trapped him.' Glyn grinned. 'You and me. Hey, that was a scarily brilliant stroke of genius, of yours, that story you invented.'

'What story?'

'That story you put in about me being the one who crashed the car into Randall's girlfriend...'

'Right.'

'Because you do know that Nick was driving that car, right? On Mulholland Drive? It was him that caused the accident...'

'Ah.'

'Just thought I'd set the record straight.'

'Fair enough.' There was a big awkward silence.

'As for that nonsense you overheard in the toilet?' Glyn made a dismissive 'pfft' noise. 'Ah, Nick helped me out in lots of ways, keeping me on the straight and narrow. If he hadn't been my Jiminy Cricket over the years I would have probably ended up in prison. You know what I mean.'

'Yes.'

There was an even bigger awkward silence, which punched the last big awkward silence just for looking at it in a funny way.

'Hey, we make quite a team, don't we?' Glyn said suddenly. 'You and me. Perhaps we should collaborate a bit more. Work together on all our projects from now on. We could be a drama powerhouse. The next Coen brothers. The next Clement and La Frenais, the next...'

'Joe Orton and Kenneth Halliwell?'

'Exactly.'

Glyn looked at Mervyn. He was being deadly serious. Glyn was going places, Mervyn could see that, and Mervyn was going nowhere, he could see that even more clearly. It was a most incredibly generous offer. Well, it *seemed* like an incredibly generous offer...

He wondered if Glyn had made the same offer to Nick. What would be a better way to keep someone with an inconvenient incriminating secret close by than weld his career to yours? Engineering the destruction of one career would lead to the destruction of the other. Perhaps – irony of ironies – by killing Nick, Randall had done Glyn a favour.

Perhaps he was just being ungracious; a tad too suspicious. Even so...

'That's very flattering, but I'm really in the middle of my novel at the moment, and that's currently where my head's at, so to speak.'

'Okay. No worries. But surely my lovely, you have to write the new episodes of *Vixens from the Void* with me? You just have to. How could you not?'

Mervyn weakened...and surrendered.

'You're right. How could I not write them with you? Of course I'd love to...'

I can't resist. How funny. Just like Nick. I'm just as weak as Nick. He's offering me too much. It's every old writer's dream to get back in the big leagues again. It's the offer to end all offers.

Literally.

I could die, yes, but I'd least I'd die writing...

Glyn grinned, and slapped the table. 'Excellent!'

Mervyn left the pub, wondering if he'd ever feel truly safe again.

CHAPTER SIXTY-TWO

The pilot for the new *Vixens from the Void* was finally completed. It was now entitled *Space Vixens* because one brand manager at Product Lazarus thought the audience wouldn't know what a 'void' was. Mervyn knew that the television audience would only have to meet a brand manager to fully understand what a void was.

Mervyn thought the pilot wasn't half bad. It was slightly glib, the characters seemed a bit obsessed with throwing out one-liners when they should be running for their lives, but that was modern television for you. And the blonde one really, *really* couldn't act. But essentially, when Mervyn saw it, he liked it.

Unfortunately, Mervyn was about the only one who had seen it. He'd been sent a DVD in the post from the production team and six months later there was still no sign of it on the television screens.

If there's one thing that any TV company hates it's uncontrolled controversy. And two murders, a suspicious death and an armed siege just about counted as controversy. Under pressure from the fans, the BBC made a coy statement to say they hadn't yet bought up the pilot, because they couldn't decide 'where it fitted in the schedules'. Mervyn's guess was either one day after the twelfth of never or whenever hell froze over. Whichever came later.

Shame really. The ratings would have been terrific.

Even if it ever got shown, and in the unlikely event a new series ever got green-lit, Louise Felcham would not be on board. One of her hairy-handed Cornishmen had got her pregnant. After a career devoted to avoiding making any product whatsoever, she was finally going to produce something that was definitively hers, and hers alone. She was thrilled (but not as thrilled as those working under her, who were salivating at the prospect of her maternity leave.)

In the same post as the DVD, he'd had a letter. From the US.

Dear Mervyn

I'm sorry I deceived you. As you will probably know, my name isn't Maggie, and I'm not even English. Well, I was born in England, but I spent most of my life in the States.

You might already know I'm an actress. I've done stuff for a few TV shows, some off-Broadway, but nothing major. I've also done other stuff to make ends meet. Stuff I'm not proud of. More on that 'stuff' below.

I'm sure you've guessed most of it. Randall approached me and asked me if I could do something for him; come to England, take on a role, introduce myself to a guy, charm him, keep him entertained, make him feel like he didn't want to leave.

'It's one of those murder games,' he said. 'The guy's paid to have an adventure,' that's what he told me. 'Excitement, death, romance... that kind of stuff. Don't let on you're not real. He's in it just for the experience.'

It's not what I wanted to do, but I was desperate to keep working, and Randall is – was – a very powerful man. You didn't say no to Randall if you ever wanted to keep working in this town. I didn't want to go back to that old life.

So I did 'that kind of stuff'. I charmed this guy. I helped him on his detective role-play game. I talked through 'the case' with him, investigated with him, even left a clue for him to find – a note under the door.

When I ran away in Trebah Gardens? I was trying to avoid meeting Randall. The deal was, we were never supposed to be seen together.

The business about my Mom dying? Yeah, that was scripted. I was meant to make you feel sorry for me, to comfort me. I was never meant to let it get out of hand – that's what happens when genuine emotions creep in.

As I said, you probably guessed all that. What I'm writing to tell you is stuff you probably don't know; I had no idea that Randall was going to murder those people. I didn't know you were his patsy. I didn't know you weren't in it 'just for the experience' (though reading about my fearless detective Stone on the internet, I think you would have stayed without my charms!) When I realised what was going on, when you told me there had been a real murder, I realised I'd been played for a patsy too. I just got scared. I ran. I took my plane ticket and ran home.

Anyway, the cops haven't come knocking at my door, so I'm grateful to you for not landing me in it. I'm also grateful to you for sorting out Randall. I'm guessing, if he managed to get away with what he was doing, I wouldn't have been left alive. What do you think, Sherlock?

I'm ashamed of what I did, and I'm ashamed of what I was (unwittingly) a part of. Maybe when the guilt's stopped eating into my heart, I'll contact you again, and take a chance that you've forgiven me. Perhaps I'll give you my real life story rather than something I memorised from a ring-binder.

Sorry Mervyn. Actresses can be a bit batty. You wouldn't believe the things they're prepared to do if they think it might help their career.

I really liked you Mervyn. No act. No fake. No pretend.

See you around.
'Maggie' x

There was no address on the letter. Mervyn considered ringing her agent, try to get a message to her. He could forgive her, he knew he could. Perhaps they could rekindle what they had in Cornwall? Have some more laughs, more breakfasts, another walk in the garden?

But no.

He thought better of it.

It was never a good idea, recreating the past.

The Mervyn Stone Mysteries Book One

❖

GEEK TRAGEDY
by Nev Fountain

Mervyn Stone does not look like a special man. However, he is special in one very important respect. He has *Vixens from the Void* on his CV. This is why, 20 years later, Mervyn reluctantly finds himself at ConVix 15.

It's a funny thing; everywhere Mervyn's dormant career takes him, there are murders. Here's another funny thing. Mervyn, with his script editor's eye for sorting out plot holes, seems to be the only one able to solve them.

❖

The Mervyn Stone Mysteries Book Two

❖

DVD EXTRAS INCLUDE: MURDER
by Nev Fountain

Mervyn Stone is invited to take part in a DVD commentary discussing one of the more controversial (and, let's face it, blasphemous) episodes of *Vixens from the Void*. And he's about to turn amateur detective. Again.

The whispers begin as the bodies pile up: 'Act of God?' Mervyn's pursued by crazed fans, mad actresses, suspicious policemen and mental fundamentalists. And he's starting to feel like God's got it in for him, too...